PERSONAL
Secrets

—— THE *Personal* SERIES ——
K.C. WELLS

Personal Secrets

Island Tales Press

Copyright © 2014 by K.C. Wells

Editor: S.A. Laybourn

Cover Photo: Ron Amato

Cover model: Dirk Caber

Cover Designer: Meredith Russell

Ed Fellows isn't sure how he got from being covered in mud from playing rugby and drunk out of his skull, to finding himself giving head to Colin Reynolds, but he isn't complaining. Not the first time, right? Even if that was a long time ago. Team-mate Colin had been the Good Samaritan who'd driven him home, but waking the next morning to find him nearly-naked and asleep on his sofa – and all too clear memories of what they got up to the previous night – launches Ed onto a completely unfamiliar road, as he struggles to accept that maybe the line he is walking isn't as straight as he'd first imagined.

Colin's been in lust with Ed since Ed joined the rugby team some fourteen months ago. Only thing is, Colin's assumed up 'til now that Ed is straight. Except the man on the couch last night certainly didn't *seem* straight. Asking Ed on a date leads to another hot encounter, and another, and suddenly Colin realizes he could fall for this guy so easily. The sex is hot, and Ed's reactions are honest. But Colin watches him wrestle with questions and issues as Ed is forced to acknowledge his sexual identity and come out to his friends and family. And Colin will be there for him.

Personal Secrets is a low-angst, sweet and hot tale containing first times and fierce friendships. Passion, heat, emotional bonds, self-discovery, and two men who complement each other in so many ways... A whole new world of experiences is about to reveal itself.

Dedication

Dedicated to Max Vos
who told me that I had to write Ed's story,
and then supported me while I wrote it:
For finding THAT photo which allowed me to see Ed so clearly:
For being there.
Max—you rock.

My thanks, as always, to my wonderful betas,
Tina, Lara, Mardee and Will.

Trademarks Acknowledgments

The author acknowledges the trademarked status and trademark owners of the following wordmarks mentioned in this work of fiction:

Coke: The Coca-Cola Company

Facebook: Facebook, Inc

Sleeping Beauty: The Walt Disney Company

Harley: Harley-Davidson

Doc Martens: Dr. Martens

Levis: Levi Strauss & Co.

Legends: Legends Hotel - Brighton

Jägermeister: Mast-Jägermeister SE

Gay Hussar: The Gay Hussar restaurant, Soho

Johnnie Walker: Johnnie Walker

Etch-a-Sketch: Etch A Sketch

Doctor Who: Doctor Who, BBC

CHAPTER ONE

Something was definitely wrong with Ed Fellows.

Okay, so he hadn't come out and said anything, but ever since he'd stepped outside the Elephant & Castle pub to talk on his phone, Ed had seemed preoccupied. Colin couldn't help but notice the incessant glances at his phone, the restless checking and re-checking of his messages, Ed's furrowed brow as his fingers did their best to tap the virtual keyboard. Colin had chuckled to himself at first when he'd caught the frequent, under-the-breath swearing when Ed made mistakes.

I suppose it's hard to text when you're pissed.

Not that Colin would know. He was stone-cold sober. *Bloody antibiotics.* He only had to take them for one more day, but that still meant he was on Coke for the night.

Talk about torture. He wasn't sure why he'd gone with the rugby team to the pub after the match. They'd spent hours getting increasingly hammered, while Colin had sat there nursing his Coke, smiling at the drunken jokes and slurred speech.

Come on. You know *why you came. The reason is sitting right next to you.*

Colin sighed internally. Ed was leaning forward, bleary eyes fixed on his phone, thankfully oblivious to Colin's crush. Colin glanced around the cozy pub at his team-mates, careful not to focus his attention wholly on Ed. He'd noticed Ed had drunk less since the phone call, and that expression of concern hadn't diminished.

When ten-thirty arrived and the team was finally showing signs of bringing their binge to an end, Colin couldn't take any more. He tugged at Ed's elbow.

"Want to tell me what's wrong?"

Ed twisted in his chair to regard him, forehead smoothing out almost instantly as he pasted on a bright smile. "Wrong? Nothin's wrong." His voice slurred slightly.

Colin snorted. "Yeah, pull the other one, mate. You don't fool me."

Ed stared at him in silence for a moment and then heaved a heavy sigh. The mask slipped from his face. "Okay, me boss Blake an' 'is 'usband are expectin' a kid, yeah? Well, Blake rang me about four hours ago to say their surrogate had gone into labour three weeks early."

Colin was impressed. "He must be a damned good boss if you're worried about him." Better to react like that than to the news that Ed's boss was not only gay, he was married.

Ed cackled. "God, me an' Blake go *way* back. We were at school together." His gaze returned to his phone. "Thing is, I've been textin' 'im an' the sod isn't answerin'."

"Maybe there's no news," Colin suggested. "Surely he'd get in touch if there was."

Ed looked glum. "You didn't 'ear 'is voice, Col. That man was worried."

Colin could almost feel the concern rolling off his friend in waves. And just like that, he wanted to be the one to help him. He got to his feet and tugged Ed to stand up beside him.

"Come on," he told his now puzzled team-mate. "I'll take you to the hospital. I'm assuming you know which one, right?"

The look of relief on Ed's face made Colin's insides quiver. *You don't have a fuckin' clue what you do to me, do you?*

"Seriously?"

"Well, no other bugger here is going to drive you, are they?" Colin grinned. "'Course I'm serious. Now let's get you there so you can put your mind at ease, okay?"

Ed's expression softened as a smile lit up his face. "Thanks, mate," he breathed.

In that moment, having the man rely on him felt damn good.

Colin was still reeling from the shock, although he was doing his damnedest to hide it. They'd gone straight to St. Mary's hospital in Paddington and after some wandering around they'd eventually found Ed's boss Blake and his husband. And it was then that Colin had done a double take.

Oh my God—that's Will Parkinson. He knew the face so well from his frequent trips to Will's Facebook page where Colin would read what his favorite gay romance author was up to. Then he'd schooled his face pretty quickly. Admitting he knew who Will was might lead to some awkward questions, which Colin wasn't prepared to answer just yet. This wasn't the time or the place—not that he had any qualms about telling Ed he was gay.

Blake was clearly surprised to see them and wanted to know why they were there. For the first time, Colin gave a thought to how they must have looked. They were still in their rugby gear, which was covered with about half the mud of the playing field. *God, we look a sight!* The two men ushered Colin and Ed into a little waiting room furnished with a sofa and a couple of armchairs. It had taken all Colin's effort not to fangirl all over Will. He must have called on hitherto undiscovered acting abilities, because Will didn't appear to notice anything. Then again, the poor guy did have a lot on his plate just then.

Ed collapsed into an armchair and addressed Blake. "Well, I've bin sendin' yer texts an' got no effin' answer, so I got a bit worried." He indicated Colin with a flick of a hand. "This is Colin, one of me rugby mates. Seein' as he's been on the Coke all night 'cause he's on antibiotics, he volunteered to bring me 'ere." He peered at Blake. "Be an absolute angel an' find me a coffee, would ya? Me 'ead's bangin.'" He paused for a second or two. "On second thoughts, you couldn't chase up some asp'rin, could ya?" He gave Blake a hopeful look.

Blake snickered. "I'll see what I can do." He went toward the door.

"I *'ave* told ya recently that I love ya, ain't I, boss?" Ed batted his eyelashes.

Blake laughed. "Every time I have coffee waiting for you, yes." He exited the room, his shoulder shaking with laughter.

Will stared at Ed in amazement. "Have you all been in the pub since Blake rang you?"

Colin snorted. "That's nothing. When we left, half an hour ago, they were still at it." He shook his head. "I should have just left them to it, instead of sitting around, torturing myself, watching them downing pints like they were about to be rationed." He sat on the sofa and sagged back. "And it's not as if *this* one"—he gestured toward Ed—"could drive, the state he was in. Although," he added grudgingly, "he did stop downing his pints as fast once you'd called."

Ed blew him a kiss. "Mwah! Ya know you only do it 'cause I'm bleedin' adorable, Col."

That casually thrown-out remark, so typical of Ed, almost made Colin's heart stop. *You have* no *idea*. Ed was brash, loud at times, a bear of a man with a generous heart—and Colin had been in lust with him virtually from the time Ed had turned up to play with the team. He'd lost count of the number of times he'd berated himself for falling for a straight guy, but there was something about Ed that was compelling.

With a start Colin realized he'd been staring at Ed for far too long. He was suddenly conscious of Will's gaze on him and hurriedly turned away. Will's expression had been all too knowing. Colin kept his gaze trained steadfastly in any direction except Ed's.

Blake returned to the room, carrying a clear plastic cup and a couple of tablets. He nudged Ed with his knee. "Here. Take these." He handed them to Ed who swallowed the pills quickly, chugging the water after them.

Ed peered at Blake's now empty hands. "Coffee?" he pleaded. Colin had to smile at that. Ed was like a little needy kid sometimes.

The door opened and a couple entered, carrying two small children. Colin got lost in all the greetings and conversation that followed. Ed leaned forward to speak in a low voice.

"That's Lizzie an' 'er 'usband, Dave. Lizzie works at Trinity—well, she did, until the birth of that little tyke." He pointed to the toddler who was at present taking shaky steps toward Blake. "An' Dave is Blake's best mate from uni. The kids are Blake and Will's godchildren."

That explained the closeness which permeated the little group. Colin felt awkward for a moment, as though he were intruding on a family gathering. Such thoughts disappeared rapidly when the door opened and a diminutive woman in a white doctor's coat entered. Judging from the speed with which Will and Blake followed her out of the room, Colin guessed all was not well with the baby. He glanced at Ed, whose eyes were trained on the door, his brow furrowed once more.

You're a good man, Ed Fellows. It wasn't the first time such a thought had crossed his mind.

Blake and Will came back into the little room, their faces drawn. Just the sight of them had everyone sitting up straight, Colin included.

"The baby's in distress," Blake explained, "so they're doing an emergency Caesarean. Donna will be going into the operating theatre in the next few minutes." Will slipped his arm around Blake's waist and kissed his cheek.

Ed's face fell. "Does the doc think the baby'll be okay?"

Will looked to Blake before replying. "She seems pretty confident, and it's a fairly quick op."

"Then come an' sit down, the pair of ya." Ed gestured to the space next to Colin on the sofa. "Just let 'em do their stuff, yeah?"

In spite of Ed's confident air, Colin could see the tension in his body. Blake sat down next to Colin, Will beside him, and the two men held hands. For a brief moment, Colin felt envious. Blake and Will had each other, not to mention these great friends who loved and accepted them. Then he brushed it aside. A relationship like theirs was what he wanted, but it wasn't as if it was constantly at the forefront of his mind. Colin's philosophy was that if it happened, it happened. And if it didn't, well, he was good with that too. There'd been one, fairly long-term relationship in his past. He and Matthew had been together for three good years, before things had started to go sour. When push came to shove, they weren't a good fit. They'd parted amicably, and since then Colin had dated, but nothing special. In the last few years there'd been no time for anything else, as he'd concentrated on his career as a graphic designer. He had a close-knit circle of friends, his team-mates, and that had been enough.

Colin gazed at Ed who perched on the sofa, elbows on knees, hands hanging down between them. Ed's attention was focused on the floor, affording Colin the opportunity to observe his team-mate. That body had formed a frequent component in Colin's masturbatory fantasies of the last few months. Ed's short, dark brown hair was a mess, and was even starting to thin a little, but Colin didn't care. He loved those clear, green eyes and firm jaw, now covered in a scruffy beard—something which was a recent addition. And that mouth. God, the nights he'd lain in bed, fantasizing about kissing those full lips until they were red and swollen. Ed's neck was thick, and Colin let his gaze drift lower to where a layer of dark hair was visible under his rugby shirt.

Fuck, hairy men do it for me every time.

Each time he'd glimpsed Ed in the showers after a match, it had been all he could do to keep his erection under control. He knew those shorts hid heavily-muscled thighs, the hair becoming denser on his calves. The wide chest and thick, rippling biceps were all evidence of Ed's workouts. Hell, he *had* to be that size. Being the prop for the team meant he needed every inch of muscle.

Once more Colin became aware of Will's eyes focused on him, and he quickly shifted his gaze. God, how long had he been staring at Ed? He'd completely lost track of time.

The door opened and the doctor entered, smiling. Will and Blake were on their feet in an instant.

"Gentlemen, you have a daughter. And mother and baby are both doing well." She beamed at them.

Will turned to face Blake. "A little girl. Blake, we have a little girl." Colin loved the note of wonder in his voice. The two men held each other, exchanging soft, loving kisses as their three friends got up to hug them, voices raised in congratulation.

"Would you like to see Donna and your daughter?"

Colin had to smile as the doctor's words broke through, her amusement apparent. Will released Blake and met his husband's gaze. "Let's go see our little girl."

Ed cleared his throat. "Okay, now I know everythin's fine an' dandy 'ere, I'm gonna go 'ome." He speared Blake with an intense stare. "An' I don't expect to see you at work, okay?" He gave Blake a cheeky grin. "'Ave a day off on me. In fact, 'ave several. It's called paternity leave, so I'm reliably informed." Ed winked.

"Done," Blake replied promptly. Both Colin and Will chuckled to see the look of faint surprise on Ed's face. "What—you expected me to argue?" Blake snickered.

Colin got to his feet. "Come on, Ed, I'll take you home. You need to sleep it off or you'll be in no state for work tomorrow, Mr. Office Manager." He grinned good-naturedly.

"That shows 'ow awake *you* are," Ed cackled. "Tomorrow's Sunday." He was still beaming as he clapped Will on the back and gave Blake a brief, manly hug before heading for the door. Colin gave a nod to the group and followed him out. They made their way along the now quiet corridors to the elevator. Ed leaned back against the elevator walls and sighed.

"Thank God everythin' worked out all right." He closed his eyes.

"Will and Blake seem like a nice couple." It felt like a safe enough remark to make.

Ed opened his eyes. "Yeah, I didn't see *that* one comin'. First we all knew about it was the office Christmas party when the coppers turned up to arrest Will for assaultin' our receptionist, Karen."

Colin stared. "You're kidding."

Ed shook his head. "God's honest truth. 'Course, it was a crock o' shit, but when Blake told the ol' Bill that Will couldn't 'ave done it 'cause they'd spent the night together..."

The doors to the elevator opened and they exited. They walked out of the hospital into the dark night, heading toward the car park. Colin was still ruminating on Ed's words.

"Wow, talk about a dramatic way to come out of the closet."

Ed guffawed. "You can say that again. Then blow me, a week later, during the New Year's Eve party, Blake goes an' gets down on one knee in front of everyone and proposes." He shook his head once more. "An' we never 'ad a bloody clue that Blake was even gay! Just shows, you never can tell about people."

They reached Colin's car and got in. Ed sank his head against the support and closed his eyes.

Colin smirked. "Yeah, close your eyes, Sleeping Beauty. I'll get you home." He switched on the engine.

"You're a real prince," Ed murmured. It wasn't long before Colin could hear the change in his breathing as Ed fell asleep.

Good job I know where you live, eh, mate? It wasn't the first time he'd driven to Ed's place to pick him up for rugby practice or a match. Smiling to himself, Colin pulled out of the parking bay and started on the forty minute or so journey to Ed's flat. As he drove along, he glanced down at Ed's muscled legs and thick calves, still spattered with mud, as were his own.

God, I need a shower, he thought. It would have to wait until he'd deposited a sleepy Ed back at his flat. He grinned to himself. *Wonder how Ed would feel if I offered to tuck him up in bed?* He barely held back the snort.

Yeah, like *that* was going to happen.

CHAPTER TWO

"You're not goin' 'til you've 'elped me wet the baby's 'ead," Ed insisted for the fourth time, reaching for two glass tumblers from inside a cabinet in his living room. He'd already pulled out the bottle of whiskey and set it down on the polished wooden surface. He weaved slightly as he stood there, clearly not sober.

Colin laughed. "Er, why was I on Coke all night? Antibiotics, remember?" He sat down where Ed had pushed him and glanced around. The living room was small and cozy and the sofa was extremely comfy.

Ed snorted. "So 'ow long 'ave you got left on 'em? I thought you said you finish 'em soon. Besides, one drink isn't gonna 'urt, is it?" He poured about four fingers of whiskey into each tumbler.

Colin gasped. "Bloody hell, Ed, are you *trying* to get me arrested for drunk-driving?" It was no use. Ed wasn't taking no for an answer. And it amused the hell out of Colin.

I don't suppose it will make much difference in Ed's case, he thought. *He's had that much alcohol already today.*

Ed handed him a glass. "Then stay 'ere, mate. You can sleep on the sofa. It's dead comfy. Besides, tomorrow's Sunday." He peered at Colin with unfocused eyes. "Oh, c'mon, Col. 'ave a drink with me, yeah?" There was a definite puppy dog look in those eyes.

Like there was any way Colin could refuse *that* look. And sleeping on the sofa wouldn't be a hardship.

"Fine, let's wet the baby's head," he said with a resigned sigh, taking the whiskey from Ed.

Ed beamed as he raised his glass. "To Baby Davis, whatever 'er name turns out to be. Long life and much 'appiness to 'er." He winked. "Though with those two for fathers, that little girl is goin' to be spoilt rotten." He knocked back a third of the tumbler and then looked at Colin with an expectant air.

Colin laughed and drank a quarter of the whiskey. He stared pointedly at Ed. "There. You happy now?"

Ed chuckled. "An' I've got just the thing we can watch on TV 'til we're ready to sleep." He put down his glass on the low coffee table which stood beside the sofa and lurched over to the bookshelf. He scanned the DVD cases, hands resting on the shelves to support himself.

Oh God, please *don't let him want us to watch het porn,* Colin prayed in his head. But when Ed turned to face him, DVD in hand, Colin cracked up.

"Oh Ed, you really are a one-off, do you know that?"

Ed frowned and looked down at the DVD in his hand. "So whass' wrong with it?"

Colin laughed. "Only you could celebrate a birth by watching the Australia vs England 2003 rugby test match."

Ed seemed perplexed. "What—you don't like this one?" His hand scrubbed across that sexy-as-fuck beard.

God, he's hot even when he's drunk.

Colin was *so* screwed.

He straightened his expression. "It's fine. Put it on." *Anything's better than the prospect of suffering straight porn,* he decided. And there was also the fact that it was one of Colin's favorite matches. Ed put the disk in the player and then sprawled out on the sofa next to Colin, glass in hand. It didn't take long before they were really into it, yelling at the TV screen. What made it more fun was that Colin was supporting the Australian team, although he wasn't prepared to share the reason for this unpatriotic behaviour.

Colin was impressed. Ed had put away a fair amount of beer since the match, and yet here he was, downing whiskey. If anything, the match on the screen seemed to energize him once more. He chuckled when Ed began shouting abuse at the referee. Colin was in complete agreement on that score. He didn't hold the New Zealand ref in high regard either.

"Less 'ave another, eh?"

Colin stared in amazement as Ed poured them both another glass of whiskey and then knocked his back.

Where the hell does he put it all? And how is he still able to function?

Colin took a cautious sip and then put his glass down on the coffee table. He was warm and relaxed, and life had taken on a nice, blurry edge.

Toward the end of the match, when Josh Lewsey performed an absolutely tremendous tackle on Matt Rogers, Ed let out a triumphant cry and flung an arm around Colin's neck. He dragged Colin's head down into his lap, whereupon he rubbed his knuckles over Colin's head, causing him to yelp in surprise.

"Ha! Looks like you chose the wrong team to support, mate," Ed said gleefully into his ear as he bent over Colin. Colin barely heard the insult. He was transfixed. His mouth was inches away from Ed's shorts, where it was easy to see the outline of his dick —his *half-hard* dick.

Oh my God—just kill me now. Then he thought about it. *How the fuck can he be semi-hard in his state? The man must have the constitution of an ox.*

Colin bit back a groan and struggled to right himself. Ed pulled away and sat back, chuckling, drinking the rest of his whiskey. He switched off the player and TV.

"You gotta admit, England were somethin'," Ed said with a grin.

Colin laughed. "Oh come on—they were already on a run of what, thirteen wins before this game? It was almost a foregone conclusion." Then he grinned. He couldn't resist the temptation. "And aren't *you* full of surprises?"

Ed tilted his head. "Whatcha mean?" The look of confusion on his face was adorable.

Colin gestured to Ed's crotch. "Well, I knew you loved playing rugby, but I never realized *watching* it gets you hard, too."

Ed glanced down to his erection and then met Colin's gaze. His eyes glazed over.

"So? You wanna give me an 'and with it, or what?" He lowered his eyes and grinned. "'Cause it looks to me like you got the same problem, mate." He waggled his eyebrows. "You do me, I'll do you. S'only fair."

It took a second or two for Ed's words to filter through to Colin's brain.

He's...he's not suggesting what I think he's suggesting—is he?

As if privy to Colin's thoughts, Ed stuck his hand down his shorts and pulled out his semi-erect cock. He held it around the base and waved it at Colin.

"Well? What about it?"

Colin was stunned. Even more so when Ed leaned against him, reached into Colin's shorts and briefs, and grabbed hold of his dick.

Oh my fucking God.

Ed let go of his own cock, grasped Colin's hand and pulled it across to his lap to press it around his shaft. Then he began to move slowly up and down Colin's length.

Colin stared for a moment, mesmerized by the slow, almost hypnotic movement. Then he grinned.

Oh, for God's sake—what more do you want? A written invitation?

And that was all it took to get his hand moving.

Colin stroked the hard column of flesh, relishing the feel of silky skin beneath his fingertips, while he made minute thrusts with his hips, pushing his dick through Ed's fist. Colin did his best to edge his shorts lower with one hand, unwilling to let go of Ed's ever-hardening shaft. Ed copied his movement and then spread his legs, sighing in contentment as Colin speeded up the sensual motion.

God, it's like being back in high school in the locker room. Colin remembered the mutual hand jobs of his youth, only this was infinitely better. He loved the feel of Ed's uncut cock as he tugged and pulled at it, Ed's hips rocking as he chased the sensations eagerly, his breath leaving him in short, sharp gasps. And Colin loved every minute of having Ed jack him off. The logical part of his brain was making a lot of sense. *Look, it doesn't mean anything. He's just drunk, so go with it. Enjoy it for what it is, because you may never get this chance again.*

Oh, Colin intended to enjoy it, all right.

Ed suddenly freed Colin's dick, pushed Colin's hand away from his own and then bent over his crotch to take Colin's hard dick into his mouth.

Colin's world came to an abrupt stop. He couldn't help the loud groan that rolled out from between his lips as Ed sucked him deep like he'd been sucking cock his entire life.

Oh FUCK, he's good at that.

Colin went onto autopilot. He placed his hands lightly on Ed's head and held him there while he pushed up with his hips, thrusting into that hot, wet cavern. *Sheer fucking heaven.* The appreciative noises escaping from around his dick told him in no uncertain terms that Ed was enjoying his task. Ed's fingers dug into his thighs as he bobbed up and down on his shaft, and Colin gasped as he was brought to the edge of orgasm within minutes.

"Gonna come," he fired out, and Ed pulled away immediately just as Colin's cock erupted, spattering come over his rugby shirt. Colin sagged back into the sofa, panting. That had been the hottest blowjob he'd experienced in a hell of a long while. He glanced toward Ed, unable to keep the smile from his face—and then stared in shock as Ed leaned against the cushions, hand around his rock-hard cock.

"Now it's your turn," he said with a wide grin.

Colin hesitated, even though a voice inside his head screamed *very loudly* at him to *get the fuck on with it.* As much as he wanted to get his mouth on that luscious dick, he knew Ed wasn't thinking clearly in his present state. *You'd be taking advantage of him, pure and simple.*

Ed raised his eyebrows. "Aw, come on. Fair's fair, right?" He pulled back the silken foreskin to reveal that wide, flared head, already wet with pre-come.

Oh, sod it.

Colin leaned over, wrapped his hand around the base of Ed's dick and took him deep.

"Fucking *HELL!*" Ed arched his back off the sofa, eyes wide as Colin went to town. His cheeks hollowed as he sucked on his cock, moaning quietly at the taste of him, the rich, manly smell emanating from Ed's pubes, a scent which filled his senses. He was oblivious to everything but giving Ed the blowjob of his life.

God, the noises he makes. It was such a turn-on. Colin licked and sucked for all he was worth, tightening his lips around the thick shaft as he went lower. Ed pushed up enthusiastically, hips pumping as he thrust into Colin's mouth with increasing speed. Colin moved his hand along the stony length as he took Ed deeper, and then stroked his fingers over Ed's fuzzy balls, savouring the weight of them in his hand.

"Oh fuck, I'm comin'." Ed's breathless cry had Colin releasing him, and mere seconds later Ed shot his load, come narrowly missing Colin's face. Ed grabbed his cock and squeezed it, shuddering as the last drops of come pulsed from it. Colin sat back and took in the sight of Ed in the full throes of orgasm.

Fuck, he's gorgeous when he comes.

Ed lay back, breathing heavily for a moment and then grinned at Colin. "Nice one, mate!" He pulled his shorts up and fastened them. Then he got to his feet and staggered into another room, returning a minute later with a light blanket and a couple of pillows which he dropped at one end of the sofa. He winked at Colin. "'Bout time we got rid of all this mud, wouldn't ya say? I'll grab a shower, an' then you can 'ave one. I'll leave out some towels for ya." And with that he walked, unsteadily, to the bathroom and closed the door behind him. The sound of the shower running followed shortly after.

Colin collapsed back against the cushions, staring at the ceiling. *That was a dream...right?*

Then he glanced down at his come-spattered shirt. *Er, apparently not.*

He closed his eyes and focused on the sensations he'd just experienced, trying to fix the details in his mind. The smell of Ed, rich and earthy. The feel of that silken flesh under his tongue. The taste of that thick, long cock. The noises—oh *God*, he'd never forget those sounds that poured out from Ed's mouth as he came.

I can't believe we did that. Even with the evidence on his clothing, and the smell of sex in the air, Colin still felt the whole situation had an unreal quality about it.

Look, stop analysing the shit out of it. It happened, yeah? And it was fucking AMAZING. So leave it at that. It's not like it's going to happen again, right?

He was stopped in the middle of his thought processes when the bathroom door opened and Ed strolled into the living room, a white towel wrapped around his hips.

"Bathroom's all yours, Col. You should 'ave everythin' you need in there. Good night, mate. Sleep well." Ed gave him a sleepy grin and then entered his bedroom and closed the door.

Colin stared at the closed door, shaking his head in astonishment. Then he sighed and headed into the bathroom.

He sagged against the tiled wall of the shower and let the jets pummel away the dirt and grime of the day, his eyes closed, mind replaying the scene on a loop.

The sad thing? Ed's probably not going to remember half *of this in the morning.*

Whereas Colin would find it difficult to forget.

Ed yawned and stretched out under the white sheet. Another warm June night meant that at some point during the night he'd kicked off the lightweight summer duvet. His bedroom window was open, and the noise of the street below filtered through, annoying the hell out of him. His head throbbed.

Oh God—just how much did I drink last night?

He glanced at the clock beside his bed and then stared at it in disbelief. It was already gone ten o'clock.

He sat up in bed and rubbed his aching head, yawning widely. Coffee was the first thing on the agenda. Ed got out of bed and padded naked to the door—and then stopped dead.

Oh bloody 'ell.

He'd totally forgotten he had a guest.

Colin Reynolds lay face-down on the sofa, fast asleep, the light blanket thrown to the floor, leaving him in just a pair of white briefs. Ed stood in the doorway to his bedroom, his gaze traveling over Colin's wide back and muscular thighs. Colin wasn't skinny, but then again he wasn't as muscular as Ed.

He's got a great arse, though. Look how tight those briefs are, stretched across those firm cheeks. God, you can even see his crack through 'em.

Ed froze, stunned that he'd even notice such things. And then it all came flooding back to him. The hand-jobs. *Oh fuck—the blowjobs.* His mind wasn't exactly firing on all eight, but it was awake enough to recall his mouth around Colin's cock. Not to mention Colin sucking him off—at Ed's insistence. His cheeks burned at the memory of Colin's initial hesitancy.

How the fuck can I face 'im this morning?

Okay, so it wasn't Ed's first blowjob with a guy, not by a long shot, but that had been a bloody long time ago and this was his *mate*, for fuck's sake.

Oh God, just kill me now...

There was no way Ed could get his brain around this without coffee. He stepped back into the bedroom and pulled on a pair of shorts, and then crept quietly past the sleeping Colin into the kitchen. He wasn't ready to face him, not just yet—and definitely not without at least two mugs of coffee inside him.

Ed stood in his little kitchen, staring out of the window as the coffee machine did its thing. The view wasn't particularly pretty—just blocks of flats and office buildings—but it wasn't as if he was registering it anyway. His mind was fixed firmly on what the hell he was going to say when Colin woke up.

Ed poured himself a mug and took a long drink. He sighed at that first hit of caffeine. *God bless the humble coffee bean.* Standing in his kitchen, the rich aroma of the coffee pervading the air, he tried to focus his thoughts on the best solution.

And that was when he decided that the best course of action was to say...nothing.

Yeah. Much better idea.

Ed poured a second mug and walked into the living room. He placed the mug on the coffee table and gave Colin a gentle shove on the shoulder. When that got little reaction, he gave a slightly more forceful push.

Colin turned his head slowly to stare at him. "What time is it?" He blinked.

"'Bout ten thirty. There's a coffee for ya," he said, pointing to the mug.

Colin sat up, stretching his arms high above him and yawning. Ed perched at the other end of the sofa and sipped his coffee, keeping his eyes fixed on the floor. The silence felt awkward.

Colin took a drink of coffee and then cleared his throat. "Look, if you're feeling embarrassed about last night, it's—"

"Well, I certainly 'ave an 'angover this mornin'," Ed said, cutting off Colin's words as neatly as if he'd used a knife. "I don't suppose you feel all that bad, considerin' you 'ad far less to drink." He didn't miss the flash of hurt in Colin's eyes, but there was no way he wanted to talk about it. He only hoped to God he hadn't fucked up their friendship.

His words definitely had an effect. Colin grabbed his rugby gear from the previous day and got dressed in front of him, without a word. He drained the mug and gave Ed a smile that didn't reach his eyes.

"Actually, I think I'll be going now. Thanks for the use of your sofa and for the coffee, but I really need to go home and get on some clean clothes." He made no effort to approach Ed, but instead went toward the door. "I'll see you next Saturday at the match, all right?" One last half-smile, and then he was gone.

Ed let out a groan. Colin had never been one to shy away from physical contact with Ed, even if it was just a slap on the back when they parted company. This uncharacteristic aloofness made Ed's heart sink.

God, I really fucked it up this time.

He sank into the sofa and stared at the ceiling. He tried closing his eyes, but all he could see was the action replay of the night before.

"No!" With an even louder groan, he opened his eyes. He had to get out of the flat and find something to occupy him. The he remembered. It was Sunday, and that meant only one thing—lunch at his mum's house. Ed normally tried to go to Sunday lunch twice a month, and he was overdue.

Lunch with his mum—just the thing to keep his mind off where his mouth had been last night. And as for Colin's efforts?

Nope. Not gonna go there.

CHAPTER THREE

Ed clambered off his Harley and then locked the garage door, grateful as always that Mum had somewhere secure to store it. Hackney wasn't the most salubrious of boroughs, and Ed had lost count of the number of times he and his siblings had begged her to move. Of course, that was about as likely as the next Pope being called Isaac.

Yeah, well, you should know. You inherited that stubborn streak from somewhere.

He gazed at the three-bedroom council house where he'd grown up with his brother and three sisters. They'd all left home by now, except that his sister Deborah, the youngest at twenty-one, had recently moved back in. Her excuse had been that she needed support while she was studying to be a nurse. All the kids knew this was bullshit, however. Debs was there solely to make life a bit easier for Mum. Things had been tough since Dad had died of a heart attack in his mid-fifties a few years ago.

Ed pushed open the back door that he knew would be unlocked and stepped into the kitchen. As usual, everything was gleaming. Woe betide any dirt that dared to show itself in his mum's kitchen. He sniffed the air appreciatively.

"Hi, Mum!" he called out. "Lunch smells good."

Mum appeared in the doorway and smiled. "Thought you were gonna give me a miss this month," she said in a quiet voice.

Ed crossed the room and wrapped her in a tight hug. "As if," he said into her ear, and then kissed her cheek. He released her and stepped back, scanning her features. He frowned. "You look tired, Mum." Her grey hair was pulled back from her face, and he couldn't help noticing the lines around her green eyes.

She waved a hand at him and huffed. "No more tired than usual." She walked over to the teapot and poured herself a cup. Ed pulled back a chair from under the kitchen table and sat down. The house was quiet.

"Where's Debs?"

Mum pointed toward the ceiling. "She's in 'er room, revisin'. She's got exams this week." She shook her head, smiling fondly. "She works bloody 'ard, that girl."

"An' who else is comin'?" Ed wanted to know. He hoped more of his siblings were on their way. Maybe it was time for a talk about giving Mum more money. Ed sent her money every month, they all did, but she still insisted on carrying on her job as a cleaner, something she'd done ever since Ed was old enough to ask what she did when she left the house.

Come on, Mum, he said silently. *Surely it's time to retire, right?*

It would be no use saying this to her face. Mum could be bloody-minded when she wanted to be. No, to tackle this, he'd need back-up. They all earned enough to provide her with an income so she didn't have to clean anymore.

"Phil can't come, he's too busy, but Tracy and Yvonne will be 'ere." Mum pierced him with a look. "You *do* know I can read your mind, yeah?"

Ed feigned innocence. "What are you on about?"

She snorted. "Don't think I don't know what you all talk about behind me back." Her expression became wistful. "Look, workin' keeps me occupied. If I was at 'ome all day, I'd 'ave too much time on me 'ands."

And he knew exactly how she'd pass that time. Dad had been gone for about five years, but Ed knew she still missed him, like they all did. He could understand her wanting to keep busy. Anything so that she wouldn't dwell on thoughts of Dad.

"Mum, there are loads of things you could be doin' with your time, ya know?" he said with a sigh. She'd worked hard her whole life—hell, so had his Dad—and he really wished she'd take it easy. After all, the only reason he was able to send her money was because they'd pushed him when he was younger. Not many kids from his neck of the woods made it into the local grammar school, but his parents had been determined when they'd seen his achievements in school. Ed had sat the entrance exams for the grammar school and then had been given a full scholarship. Not that life there had been all that pleasant—there were always going to be kids who looked down their noses at a boy from Hackney whose dad was a binman and whose mum was a cleaner. Thank God for Blake.

"Why don't you make yourself useful an' lay the table?" she suggested, handing him the cutlery.

And that's the end of that conversation.

Ed couldn't wait for his sisters to get there. Even though their chatter was sometimes annoying, anything was better than what was going on in his head right at that moment. All he wanted to do was tune out the thoughts that wouldn't leave him alone.

Ed let himself into the flat and went straight to the cabinet where he kept the alcohol. He poured himself a glass of whiskey and then downed it, gasping as the fiery liquid hit the back of his throat. Lunch had been good, but he'd been unable to shake himself free of the thoughts which had plagued him ever since he'd walked into his living room that morning. He'd stayed longer than usual at Mum's, chatting with his sisters, catching up on their lives, all in the hope that it would help clear his head.

Yeah, an' that really worked, huh?

The events of last night nagged at him. Two things in particular disturbed him about the whole thing. One, that he'd enjoyed the blowjob as much as he had. Okay, so it had been a while, but bloody hell, it was way better than he remembered. And that *was* disturbing. But what was infinitely worse was that he'd walked into that room, seen

Colin's arse, and *really* appreciated it—when he was sober. Hungover, but definitely sober.

There is no WAY I'm gonna start lookin' at guy's arses, he told himself. *I am not fuckin' GAY. Never mind what I got up to in the past. That was just experimentation, right? It didn't mean anything...right?* The thought had him pouring another glass and knocking it back just as quickly as the first.

Panic bubbled inside him. He had to do something—and fast. He opened the drawer in the cabinet and fished out his address book. He flipped through the pages until he found Michelle's number. *God, how long has it been since I saw her? Eleven months at least.* For all Ed knew, Michelle could be happily married by now. They'd dated off and on—more off than on if he were honest—and it had been mostly for the convenience of sex. Neither of them had been looking for anything permanent.

He dialled her number, silently praying she hadn't changed it, and that she was still the little horny bunny he remembered. When Michelle answered after a few rings, he had to fight hard to bite back his sigh of relief.

"Hey, babe, 'ow's it goin'?"

"Bloody hell, Ed Fellows! Where you been, you bastard?" Michelle sounded delighted to hear him.

He snickered. "Yeah, I've missed you too. Listen, you doin' anythin' tonight?" His stomach churned and his chest was tight as he awaited her response.

"Aww, you in need, babe?" Her chuckle lightened his anxiety. "Well, as it happens, I *am* free this evening. You wanna pop round? God, I must be psychic—I bought a bottle of that whiskey you were always so fond of, just yesterday." She cackled. "I must've known you were coming."

Oh, thank God for that. "What time?"

"Eight o'clock?" Michelle suggested. "That'll give me time to tidy up the place." That chuckle reverberated through his head once more. "Not that it matters—you just want to see the inside of my bedroom, don't you, babe?"

Thank fuck she hadn't changed. Ed laughed. "God, you know me far too well."

Michelle joined in with the laughter. "Yeah, well, life's too short to mess about. I'll be waiting, okay? Just make sure you come packing that horse dick of yours. I've missed him." She hung up.

Ed pocketed his phone and gave the whiskey bottle a glance. Then he gave himself a quick mental shake.

You've 'ad enough, mate. Besides, brewer's droop is the last thing you need right now, eh?

Oh God, yes.

Ed got out of the foul-smelling elevator as fast as he could and walked briskly to Michelle's door. *Fuck, why do people feel the need to piss in elevators?* He shuddered as he rang her bell. When the door swung open, Michelle poked her head around it and grinned.

"Get in here. Don't want the neighbours seeing me in this state."

Ed stepped into the little hallway and burst out laughing when he caught sight of her. The almost transparent negligee left little to the imagination. "Oh, you're rarin' to go, ain't ya?"

She returned his grin and reached out to grab his crotch and squeezed hard. Her eyebrows lifted in obvious surprise. "Yeah, but *you* aren't, that's for sure." Then she winked. "I'd better see what I can do about that, eh?" She grabbed his hand and led him into her bedroom.

Warm lamps lit the room. Michelle wasted no time undressing him and throwing his jeans and T-shirt over a chair.

"Bleeding hell, Ed, I swear you've got even more muscles than the last time I saw you. You living in a gym or what?" She stroked his biceps and then ran her fingers over his pecs, brushing lightly across his nipples, making Ed catch his breath. She caressed his abs and turned admiring eyes up to gaze at him. "Talk about a six-pack. And thank God you haven't gone for the shaven look. I like a man with hair." She stroked his beard. "And I really like this."

Ed chuckled. "God, just think 'ow long it would take me to get rid of this lot," he said, gesturing to his body. He caught his breath once more as she trailed her fingers lower, to where his dick lay against his thigh—flaccid.

Oh fuck.

Michelle pushed him back onto the bed and then knelt in front of him on the soft-looking rug. She took his dick in her hand and grinned up at him.

"Oh, don't you worry, babe. All he needs is a little encouragement." And then she took him into her hot, waiting mouth.

Ed dropped onto the bed and closed his eyes, concentrating on the sensation. For the first time in his life, his cock took its time to harden. He squeezed his eyes tight shut, focusing on the feel of Michelle's tongue as she worked his shaft.

Come on. You always said that mouth of hers was sheer heaven.

Not now, it wasn't. Heaven was rougher, faster—and with a hint of stubble.

Ed opened his eyes wide. What the fuck…?

He sat up and grabbed Michelle roughly, pulling her up onto the bed and then rolling on top of her, kissing her hungrily. She responded, and he ground his crotch against her, loving the moan that escaped her lips.

That's it. That's better.

Their kisses seemed to ignite a fire in him. He propped himself up on his hands and thrust against her. She reached down and grasped his dick, tugging it. For a moment he saw her expression falter, but then she recovered. She opened a drawer beside the bed and pulled out a condom. She tore it open and rolled the thin latex over his length.

Ed pushed into her hand, relieved to find his shaft at least half-hard.

Michelle spread her legs wide. "C'mon, Ed. Fuck me," she whispered, guiding his dick to her entrance.

Ed froze. He stared down at her face, her eyes wide, incredulity plainly written there.

What the fuck is wrong with me?

With a loud groan he grabbed her by her hips and flipped her onto her stomach. He pulled her hips toward him, before pushing up the negligee to bare her arse. She gasped, before spreading her legs once more.

For a moment he gazed down at the smooth globes of her arse—except it wasn't her arse he was seeing in his head. It was Colin's. Those firm cheeks. The way he filled those tight briefs. The shadow of his crease through the stretched fabric. Ed's cock began to fill.

Then he looked down at Michelle as she lay before him, arse tilted, her breathing rapid. He thought of sliding into her warmth.

And it was then that his dick decided it wasn't going to play anymore.

"Look, it happens to all blokes, right?"

Ed knew she was trying to make him feel better, but the point was, it had never happened to him. Ever. Not. Fucking. Once. He sat on her sofa, back stiff, uncomfortable as hell. And definitely *not* in the mood for a post-mortem on his spectacularly abysmal performance.

"Well, you'd already had a drink before you got here, hadn't you? I could smell it. Maybe that was it." She leaned forward and lightly stroked his forearm.

No, definitely not helping. The one thought burning into his brain was that he'd been totally smashed last night, and yet he'd had no problem getting it up for Colin. Hell, he'd almost come just from the feel of that mouth on him. So blaming it on the booze? Wasn't gonna work.

"You know what?" he said, getting to his feet. "I think I should just leave."

Michelle's mouth fell open. "What? Don't you want to stay a while?" The sympathy he saw in her eyes was too much to bear.

He shook his head and tried to force a smile. "Let's leave it, okay? I just wanna go 'ome." He slunk to her front door, conscious of her following him. He turned at the threshold and kissed her on the cheek. "Sorry if I spoiled your evening." When she opened her mouth, undoubtedly about to protest, he covered her lips with a single finger. "Leave it, please, okay, Michelle? Just...leave it."

Eyes troubled, she nodded and held the door open for him. He exited the flat and walked slowly to call the elevator. As it arrived he looked back. Sure enough, Michelle was watching him, a plain robe clutched around her. The expression of sadness and concern on her face tugged at his heart. He turned his head away and entered the elevator.

Just get me out of 'ere.

He sat in the taxi, oblivious to the sights and sounds as the cab made its way through the busy, noisy streets. All he could think of was Colin. That image rose up once more in his head, and he groaned as his cock twitched.

Oh FUCK.

There was no getting away from it. He couldn't blame his reactions on the alcohol anymore. Once? Possibly. Twice? No fucking way.

He leaned forward, elbows on knees, head in hands.

Colin, mate...what the fuck have you done to me?

CHAPTER FOUR

It was no good. No amount of coffee was going to improve his mood this morning.

Ed stomped out of the office kitchen, mug in hand. Of course, it had only made matters worse that he'd had to make his own coffee that morning, what with Blake being on paternity leave.

Funny the things you take for granted. Like walkin' into the office and smellin' the coffee 'cause your angel of a boss got there before ya, like he always does, and got the machines workin'.

Not that he begrudged Blake the time spent with Will and the baby, who, according to a text that morning, now had a name—Sophie.

Ed was doing his best to start the day right, but it just wasn't happening. For one thing, he'd had hardly any sleep. He'd lost count of the number of times he'd gazed at his clock and groaned because the slumber he craved was eluding him. By the time the alarm had gone off at six-thirty, Ed was exhausted and grouchy as hell.

He stayed in his office for as long as possible, trying to deal with his emails, but just looking at the screen made his head ache. The prospect of leading the team meeting at nine made his heart sink.

I just wanna be on me own today. Is that too much to ask?

He already knew the answer to that one.

At eight-fifty, Ed walked into the conference room and stopped. Sitting at the table, mug in hand and with a huge, shit-eating grin on his face, was Rick. In spite of his mood, Ed broke into a smile.

"Hey, mate, you're back!" He pulled up a chair next to Rick and sat down.

Rick positively glowed. He put down his mug and leaned back in his chair, hands laced behind his head. "Yeah, we got back last night. How's it going here in the real world?" His eyes were bright, skin tanned a warm shade of brown. "I gather from Beth I missed all the excitement on Saturday."

Ed snorted. "Trust you to be out of the country when shit 'its the fan. Don't worry, though—we coped. And Blake says the baby is beautiful."

Rick nodded. "Will sent me a pic." He got his phone out of his pocket and scrolled through. He handed the phone to Ed, who gazed at the gorgeous photo of Blake cradling the sweetest little baby he'd ever seen. And Ed didn't 'do' babies, so that was saying something. The adoring look on Blake's face was beautiful to behold.

Rick sighed. "That kid is going to be *soooo* spoiled."

Ed handed the phone back with a nod, then gave Rick a speculative glance. "So, 'ow was Italy? Did Angelo tan your arse for eyeing up the fit blokes?"

Rick snorted. "He could try." There was that happy look again. "Oh Ed, it was great. We went to Florence, Rome, Naples, Pompeii, Siena...I tell you, going around a foreign country with someone who speaks the language is a definite plus in my book. And Oh My God—Venice. It was...beautiful."

Ed couldn't get over how relaxed Rick looked. It had been his and Angelo's first trip to Italy, and Ed knew it was a big thing. Although the two men had been together for over six years, it had taken Angelo that long to work up enough courage to take Rick to meet some of his family. Not all of them, certainly—there were still loads of more traditional family members who wanted nothing to do with the lovers. But Angelo's younger cousins were a different generation and Rick had been so excited at the prospect of meeting them. He'd talked of little else in the months leading up to the trip.

The door opened and the rest of the team filed in, everyone breaking into excited chatter when they caught sight of Rick. Ed had to admit, the office had been quiet without the voluble Head of Marketing and Sales. Rick was hugged and patted while he answered question after question. Ed let it go on for a few minutes until the noise level began to make his head throb.

He cleared his throat. "'ow 'bout we get this meetin' started, eh, people? Then we can get around to doin' some actual work in 'ere." He gave them all a hard stare, but it was no use. They were far too used to him by now. Still, they sat down and let him lead the meeting with the minimum of interruptions. After thirty minutes or so, Ed had gone through everything Blake had sent his PA, Shane, via email and the team dispersed. He grabbed more coffee and retreated to his office, where he sat behind his desk and stared out of the window while he sipped the hot, aromatic brew.

God, Blake, where are ya when I really need to talk to ya? Your timin' sucks.

He didn't mean it. His head was a mass of confusing thoughts in chaotic collision. All he could think about was Saturday night—and Colin. He tried looking at it logically, but logic didn't seem to be working. And as the morning wore on, his frustration only increased. By lunchtime, things were no better. He'd spent most of the morning trying to focus on the applications Blake had asked him to go through for his new PA, since Shane would be leaving them within a few weeks.

And that was another thing that was pissing him off. Shane had been Will's replacement, and things had worked out great. He was a lot quieter than Will—although he was coming out of his shell more and more lately—and tended to fade into the background at team meetings, but he was extremely capable and Blake had been delighted with him. Until the day a few weeks back when Shane had come into work and told them all that his fiancée had just got a new job as a pharmaceutical chemist—in Australia—and the two of them were going to be moving out there as soon as everything was sorted out.

Talk about droppin' us right in it.

Ed had a pile of forms on his desk to go through, so he could invite prospective candidates for interview. Blake had made it clear that he trusted Ed's judgment implicitly. The most experienced applicant was female, however. Ed snorted at the thought of another female PA.

Blake's track record with the fairer sex was the reason why he'd gone for a male PA in the first place.

And look 'ow that worked out, Ed thought wryly. *You ended up marryin' 'im.*

At least sorting through the applicants kept his mind away from...other things.

Yeah, right. Colin never left his thoughts. Not once.

When lunchtime came, Ed went into the kitchen to pour himself another coffee. Rick was there, munching enthusiastically on chicken salad. When he saw Ed, he put down his fork and sighed.

"Okay, give it up. What's going on with you today?"

Ed stared at him in dismay. "What makes you think anythin's wrong?"

Rick opened his eyes wide and barked out a laugh. "Oh come on. You think I'm *that* blind?"

Ed's retort was on the tip of his tongue, but Beth chose that moment to wander into the kitchen, and Ed used the diversion to escape to the haven of his office. He sank into his chair, leaned back and closed his eyes.

How could a little thing like a blowjob screw up me mind like this?

Except, of course, he knew it wasn't the blowjob.

After lunch things were no better. The lack of sleep began to catch up with him, and unfortunately it affected those around him. Conversations were abrupt, nothing like his usual breezy manner, and they grew shorter as the afternoon wore on. He could see the surprise on the faces of the team. Ed told himself that he'd make it up to them the next day, providing he got a decent night's sleep. But at this rate, he'd be taking them *all* for a drink on Friday after work, to apologize. Thank God the day was nearly over.

Karen stuck her head around his office door. "Ed, the Frankfurt printers have emailed us. There seems to be a problem with—"

"Oh, for God's sake, just forward me the email, okay?" Ed barked at her. "You don't 'ave to come 'ere bleatin' at me. I've got better things to do, all right?"

Karen paled. "I...I'm sorry I disturbed you." She withdrew hastily.

Ed put his head in his hands. Now *look what you did.* He'd never spoken so harshly to Karen before, and what made it all the worse was that he knew she had a soft spot for him. She always greeted him with a smile. In the years since she'd kicked her rat of a boyfriend into touch, Karen had changed considerably. Gone was the whole man-eater look, the heavy make-up, the excessive jewelry. Karen had become like a mum to the team, someone they relied upon.

And that makes it even worse. God, the look on her face....

Ed sighed. Time for a last coffee. He got up, left the office and entered the small kitchen. Thankfully, no one was there, and there was just enough coffee left to fill a mug. Ed poured it out and then cleaned the jug and emptied the machine, ready for the following morning.

"Can you come with me for a minute?" Rick stood in the doorway, his brow creased.

It was on the tip of Ed's tongue to make an excuse, but the expression on Rick's face gave him pause. "Sure."

He followed Rick along the corridor and into the conference room. Rick closed the door behind them, and then gestured for Ed to take a seat. Ed sat, his gaze trained on the unusually serious Rick.

Rick regarded him intently for a moment and then sighed. "Look, I don't know what's been going on with you today, but you've pissed off a lot of people. You've had Karen in tears, and over nothing, by the sound of it." He locked eyes with Ed. "If you don't straighten up and get over this, whatever this is, I'm gonna call Blake."

Ed froze. The last thing he wanted was for Blake to start worrying about Ed's ability to do his job. *Christ, he relies on* me *to keep things runnin' smoothly around here.* And then it dawned on him. Okay, so he couldn't talk to Blake. But sitting in front of him was a good friend—who happened to be gay.

And possibly the only bloke I know right now who has a fuckin' clue what I'm goin' through.

That decided him.

"Look, I think I need to talk to you, but not 'ere."

Rick said nothing, his expression unchanged. Then he pulled his phone from his jacket pocket and punched in a number. "Babe? Listen, I'm going to be a bit late, okay? There's a crisis at work. I'll call you when I'm on my way home, all right?" He listened intently and then smiled. "I love you too. Keep it warm for me." He hung up and then got to his feet. "We're the last. Everyone's gone home. So go grab your jacket and we'll get out of here. You can come back for your bike later."

Ed nodded and went into his office to pick up his leather biker's jacket. Rick was waiting for him by the main doors. Ed made sure everything was switched off and then locked the doors. The whole time, his heart was pounding.

What the 'ell is Rick gonna say?

The quiet little pub was just around the corner from the Trinity building, and it was the favorite haunt for after-work drinks for most of the team. Thankfully it hadn't started filling up yet.

Rick leaned back into the corner booth, pint glass in hand. "Okay. Spill it."

Ed took a deep breath, and then it all came tumbling out. The hand-jobs. Blowjobs. The way Colin had looked that morning. Ed's failure to perform with Michelle. The way his dick hardened when he thought of Col's arse. Ed didn't spare him any details—this wasn't the time for being coy.

Rick sat there, saying nothing. When Ed finally finished, he met Rick's gaze. "That's everythin'."

Rick took a good, long, deep breath. "There's a chance you're bi. Or maybe you just have a thing for this particular guy. I mean, it's not like you've done this before, right?"

Ed's cheeks burned. He cleared his throat. "Yeah, about that…"

Rick's eyes widened. His mouth dropped open. "Oh my God. When Angelo and I got together. You, me and Blake talking. Me making some joke about how maybe you were working with the wrong plumbing. And Blake snorted." He started laughing. "I thought at the time something was up." He arched his eyebrows. "You might as well come clean, Mr. Fellows. You've told me everything else."

"Look, it's no big deal, all right?" Ed spluttered. "It's just…. Well… you know Blake and me were at the same school, yeah? Well, we both played on the school rugby team. Anyway, one day after a match, Blake walked in on me and Derek Melling givin' each other an 'and-job in the changin' room when we thought everyone 'ad gone." He sighed, his cheeks flaming red. "The bastard teased me about that for bleedin' years afterward."

"Well, that's not so bad," Rick conceded. "All boys probably experiment like that at some point or other." He narrowed his gaze, his lips twitching. "There's more, isn't there?"

Ed nodded. "When I was at uni, one night my room-mate and me got pissed, and ended up givin' each other blowjobs. Only, it got to be a regular thing, see? And yeah, it 'appened when we were sober, too." He stared at Rick. "But that was all I did, all right? Nothin' else. I 'aven't 'ad sex with a bloke."

Rick snorted. "I hate to tell you this, but a blowjob *is* oral sex. Unless your name is Bill Clinton, of course." His expression softened. "Okay, maybe you're bi, maybe not. If you *do* have a thing for this guy, that could explain why things didn't go as well with Michelle."

Ed stared at him in despair. "What am I gonna do?" His chest was tight, his mouth dry.

Rick smiled. "You're gonna figure it out, that's what. Ed, I've known you all these years. We're mates, yeah?" Ed nodded. "I've never seen you run from *anything*. You're just going to have to take the bull by the horns and deal with it. That's how you deal with everything else—why should this be different?"

Ed became very still. "What do you mean? How can I deal with it?"

Rick shrugged. "Ask this guy out."

Ed boggled. "Like, a date?"

Rick nodded. "It could be for something as simple as a meal and a drink. But when you meet him, think about how you feel. Are you still attracted to him? Do you want to shag him, or would you rather go off and shag a girl? Because either way, mate, this is going to eat at you until you face up to it."

Ed knew he was right. God, it was already gnawing into him after only two days. If only it were that simple. "But he's straight."

Rick regarded him calmly. "You don't know that." Ed opened his mouth to say something, but then snapped it shut. Rick grinned. "I'm right, aren't I?" He folded his arms across his chest. "So you need to go home and think about what you're going to say to this bloke. Only, don't leave it too long. I'm not sure my nerves could take another day like today." He levelled a firm stare at Ed. "And you have got some *serious* grovelling to do tomorrow morning."

Ed let out a sigh. Life had suddenly gotten a lot more complicated.

CHAPTER FIVE

Ed arrived at work the following morning, his arms full. He left the large bouquet of flowers on Karen's desk, along with the pretty card bearing his apology. In the kitchen, he put the freshly made croissants and *pain au chocolat* onto plates, with a sign telling people to help themselves. And finally, he nipped into Rick's office and left a *very* large bar of his favorite chocolate on top of his keyboard.

Satisfied that he'd begun to make amends, Ed got the coffee machines going and then stood impatiently awaiting the first mugful. He'd spent all Monday night dwelling on Rick's advice. His first reaction had been one of panic.

But I'm not gay.

When he'd had time to think about it, the panic subsided, but only a little. Rick had been correct, of course, in his comment about oral sex. And maybe it was time for Ed to be truthful with himself. *Goin' back for repeated blowjobs isn't exactly the action of an entirely straight guy, is it?* There was no doubting he'd enjoyed them, too. His roommate, Don, had been very...enthusiastic.

Yeah. Maybe not so straight after all.

And considering he was about to ask a guy out on a date? Yeah, not so straight.

So...giving and receiving blowjobs? No problem. Thinking that he might be gay or bi? Yeah, that part didn't sit so easily.

His contemplative mood lasted throughout the morning. He apologized individually to each team member, and was relieved when they hugged and patted him, apparently with no ill-feeling. Karen loved the flowers—that was for sure. But Ed still wasn't feeling himself. He put up with the churning in the pit of his stomach until after lunch, and then he couldn't stand it any longer.

Ed pushed his office door shut and then got out his phone. The call connected, but it was several seconds before Colin spoke.

"Hi, Ed, what can I do for you?"

Ed groaned inwardly upon hearing the cautious note in his voice. Not that he blamed Colin, not after the way he'd spoken to him that Sunday morning.

"Hey, Col. D'ya fancy meetin' me for a pint an' maybe a bite to eat after you finish work this evenin'?" He kept his tone light.

"A pint? And food?" Another pause. Ed's stomach rolled over. At last Colin spoke. "Yeah, sure. Where do you want to meet?"

Oh thank God. "'Ow about the Elephant & Castle? Six-thirty sound okay?"

"Yes, that's fine. Look, you'll have to excuse me, Ed. I'm about to go into a meeting. I'll see you there." Colin hung up.

Ed let out his breath in a long exhale. One obstacle surmounted—but an even bigger one to come.

Ed entered the pub and glanced around. No sign of Colin yet. He went across to the bar and ordered a pint of lager. Nursing his glass, he grabbed a table in a quiet corner which could be seen from the bar and then sat back to wait. By the time he'd drunk half of it, Colin had arrived, jacket slung over his shoulder, white shirt unbuttoned at the collar and no tie. He spotted Ed and gestured if he wanted a drink. Ed held up his glass and Colin nodded.

Ed took the opportunity to study him as he waited at the bar. Colin was about five nine, with short, sandy-blond hair and pale blue eyes. He knew that beneath the white shirt was a wide chest with little hair on it. It was as if he was seeing Colin for the first time, only with new eyes.

Give 'im 'is due—Col's a good-lookin' man.

The thought didn't freak him out.

Colin approached Ed's table and sat down in the chair facing him. The first thing that struck Ed was his body language. Colin seemed unable to sit still. He crossed and then uncrossed his legs, fingered his collar, and then shifted his weight on his chair.

Ed sighed. *No time like the present.*

"I need to talk to you about what 'appened the other night. I know—"

Colin jumped in. "Look, we'd had a drink, and sometimes things just happen, yeah? But nothing's changed, okay? We're still mates." He took a long drink of his beer.

Ed's heart hammered as he lowered his head. He breathed in deeply. *Moment of truth.* "Maybe I want more," he murmured.

Silence. He stole a glance at Colin.

Colin gazed at him, a stunned, dazed expression on his face. "What...what did you say?"

Ed's face heated up. He raised his chin, squared his shoulders and looked Colin in the eye. "I said, maybe I want more."

Col sat there, mouth hanging open, astonished.

Ed's heart sank. *Oh fuck. Well, at least I know now.*

"I get it, you're straight. You've prob'ly got a girlfriend, too." Ed swallowed. "I know I shouldn't 'ave said anythin', but ever since we... *you* know....I 'aven't stopped thinkin' about it. I can't get it out of me mind." He let out his breath and sagged into his chair.

Colin looked distinctly perturbed. "Why do you assume I'm straight?"

Ed sat bolt upright. "Eh?"

Colin's eyes were cool. "Do you think all gay men run around with limp wrists, lisping? What about your boss, Blake? Does he act camp?" Ed shook his head, eyes wide. "Then why would you think I was straight?" Colin huffed. "You blokes kill me with this shit."

Ed stared at him open-mouthed. "But... you play rugby."

Colin laughed. "What, you think gay men can't play rugby? I've got the same equipment as you." He smirked.

Ed's mind was in a whirl. He was at a loss for words. Only one thing had gotten through.

Colin is gay.

Colin's eyes danced with amusement. "Well, you said you wanted more. How do you feel now you know? What are you going to do about it?"

Ed was sure even the tips of his ears were scarlet by now. He coughed.

Colin crossed his arms over that wide chest. "Go on then, ask me out. Let's go out on a date. You say you want more? So prove it." He leaned in close, his voice lowering. Colin's eyes gleamed. "Or do you just want me to suck your dick again?" Ed could hear the merriment in that voice.

Ed felt totally thrown off course. The one thing he did know was that Colin had just thrown down a gauntlet, and Ed never backed away from a challenge. Ever.

He straightened in his chair.

"Col, would you like to go out on a date with me?" Ed stuck out his chin, meeting Colin's gaze.

Colin didn't bat an eyelid. He sat back and crossed his arms once more. "Sure, when?" That smirk hadn't ventured off his face.

Ed swallowed. "Friday night. I'll pick you up at your place at 6.30, 'ow's that?"

Colin smiled. "That'll be fine."

Ed heaved a sigh of relief. "Okay, now we've got *that* sorted... What did you think of Saturday's game? Was it me, or is Murphy getting worse? I mean, he nearly dropped the ball twice!" *For God's sake let's talk about somethin' else—anythin' else.*

Colin laughed. "Yeah, I can't believe Trevor hasn't said anything yet to him."

Ed sat back and drank his lager, relaxed for the first time all day. This felt normal. This was him and Col, mates, discussing rugby, like nothing had happened.

Except, of course, that he'd just asked his *mate* out on a date. And his mate had said yes.

Ed was trying not to think about *that* part.

Ed stuck his head around Rick's door. "You got a minute?"

Rick looked up from his monitor and smiled. "Sure. Come on in."

Ed entered the office and shut the door behind him. He paced the floor in front of Rick's desk.

Rick laughed. "Whoa, what did *you* have for breakfast? Jumping beans?"

Ed snorted. "I was too bleedin' worked up to 'ave breakfast." He was still pacing.

Rick cocked his head to one side. "Well? Have you spoken to him yet?"

Ed turned his head to look at Rick. "Oh yeah, we spoke, all right. He only went an' said *yes*, didn't he?" The butterflies in his stomach had suddenly all taken to wearing Doc Martens.

Rick beamed. "Fantastic! So what's the problem?"

Ed stared at Rick. "What's the problem?" he mimicked. "Oh my God, Rick, I'm goin' on a date with a guy! What am I gonna do? I mean, where do I take 'im? What do I wear? Do I take 'im flowers, or what?"

Rick guffawed. "You need to calm down, mate. We'll figure it out." He scrubbed a hand across his cheek. "As for where to take him, the one to ask is Blake."

Ed stopped pacing. "I am *not* tellin' Blake. One, he's on leave, an' two, he's gonna be all *I told you so* as soon as he 'ears."

Rick snickered. "Well, there *is* that, I suppose. You don't have to tell him *who* the date is with, just that you want to impress...your date. 'Cause I'll bet you anything you like that Blake'll come up with somewhere really special if he knows it's important."

"Okay," Ed said grudgingly. Rick had a point.

"And as for what you wear," Rick continued, "make it smart-casual. Nothing too dressy, but nicely pressed, yeah?" Ed nodded. Then Rick grinned. "And never mind flowers—I'll get Angelo to recommend a really good bottle of wine. He's good at that."

Ed kept nodding, relieved to feel the panic receding.

Rick got to his feet, came around his desk and hugged Ed briefly. He stepped back, his eyes trained on Ed's face. "Feeling better now?"

"Yeah," Ed said, giving him a sheepish smile. "Sorry. I was thinkin' 'bout this all last night and I got into a bit of a panic."

Rick barked out a laugh. "Ya think?" Then his expression softened. "Okay, look. When's the date?"

"Friday."

Rick nodded. "And today is Wednesday, right? So you need to *stop* thinking about this, or you'll drive yourself nuts. Just get on with work, same as usual. And try not to think about it too much." He fixed Ed with a firm stare. "I mean it, Ed. Friday will get here soon enough without you wishing away the week."

Ed smirked. "Yes, *Dad*." He grinned as Rick pushed him out of his office. Still smiling, Ed went in search of caffeine.

Work now... think about date later, he told himself sternly.

Because Rick was right. Friday would be along all too soon.

Clutching the plastic bag containing a bottle of wine, Ed buzzed Colin's flat and then looked through the glass door at the wide, airy entrance hall to the building. He'd never been inside before. When he picked Colin up for rugby practice, he usually waited with his Harley until Colin came out. But tonight the bike stayed at home in its lock-up.

"Hello?" Colin's voice sounded metallic.

"It's me."

"Come on up. Second floor, apartment three."

Ed heard the buzz as the door clicked open. He entered, noting the polished marble floors, everywhere spotless—certainly nothing like Ed's block of flats. The elevator doors slid open to reveal mirrors on three sides. He pressed for the second floor. The ride was whisper-quiet and smooth. There was a familiar feel to the building, something Ed couldn't put his finger on. He stepped out of the elevator and quickly found apartment three. Before he could raise his hand to knock, Colin opened the door—and Ed caught his breath.

"Is that 'ow you're goin' to the restaurant?" he asked.

Colin laughed. "Do you want to get through the front door before you start asking questions?" He ushered Ed through into a small hallway. Ed couldn't take his eyes off Colin in his elegant suit in dark grey, pale blue shirt and matching tie.

Colin snickered. "Close your mouth, Ed, you're catching flies." His eyes were bright. "I take it you like me in a suit? Do I look good?"

Ed felt distinctly flustered. *Good*? The man looked *gorgeous*. What was *really* yanking his chain was that Ed's dick was sitting up and taking notice.

What the fuck is goin' on 'ere? One blowjob from this guy an' suddenly me inner Gay is released?

Colin's expression morphed into an empathetic look. "I'm sorry, I was running late, so I've only just got home. Give me about ten, fifteen minutes to grab a shower and get changed, and then we'll be on our way." He gestured to an open door. "Go sit down in the lounge and make yourself comfortable."

Ed went into the room, Colin behind him. As soon as Ed saw the spacious apartment he knew why the place had seemed familiar.

Oh my God—it's just like Blake's place.

There was that same minimalist feel to the place, the same elegance. And it was a world away from Ed's humble little flat in Lewisham. Despite the fact that he'd played rugby and drank with Colin most weekends for the past fourteen months, for the first time Ed felt out of his league.

"Do you want to tell me where we're going?" Colin called over his shoulder as he went through another door. Ed was too busy looking down at his clothing to reply. He'd worn a pair of well-fitting jeans, and a black shirt that was casual but ironed to perfection. Ed smoothed his hand over the shirt, and then rubbed his palm over a jeans-clad thigh, conscious of his clammy palm.

Oh for God's sake, there's nothin' to be nervous about. It's just dinner.

He listened to the sound of the shower running, trying not to think about Colin's naked body under the stream of hot water, soap running down over that lean torso...

Ed shook himself. He put down the bottle on the low, glass-topped coffee table and went for a look at the bookshelves. The first thing he spotted was Will's name. Ed grinned. Colin had every one of Will's books. *Well, well, well....*

The sofa was upholstered in a warm, brown leather, with deep cushions and thick arms, long enough to stretch out fully if someone wanted to take a nap there. A gas fire, complete with coals, was set into the wall, and a thick, cream rug sat on the polished floorboards below it. Ed spied small speakers here and there, hinting at a music system.

"Do you like the place?"

Ed turned to look at Colin as he came through the door.

Oh, fuck me.

He wore a pair of stunning, skin-tight Levis that showed off his arse to perfection. A deep marine-blue shirt in silk, that clung to his toned, muscular body. Okay, so he wasn't as built as Ed, but *damn*, Colin had muscles in *all* the right places.

An' why 'ave I never noticed that before?

Remembering his manners, Ed picked up the bottle of wine and handed it over.

Colin removed it from its bag and nodded in approval. He raised an eyebrow. "Is this for now, or maybe later?" His eyes twinkled, and for a second or two, Ed felt thrown off balance once again. Colin smiled. "Well, if you're driving, maybe later." He smirked. "And you still haven't told me where you're taking me."

Ed recovered himself sufficiently to grin. "It's a surprise."

Colin laughed and led the way to the front door. "In that case, let's be on our way."

Once they'd exited the building, Ed hailed a passing black cab. They got in and he rattled out the address of the restaurant in Soho.

Colin's eyes widened. "That's Daniel Farrington's new restaurant."

Ed blinked. "Er, yeah." The name obviously meant something to Colin. Ed had been none the wiser when Blake had mentioned it to him.

Colin whistled. "I'm impressed. From everything I've heard, it's difficult to get in there."

Ed gave a modest shrug. "Depends who you know." The restaurant was fairly new, but so far, according to Blake, it had received rave reviews. Apparently the dress code was casual, but Colin had been right about one thing—booking a table was a nightmare.

Thank God for Blake. His boss had pulled a few strings to get them in there.

It wasn't long before the cab pulled up outside the smart-looking restaurant. The two men were shown to their table and given the menus to peruse.

Ed glanced around. The lighting was subtle, as was the background music. Nearly every table was taken. The patrons ranged from couples, to the occasional groups of businessmen.

The waiter handed Ed the wine list. He looked at it for a moment, cleared his throat and then handed it to Colin.

"Why don't *you* choose somethin'?"

Colin smiled and then he gave the waiter his choice, before sitting back, looking completely at ease in his surroundings.

While I feel like a bleedin' fish out of water, Ed thought glumly. He was trying desperately to make a good impression, but he couldn't shake the thought that Colin was *way* out of his league. *I mean, that suit he wears to work, for a start.* Which got him thinking....

"Colin, I know I've never asked, 'cause it's never come up, but what is it you do exactly?"

Colin smiled. "I'm a graphic designer for a firm of architects. I do all their CAD work."

Ed was impressed. Colin had to be a bright guy to do that job. And judging from his clothes and his apartment, he was damn good at it, too.

"And you're the office manager for Trinity Publishing?" Colin asked him. "That sounds like an interesting job." He was trying desperately to get Ed to relax, because it was obvious his date felt out of his element. Colin still couldn't believe they were there. It had taken him a day or two to get over his shock at Ed's revelation. But now they were there? Colin was determined to make sure they had a good time—and that included his plans for after dinner.

If we ever get through this and make it back to my apartment.

Because Colin intended to blow Ed's mind.

He relaxed into his chair, his gaze focused on the man sitting opposite, who twisted his napkin in his hands.

"Listen, Ed. I'm the same guy that you showered with, sweated with, played rugby with, got drunk with..." Colin smiled. "I'm still the same guy."

To his relief, Ed's face cleared at his words. While they ate, they began to talk more, even tell jokes and share a few laughs. Colin was pleased to find out they had more things in common than he'd previously thought, especially when it came to music and films. When the subject got around to books, Ed grinned.

"Yeah, well, I couldn't 'elp but notice your book collection." His eyes sparkled.

Colin was confused by this for a moment, and then the penny dropped. He blushed.

"Oh God. You saw my collection of Will's books, didn't you?" Ed chuckled. Colin shook his head, cheeks hot. "You have *no* idea how hard it was to sit in that waiting room, on the same sofa as *Will Parkinson,* for God's sake, and not say anything!"

Ed snickered. "I bet you were dyin' to ask for 'is autograph, weren't ya?"

"Yes!"

Ed laughed, and the sound warmed Colin's heart. It was good to see Ed relax at last. Dessert came and went, as did the coffee, and Colin decided it was time to lead Ed into new waters.

He leaned across the table and lowered his voice. "Maybe we should go back to my place and break open that bottle of wine." He sat back and waited.

Ed stared at him for a moment, doing a favourable impression of a deer in headlights. And then he smiled.

"I'd like that."

Colin heaved an internal sigh of relief. *And now on to what I have in mind.*

A frisson of excitement danced up and down his spine at the thought of what was to come.

Hopefully.

CHAPTER SIX

As they went up in the elevator, Ed's heart was pounding nineteen to the dozen.

Come on, you're gonna have a glass or two of wine. Stop panickin'.

Except since when did a date end with a glass of wine?

And there went his heart, pounding away again.

Colin let them into the apartment and headed straight for the kitchen, returning with a corkscrew and two glasses. After opening the bottle, he poured it out and handed Ed a glass.

He watched as Colin swirled the ruby liquid, looked at it, smelled it.

Oh fuck—the man knows his wine. Angelo, you better 'ave done me proud...

Colin took a sip and then smiled. "Oh, that's good."

Ed could have wept with relief. He mentally promised to thank Angelo profusely the next time he saw him. Colin gestured to the sofa and they both sat, drinking their wine. The alcohol warmed Ed nicely. Gradually he began to relax again, as they chatted about upcoming matches, and the teams they'd be facing. Ed's nerves had all but dissipated by the time Colin asked if he wanted a refill.

"Sure." He handed Colin the glass, who filled it. Then his heart almost stopped when Colin handed him the glass—and then straddled his lap, facing him.

Ed froze. His mouth was suddenly as dry as the Sahara. He stared up at Colin, heart now beating so fast he was sure it would explode out of his chest.

Colin gently took the glass from his hand and stretched back to place it on the table. Then he leaned forward and kissed him on the lips, soft as a whisper.

Ed sat there, unable to move for a moment, startled by the feel of a definitely masculine cheek against his, a manly scent pervading his senses. Colin didn't even falter. He went right on kissing him, hands cupping his face now, big, strong, capable hands that left Ed in no doubt as to exactly *who* was kissing him.

And fuck, it felt good.

So good, in fact, that Ed began to kiss him back.

Colin smiled against his lips. "That's it. Just go with it." He moved to Ed's neck, sliding warm lips over the skin, kissing, sucking.

And Ed just...melted.

"Oh fuck," he whispered, letting out the tiniest moan as Colin sucked harder. Ed's cock hardened. God, this was nothing like he'd expected. And it really turned him on. As good as it felt to have Colin's mouth there, Ed knew what he wanted. He reached up and put his hands to the back of Colin's head, guiding him back to where he wanted him to be.

He wanted Colin's kiss.

Colin moaned appreciatively as he kissed Ed, his hands on Ed's shoulders. Ed gasped when Colin ran his tongue over Ed's lips, licking along the seam. Colin murmured softly. "Open for me, Ed."

Ed groaned and let him in.

Colin's tongue went deep, exploring him, tasting him. And fuck, Ed wanted more. He sucked on Colin's tongue. He slid his tongue into Colin's mouth, the kiss becoming wet, just perfect, as they devoured each other, their moans and low cries increasing. Ed could feel Colin's erection as he began to move, hips rolling. Ed let go of Colin's head and slid his hands lower, stroking his back, feeling the warm skin through the silk. Lower still, until he reached the waistband of his jeans. Colin's tongue went deep and Ed groaned into his mouth as he cupped that firm arse and squeezed.

Making out with a woman had never felt *this* fucking good. And Ed didn't want it to stop.

Colin kissed him hungrily, hands moving to undo the top buttons of his shirt, before sliding under the fabric to stroke his chest, fingers curling in the hair there. Ed moaned, wanting more—no, *needing* more.

"Please," he murmured, breaking the kiss. "Please, Col." He didn't know exactly what he needed, only that he did.

Colin stopped and looked down at him, lips reddened, eyes like liquid fire. He lifted himself off Ed's lap and held out his hand. Ed took it without hesitation and Colin pulled him to his feet and led him out of the lounge—and into his bedroom.

There was no time for nerves as Colin began to undress him, nibbling on his neck as he slid the shirt off Ed's shoulders. Ed threw his head back and gasped as Colin flicked his tongue over Ed's nipples.

Fuck, why has no one ever done that to me before now?

It was as if there was a direct connection from there to his dick—his increasingly rigid dick. And Ed made sure Colin knew how he felt about what was taking place.

"Fuck, yeah."

Colin grinned as he undid Ed's jeans and tugged them lower. He pushed Ed backward onto the bed and then pulled them from his legs. Ed moved farther up the bed and stared, eyes wide, as Colin stood before him, slowly undoing his shirt, revealing that glorious expanse of skin—that Ed couldn't wait to trace over with his tongue. He gazed at the firm, muscled thighs, the gorgeous cock which jutted out. Ed's dick rose, hard and aching, and he wrapped his hand around the base, stroking it slowly, his eyes fixed on Colin who got onto the bed and crawled toward him on hands and knees, still grinning.

Colin bent down and went straight for Ed's neck, stopping to suck at his earlobe. Ed shivered, unable to lie still as Colin moved down his body, kissing, licking, sucking, taking his time. As he neared Ed's dick, Ed whimpered, desperate to have that perfect mouth on him once more. Colin paused and looked up at him from under sandy-blond eyelashes, and then licked a firm line up from root to slit. Ed moaned.

But instead of taking the head of his dick into that hot heaven, Colin paused once more.

"Roll over," he said, his voice hoarse with desire.

Shaking, Ed did as he was told. He lay on his belly, gasping as Colin grabbed his hips and pulled them toward him.

"Spread your legs—wide."

Ed shifted his legs apart, body trembling now as he waited. Colin's cheek was rough as he kissed the globes of his arse. Ed caught his breath as Colin spread him wide and bit gently at his cheeks, before kissing where he had bitten.

And then all the breath left his body in a heady gasp at that first contact with Colin's tongue.

Oh Holy Fuckin' Mother of God. That feels...incredible.

Ed groaned into the pillow, clutching the sheets in tight fists as Colin licked around his hole, fluttering over it, and sucked it for what felt like hours. Colin's breath was hot against his crease, and Ed howled when he pushed at Ed's tight pucker with his tongue.

Ed let go of the sheet and reached back to grab Colin's head, forcing him to bury his face between Ed's cheeks. "Oh fuck, don't stop," he groaned. Colin chuckled as he pushed his tongue into Ed's body. Ed loved the rasp of Colin's rough cheek against his arse.

Ed pulled his knees under him and pushed back onto that agile tongue which was fucking his hole. Colin pulled his cheeks apart as he dove deeper, and the sounds he made were so fucking sexy.

Fuck, I could let 'im do that all fuckin' day.

And then everything stopped, as Colin grabbed Ed's hips and flipped him roughly onto his back. Ed lay back against the pillows, panting, as Colin reached into a drawer and pulled out...a leather bootstrap, which he proceeded to tie around the base of Ed's dick, like a cock-ring.

Ed arched his eyebrows and Colin chuckled. "We don't want this over before it begins, do we?" Then he went back to the drawer and took out a condom and a tube of lube.

Ed watched with parted lips as Colin gloved him up and then slicked his hard-as-a-rock dick. Colin moved slowly to straddle Ed's hips, reaching behind him to grab his cock and position it against his hole. Colin locked eyes with Ed as he lowered himself onto that granite shaft, letting out a low moan as it filled him.

Oh my fuckin' God. Colin's heat seared him. It was so tight, so... right.

Ed stared at him, open-mouthed—and then thrust up into him in one fluid glide.

"Oh, fuck, yeah," Colin breathed as Ed grasped his hips and pulled him down onto his cock. He took hold of Ed's hand and brought it to his shaft. "Work my dick while I ride you," he gasped. Colin placed his hands flat on Ed's chest and rolled his hips, letting Ed slide in and out of that hole which gripped him so tightly. Ed jerked Colin's shaft, loving the breathless pants which came thick and fast. Hell, he loved it *all*. The sounds Colin made as he rode him, faster and faster. The feel of that solid flesh in his hand. That hot, tight heat wrapped around his dick. Everything was pushing him relentlessly toward their mutual goal. He looked up at Colin's lean, firm body, hips rocking, body undulating, a light sheen of perspiration on that wide chest, and then tugged harder on the beautiful cock in his hand.

"So close," he cried.

Colin nodded and bent down to kiss him hungrily. Ed threw an arm around him and held him firm as he fucked into him, balls slapping against Col's arse. That familiar, searing, white-hot feeling boiled inside him and he knew he was there. With a loud groan he seized Colin's mouth in a brutal kiss as he shot his load deep inside him, stiffening as he thrust into Colin's channel.

Colin moaned into his mouth and Ed felt heat as he came over Ed's belly and chest. Ed let go of Colin's dick and put both arms around him, pulling him closer, their kiss deepening as their orgasms smashed into them, a relentless, all-consuming wave of pleasure that took Ed's breath away. He shuddered through the peaks and troughs of it all, relishing the glow which spread throughout his body, filling every crevice. Colin moved gently on top of him, their kissing finally slowing.

Ed's cock slipped from the confines of Colin's body, and Colin sat up, moving slowly to untie the bootstrap and remove the condom. He dropped both items onto the floor and then stretched out on top of Ed. He propped himself up, forearms on with side of Ed's head and stared at him.

"That was—"

Ed craned his neck to stop the words with a kiss. He didn't want words to spoil the moment. Colin melted into the kiss and Ed closed his eyes, luxuriating in the feeling of holding a man in his arms. The warmth of the room was a comfort as he felt himself begin the slow descent into sleep, his arms still around Colin, his body sated.

And happy.

Ed awoke to a darkened room—and a hot, wet mouth around his dick.

"Oh, fuck, Col..."

Colin chuckled, causing vibrations around his cock. Ed groaned in disappointment as Colin released him. "You complaining?"

"Fuck, no!" Ed exclaimed vehemently. "But ya could've woken me up, ya know."

That chuckle again. "Does that mean I can put the light on?"

Ed reached for the lamp and clicked it on. He blinked in the warm light. Colin was lying on his belly between Ed's legs. As he watched, Colin slowly drew Ed's dick back into his mouth. Ed bit his lip, shuddering at the sensation. He groaned louder when Colin pulled off him once more.

"What the fuck are you tryin' to do to me?" he whined.

Colin grinned. "I have a much better idea." He grabbed Ed's legs and tugged him farther down the bed, and then swung around, so that Ed found himself staring up at a full, heavy cock pointing down at him.

Oh yeah. Ed could go for *that* idea in a big way.

Within seconds he had Colin's firm, fat dick in his mouth, and he was rubbing his finger over Colin's hot little hole.

Fuck...talk about a circle of pleasure.

The feel of Colin's mouth around him only made him want to suck Colin's cock deeper. And as he licked and sucked Colin's shaft, the groans it pulled from Colin's lips only fuelled his desire even further. When he finally slid a finger inside Colin's arse, the resultant long, low moan of pleasure that burst out of Colin made his heart sing.

I'm makin' 'im feel good. And damn, if that didn't make his heart soar. It was a heady moment, made richer by the feel of Colin's skin under his fingertips, the taste of his dick on Ed's lips, the smell of sex, earthy and so fucking hot....

And suddenly they were both coming, Ed shocked into momentary stillness as Colin pumped hot come unexpectedly into his mouth. Colin tried to pull his cock free, but Ed grabbed hold of him and held him tightly as he swallowed Colin's load, the taste bitter but not unpleasant. He shot into Colin's mouth and gasped as Colin sucked him deep, taking every last drop from him. They both rolled onto their sides, breathless.

And then Ed started to laugh. It started as a chuckle but swelled until he was holding his belly, aching with it. Colin scrambled to lie beside him, plainly perplexed. Ed let his laughter die away and then he reached up to touch Colin's face.

"Never in a million years, mate." Colin raised his eyebrows and Ed chuckled. "If you'd ever tol' me 'ow much fun sex was between two blokes, I'd never 'ave believed ya, not in a million years." He grinned. "An' as for me swallowin' spunk...." He shook his head. He'd never swallowed before. Obviously that had been a gay move too far for roomie Don.

Colin returned his grin. "I take it you enjoyed the experience?"

Ed beamed. "*Enjoyed* it? Mate, all I can say is, when do we get to do this again?"

It was Colin's turn to laugh. "How about we get some sleep first?"

Ed pulled a face. "Aw, c'mon, Col. I'm makin' up for lost time 'ere." He winked. "But I dare say I can wait 'til the mornin'. 'Specially if it means I get my fat cock in your tight arse again."

Colin groaned. "Oh God, I've created a monster." Then he grinned. "Thank fuck for that." He propped himself up on his elbow and gazed at Ed. "Let's go back to sleep. We can swing by your place tomorrow and pick up your rugby kit for the game." His eyes met Ed's. "What do you say?"

Ed smiled. "Sounds perfect."

Colin switched off the lamp and Ed spooned up behind him. Colin pulled the sheets over them and then reached back and pulled Ed's arm across him, like a blanket. Ed snuggled up, warm and sated once more, breathing in Colin's scent. For the first time in his life, Ed fell asleep holding another man in his arms.

And it felt absolutely...perfect.

CHAPTER SEVEN

Ed woke up to find his nose buried in Colin's hair. He breathed in Colin's scent, inhaling the smell of bed-warmed skin and clean hair. God, that was good. He liked the way his dick was nestled between Colin's arse cheeks.

Now there's an idea....

He began to move his hips, rubbing his cock over Colin's hole, keeping the motion slow and gentle. Colin stirred, then twisted to look at Ed. More movement. Their eyes met, and in silence, Colin handed him a condom. Ed nodded. He tore open the packet and rolled the latex over his hard morning wood. Then he reached behind him to where Colin had left the lube the previous night, and slicked up a couple of fingers. He kissed Colin's shoulder as he slid his fingers into his arse. Colin's head rolled back, eyes closed, as Ed moved inside him, stretching him. It wasn't as if he was a stranger to anal sex. But fucking a man? It was proving addictive.

Colin pushed back onto his fingers, little noises escaping his lips, their combined breathing the only sounds in the room. Ed withdrew his fingers and pushed Colin's leg forward, bent at the knee. Ed placed his cock against Colin's entrance and then slowly, so slowly, he pushed inside him.

Colin pushed out a long, drawn-out sigh, and Ed put his arm around him once more, cradling him as he rocked in and out of his body. No hurry. As far as Ed was concerned, this was heaven. The smell of the warmed sheets surrounding them. The musky wake-up smell that emanated from their bodies. Colin's broad shoulders, his cheek against them, Ed laying soft kisses there. The feel of solid muscle beneath him as he rolled slightly, Colin spreading his legs to accommodate him. The glorious curve of Colin's arse. The noises Col made. Moving his hand lower to play with Col's dick, feeling it harden in his hand. Colin turning his head, silently demanding Ed's kiss, and the feel of stubble against his cheek.

It was the same act as the previous night, and yet it was so very different. So much more. Last night had amazed him. It was nothing like having sex with a woman, and Ed had loved that. Colin begging him to pound his hole. The hard slam of flesh against solid flesh. The knowledge that Colin could take everything Ed could dish out. But this? This was languid, sensual heaven.

Ed lost track of how long he was inside Colin, sliding in and out of that soft, warm channel. He loved the way Colin began to make more noise as he got closer to his climax. Ed couldn't hold it in any longer. He pushed Colin flat onto the mattress and then began to fuck him, hips bucking as he thrust into Colin's tightness. They both cried out until they were hoarse, as Ed came deep inside him, and Colin spilled come onto the sheet below him, without a single touch but the friction of the sheets against his dick.

Ed collapsed on top of Colin, nose buried once more in his hair, breathing in that wonderful aroma of pure, unadulterated male.

Colin let out a wry, breathless chuckle. "Damn, were you taking lessons in your sleep? Because that was...." He sighed. "That was a wonderful way to wake up."

Ed eased his spent cock out of Colin's arse and dropped onto his back. "Nah, that was a fuckin' *marvellous* way to wake up."

Just then his stomach growled.

Colin laughed. "Yep, three orgasms will make you hungry, all right." He grinned. "And that's my cue to make you some breakfast." He got out of bed and then looked down at the sheet. "And I'd better remember to change the bedding, too." He winked. "Okay, a quick clean-up first, *then* I'll make breakfast." He padded naked out of the bedroom.

Ed pulled off the soiled condom, tied it off and dropped it to the floor. He laced his hands behind his head and stared at the ceiling. It had felt like the most natural thing in the world to slide into Colin. He kept waiting for the other shoe to drop, but so far he'd fucked Colin twice and it just kept getting better and better. His thoughts went back to those university blowjobs.

Why didn't I wonder at the time if I was gay, or even bi? Why did I never explore this?

He knew the answer to that one. Being gay wasn't an option. He'd been surrounded by macho rugby players, and exploring the possibility had never occurred to him. He'd seen his experimentation as just that, and homosexuality was a dirty word in his circles. Not like now. Okay, so there was still discrimination and hatred, but bloody hell, the world had come a long way in the past decade alone.

His stomach rumbled, and just then he caught a whiff of fresh coffee.

Ooh, now you're talkin'.

Ed rolled out of bed and walked into the kitchen to find Colin standing there naked, whisking eggs in a bowl. Ed could smell bread toasting, and the delicious aroma of sausages under the grill. Colin looked over his shoulder at him and smiled.

"Help yourself to coffee. Breakfast won't be long."

Ed padded over to the coffee machine and poured himself a mug. Colin stood by the hob, scrambling eggs in a frying pan. Ed came up behind him and nuzzled his neck.

Colin squirmed, but made a low noise of pleasure. "If you keep doing that, I'm going to burn the eggs. Go back to bed, and I'll bring it to you."

Ed chuckled and took his coffee mug into the bedroom. He took one look at the stained sheet and then stripped it from the bed. He pulled the covers up over the mattress and then fluffed up the pillows. Ed stretched out on top of the bed, legs crossed at the ankles, and drank his coffee. He smiled at that first sip. Colin made good coffee.

Colin came into the bedroom bearing a tray with their breakfast. After placing it at the foot of the bed, he turned on the TV and tossed the remote to Ed.

"See if you can find a news program, or some sports."

They lay on the bed, eating their breakfast and watching the morning news. Then Ed found the sports channel and they spent a good hour discussing that, both still naked. Soon it became time to get ready for their match.

"You can have a shower with me," Colin said with a gleam in his eye, "as long as we agree now, there will be no fucking in the shower. Because I don't know about you, but I don't think there's a drop of come left in my body."

Ed snorted. "You got that right." His dick felt wrung out. He noticed Colin's cheeks heating up. "What just crossed *your* mind?"

Colin grinned. "I was just thinking about showering with you. You have no idea how many times I watched you in the shower after a match, longing to touch you. God, it was such a hard task, keeping my dick down."

Ed stared at him. "Col, exactly 'ow long 'ave you been watchin' me in the showers?"

Colin stroked his chin. "Let me see. When did you join the team?"

Ed thought about it. "Last year in April."

Colin grinned. "Well, then that would mean I've been watching you since last year in...May?"

Ed was flabbergasted. To think Colin had been fantasizing about him all that time—and he hadn't had a clue.

Colin chuckled. "So, with that rule firmly understood...Want to take a shower with me?" He got off the bed and held out his hand to Ed.

Ed beamed. "Oh, I think I can manage that." He grabbed Colin's hand and was hauled off the bed. As they exited the bedroom, Ed leaned close. "Just don't bend over for the soap if you drop it, yeah?"

He loved Colin's guffaw.

Ed took off his crash helmet and stowed it in the luggage compartment of the Harley. Colin handed him the spare. Ed had lost count of the number of times he'd given Colin a ride to rugby practice, but this had to be the best journey yet. They'd taken a taxi to Ed's flat, and Ed had gone up to grab his rugby gear, leaving Colin in the entrance hall. It felt wrong not inviting him up, even though he'd already seen it. It wasn't that the flat was untidy, but compared to Colin's apartment, it felt poky and drab. Ed had lived there ever since he'd started working at Trinity. He could probably afford a better place, but sending money to his Mum every month left him a little tight. And yeah, he knew in his heart that Colin wouldn't give a flying fuck about the size of his little flat, but it was difficult to overcome his anxieties.

Ed loved his Harley. He loved the speed, the solid, reliable feeling of the bike between his thighs. He loved zipping through the London streets every morning, dodging traffic. But today was a first. Today he'd loved that moment when Colin had slipped his arms around Ed's waist and held him tight. God, that had felt damn good. In fact, all the way to the rugby club, Ed was feeling so good, he was almost giddy, and Colin's mood seemed to match his own. In the taxi going to his flat, they'd laughed and joked, kidding around with each other. Now and again Ed found himself staring at Colin, recalling their night together, and the memories had sent a rush of warmth flooding through him.

I fucked a guy. Not once, but twice.

Ed felt no shame, only a slow release of pleasurable sensations as he remembered the feel of Colin's body, the heat inside him, their kisses... Then Colin would catch his eye and grin, letting Ed know the same thoughts had been in his mind too.

Ed had never been happier.

Ed glanced around at the team which had piled into the Elephant &
Castle. Unlike the mood of the previous week, the players were quiet.
Maida Vale Rugby Club had beaten them, only by one point, and the
mood was sombre. He knew from past experience that the next hour or
so would be filled with match analysis and suggested plays for the next
match. Trevor Maitland, the team captain, took his role seriously. It was
one of the reasons Ed had left his former team to join the Kensington
Rugby club: they were a much more competitive team.

Trevor bought the first round of drinks for everyone, and the team
took over a whole corner of the pub. The management were used to
them by now, as this was their regular drinking hole after matches and
practice. Colin took a seat next to Ed and leaned forward, discussing
the match's highs and lows with Trevor and Phil Maddox, the team's
fly-half. Ed supped his pint and listened as the discussions grew more
animated.

"That long throw of Jeff's was bloody brilliant!" exclaimed Trevor.

Phil nodded enthusiastically. "Yeah, and when Dick dummied and
shot through that gap, God, I really thought he'd make it."

"Well, he did make about five metres before the ball got snaffled,"
Colin admitted. "I've got to say, when Pete was under that mound of
bodies, and Tony acted as scrum-half, passing it to Dave... Bloody hell,
Tony did a fantastic job of protecting it 'til Pete was back in position."

Phil grinned. "And that pass Pete made to you," he said to Trevor.
"That was bleedin' accurate, dead-on, if you ask me. But that kick you
took, mate, that was ace." He turned to find Pete, who was sitting in the
corner. "Nice work, son!" He raised his glass to him.

Pete mimicked him and grinned, while his team-mates cheered and
clapped him on the back.

Yeah, there'd been some good moments, in spite of us losin', Ed thought. He was suddenly aware of being scrutinized. Ed looked up to find Bill Murphy staring intently toward him and Colin. Ed bristled. Of all the players on the team, Murphy was the least liked. The man was not that great a player to start with, but on top of that, he was arrogant, pushy, and at times downright obnoxious. Ed tried to have as little to do with him as possible, but at that moment, Murphy's intense scrutiny was pissing him off, and Ed had had just about had enough of it.

"Whass up with you, Murphy?" he demanded.

"Nothing," Murphy fired back, lips narrowed.

"Maybe he's contemplatin' 'is future in this team after he dropped the ball again, which prob'ly cost us the match," Tony muttered under his breath, but loud enough that those around him murmured in agreement. Ed said nothing, but silently agreed. Tony was one of the team's Locks, and strictly speaking shouldn't have been passing to Dave in the first place—as scrum half, that was Murphy's job.

Murphy's upper lip curled. He slammed his glass down onto the table and glared at his team-mates. "What makes you think it wasn't the queers that made us lose the game?"

Ed's heart skipped a beat. He didn't dare look at Colin. The rest of the players looked at each other, frowning.

"What the fuck are you talking about, Murphy?" Trevor sounded pissed off.

Murphy pointed straight at Ed and Colin. "You mean you all haven't noticed how lovey-dovey they've been all day? And they arrived together, didn't they? Three guesses how they spent *their* morning. I bet if you got close enough, you could still smell the come."

Ed's face heated up as everyone turned to scrutinize him and Colin. He clenched his jaw, hands curled into fists, and bounced out of his chair, ready to deck Murphy. Several members of the team copied him, standing and moving closer.

Colin stood up slowly, stepped in front of Ed, and got right in Murphy's face. He lowered his voice, his gaze fixed on the sullen player.

"Okay, so I suck dick. I can *still* play better than you. Besides, I'm not the one who keeps dropping balls and missing play, am I, Murphy? Maybe if *you* got laid more often, you'd play better."

His words were greeted with gasps and snickers. Colin gazed around at his team-mates, meeting their eyes, his chin held high.

"Yeah, I'm gay. It's not like I've ever hidden it. I've just chosen not to tell you. I happen to think who I take into my bedroom is no one's business but my own."

Then one by one, Ed felt the eyes of every player turn to him. An invisible band tightened around his chest and sweat popped out on his brow. He didn't have a fucking clue what to do, how to react, what to say. So he did the only thing he could think of.

Ed grabbed his bag containing his clothes and biker jacket, cast one glance in Colin's direction, and walked out of the pub.

As he hurried along the street and into the side alley where he'd left the bike chained up, the only thing on his mind was the stricken look on Colin's face when Ed had turned to leave. A look that said Ed had just wounded his lover.

Ed got to the bike and undid the chains. He leaned on the wide seat and breathed in deeply for a few seconds. Then he got out his phone and speed-dialed Rick and Angelo's flat.

"Hi, Angelo here."

Ed tried to breathe more evenly. "Angelo, it's Ed. Is Rick there?"

"Oh, hi. No, he's just stepped out to go to the local shop, but he'll be back in a sec."

Thank God for that. "Is it okay if I come over?"

Ed could hear the smile in Angelo's voice. "Yeah, sure, no problem. Do you have the address?"

Ed didn't so he listened carefully. "I'll be there in about thirty minutes, all right?" He hung up, put his phone away and then got onto his bike. Right now he needed some advice.

Why do I get the feelin' I just fucked things up?

CHAPTER EIGHT

Murphy had the smuggest look on his face, one that Colin badly wanted to wipe off—with his fist. Yeah, the smug bastard looked really pleased with himself. And Colin was still reeling from the fact that Ed had walked out and left him there. The more he thought about it, the angrier he got.

After everything we did last night. What the fuck did that mean to him, if he can just get up and walk out?

In his head, a pissed-off voice was saying *This is what happens when you fall for a straight guy* and *I told you so*—very, very loudly.

Trevor snickered. "Well, at least we know Colin won't drop balls."

That brought guffaws from the whole team, except Murphy.

He stared at them, aghast. "You mean it doesn't bother you, having two queers on the team?"

Pete snorted. "As long as they can fuckin' play, who cares? *They* weren't the ones who nearly lost us last week's game—and maybe did lose us today's." He stared intently at Murphy. "Maybe *you* should take some lessons from *them* on 'ow to 'andle a ball." More snickers and smothered giggles followed his little speech.

Murphy spluttered and sprang to his feet. He grabbed his jacket off the back of his chair and glared at his team-mates, who merely stared back at him, faces straight. Murphy gave Colin one last, very dirty look before turning on his heel and marching out of the pub. Colin caught the words Murphy muttered under his breath just before the door slammed shut after him.

"Fucking fag."

Trevor cleared his throat. "Okay lads, another round and I'm buying."

His announcement was greeted with cheers, and then the discussion of the match continued. Colin stared at his team in amazement. No mentioned Murphy's outburst. And no one treated

Colin any differently. It was as if the whole episode hadn't even occurred. Nothing had changed

Except for the ache in Colin's heart.

Ed pushed the Harley through the wide door to Angelo's studio as instructed, and watched as Angelo locked it after him.

"The bike will be safe here," Angelo told him. "Rick's back. He's upstairs in the flat, with my sister, Maria." Angelo led him up the staircase to the apartment above. Ed looked around with interest at the home Rick and Angelo shared. The living room was large and airy with lots of natural light, and there was a warm, cozy feel to it. A deep, comfy-looking sofa, thick floor cushions, rugs everywhere: it felt like a home.

Rick was sprawled on the sofa, the TV on in the corner, showing some old black-and-white film. He sat up and grinned when he saw Ed, but the smile died on his face.

"Something's happened," he said, eyes full of concern. Ed nodded, his throat tight.

Angelo bent down and kissed the top of Rick's head. "I'll go back into the kitchen and Maria and I will carry on making the ravioli."

Rick reached up and stroked his lover's cheek, an adoring look on his face. Angelo gave Ed a quick flash of a smile and then disappeared into the kitchen.

Rick rose from the sofa and went to a cupboard. He pulled out a bottle of whiskey and a tumbler. After pouring out a generous dollop, he handed it to Ed and then gestured to the sofa next to him.

"Okay, you need to sit down, take a deep breath, calm down, and then tell me what's happened."

Ed sank into the comfy sofa and sipped the whiskey, letting it warm him.

Rick sat next to him and then regarded him intently. "Let's start with the date. Did it go okay?"

Ed nodded, relaxing a little, thanks to the whiskey. "Yeah, it was great. That restaurant was perfect, by the way. I must thank Blake. But yeah, it was a perfect first date. And the endin' was, shall we say, explosive?"

Rick's mouth dropped open. "Ed Fellows, you randy little bugger. You fucked on your first date, didn't you? Didn't you?" He grinned. "Tell me more! Details, gimme details!"

Ed snorted. "Do I ask you what you two do in your bedroom? No, I don't, so fuck off."

Rick guffawed, but then his grin faded. "So what happened?"

Ed looked down at his glass and then knocked back the remaining whiskey, gasping as it hit the back of his throat. He set the glass down on the coffee table and then told Rick about the incident in the pub, and the way he'd walked out.

To his dismay, Rick winced. "You left him there? To fend for himself?"

Ed huffed. "You didn't see 'im. Trust me, he looked like he could cope. Put it this way, he was copin' better than I was, that's for sure." Colin had seemed so confident, so secure in his sexuality.

Rick bit his lip. "Okay, there's no nice way to say this but I'm gonna say it anyway." His eyes met Ed's. "You fucked up, mate."

Ed groaned. "I know, but I didn't know what else to do." All he could remember was that suffocating feeling of sheer panic that had rolled through him like a relentless tide.

Rick looked distinctly unhappy. "You need to make a decision here. If you want this to go any further with this guy..."

"Colin," Ed interjected. "His name is Colin." And *fuck*, but it hurt to say it.

Rick nodded. "If you want this to go any further with Colin, you're going to have to make a serious decision here. Colin's got balls of brass, by the sound of it. I think it unlikely he's gonna be *anyone's* dirty little secret."

Ed listened, acutely aware of the hollow feeling in his chest.

Rick locked eyes with him. "So either man up here and decide that you're okay with being with a guy—*this* guy—or walk away. Because right now you're not doing yourself any favours and you're *definitely* not doing him any."

"I know," Ed said softly. He gazed at his hands in his lap.

"Ed, look at me." Ed lifted his chin. Rick's expression was full of compassion. "Tell me, how did you feel this morning?"

Ed smiled, in spite of his melancholic mood. "The best I've felt in a long time."

Rick returned his smile. "Tell me what was so good about it."

Ed put his head back against the seat cushion and closed his eyes. "Walkin' up behind Col while he was cookin' and nuzzlin' 'is neck. Wakin' up and smellin' 'is 'air. Lyin' in bed with 'im, so close together. The smoothness of 'is skin on 'is back, an' the feel of 'is stubble on me face when he kissed me."

Rick giggled and Ed opened his eyes to glare. "What?"

Rick pointed down to the rugby shorts that Ed still wore, where an erection had clearly begun to make its presence known. "I think that answers a lot of questions."

Ed's cheeks went from cool to flaming in seconds.

The kitchen door opened and Angelo's sister Maria came into the room, carrying a glass carafe of red wine and four glasses. Ed couldn't help noticing her T-shirt. It was black, with rainbow lettering which read *Love is Love*. Angelo followed her. He pointed to the carafe.

"Ed, this is some of my family's homemade wine that we brought back from Italy. Would you like a glass?"

Ed nodded and Maria handed him a glass into which she poured the wine. Rick smiled at him and bumped him with his shoulder.

Maria looked at Ed and frowned. "Oh, are you okay?"

Ed could only guess how he looked.

Rick gave her a smile. "Oh, there's not much wrong with Ed here, apart from the fact that he's a little love-sick puppy right now."

Ed let out a low growl.

Maria gave him a sympathetic glance. "Aww, who is she?" Ed blushed and Rick giggled. Maria looked from Rick to Ed, then back to Rick again and then rolled her eyes. "Oh hell, at this rate there'll be no straight men left for me." She sank onto a floor cushion and took a long drink of her wine.

Angelo chuckled.

Rick regarded Ed intently. "So what's it gonna be?"

Angelo sat on the arm of the sofa and put his arm around Rick. He tilted Rick's face up toward his and kissed him, paying no mind to Ed's presence. Ed glanced at Maria to gauge her reaction. She smiled lovingly at her brother and his lover.

That made his mind up, then and there.

I want to be with Colin—if he's still speakin' to me after this.

Just then, Ed's phone rang. He pulled it from his pocket and stared at the screen for a moment. *Colin. Oh 'ell.*

Rick nudged him. "You're going to have to talk to him, sooner or later."

Ed sighed and accepted the call. Colin's voice was harsh in his ear.

"You son of a bitch. How the fuck could you do that, after what we did?"

Ed winced, his heart sinking. He held the phone away from his ear, still able to hear the pain and anger in every word. And from the faces of the three people around him, they heard every word too.

Rick grabbed the phone from him. Ed stared at him in horror, but Rick held up a hand. "Is this Colin?" he asked brightly.

Ed could hear Colin's reply. "Who the fuck is this?"

"My name's Rick and I'm a friend of Ed's." Rick put the phone onto speaker phone. Colin was muttering, still angry. Rick rolled his eyes. "Look, I need you to calm down so I can explain something, okay?"

Silence fell at the other end.

Rick gave them a relieved smile. "Colin, Ed has told me everything that happened. But I have to say, I have never seen Ed so upset as he is right now."

"As he bloody should be," Colin said in a gruff tone. Ed's heart constricted.

Rick continued. "Well, you have to understand, he's still new to this. After all, you were his first date with a guy." Colin fell quiet. Rick pushed on. "You remember *your* first date with a guy? How *you* felt?"

Colin sighed. "Yeah, I do."

Rick let out a relieved sigh. "Okay. Here's an idea. We're going to have dinner shortly, *we* being myself, my partner Angelo, his sister and Ed. Why don't you join us? You and Ed can talk."

There was a moment of silence. "Yeah, okay."

Ed stopped holding his breath as Rick gave Colin the address.

"I'll be there as fast as I can." Then he hung up.

Colin got out of the taxi, sports bag slung over his shoulder, and looked at the ornate door which led to Angelo's studio. He raised his hand to ring the bell, only to have the door open before he had the chance. A guy about his height with jet-black curly hair and equally dark eyes stood there, smiling.

"You must be Colin. I'm Angelo. Come on in."

Colin stepped into a light, airy studio, redolent with the scent of wood and oils. There were two or three work benches, covered in pieces of wood in different sizes, along with chisels and sandpapers. Angelo led him up a staircase and into an apartment. A young woman was pouring wine at a table, and one glance told Colin she had to be Angelo's sister. Colin was introduced to Rick who greeted him warmly. But there was no sign of Ed.

Colin frowned, about to speak, when Ed stepped out of another room. He seemed to have trouble meeting Colin's gaze. His cheeks were flushed, hands shoved into the pockets of his jeans.

For a moment Colin didn't know what to say to him. The words he'd rehearsed in his head over and over on the journey over there, deserted him at the sight of Ed's obvious discomfort and embarrassment. And then it hit him. He couldn't stay angry. Not with Ed.

Oh shit. I have it bad, don't I?

He opened his mouth to speak but Ed beat him to it. He looked up at him through his eyelashes, and his voice came out low and cracked.

"I'm so, so sorry. I didn't know what to do, what to say. I should never 'ave left. I was a total coward an' an absolute arsehole. I really, really 'ope you can forgive me."

Anything Colin had been about to utter left him when he heard the pain in Ed's tone.

"All right," Colin huffed, "but you're gonna owe me."

Who am I kidding? He wanted to pull Ed into his arms and kiss him repeatedly until the man was dizzy, too dizzy to walk away from him like that ever again.

Ed stared at him, clearly not expecting that response, his lips parted.

Maria handed Colin a glass of wine. "You let him off way too easily. You should have had him down on his knees, begging." She winked at him.

Colin glanced at her T-shirt and sized her up pretty quickly. He leaned in close and said in a stage whisper, "Yeah, but he's *such* a good fuck."

There was a moment of startled silence, and then Rick and Angelo cracked up. Ed's mouth fell open and Maria flushed bright red, giggling. Colin couldn't hold back his smile any longer. He walked over to Ed, looked him in the eye, and then leaned forward to kiss him, no mere peck on the lips but a *by-God-I-mean-business* kiss, his arms slipping around Ed to pull him closer. Ed stiffened for all of two seconds before surrendering, and then he all but melted in Colin's arms.

Rick's voice made it through.

"Well, *that* was a bit more than I needed to know."

CHAPTER NINE

Ed finished the last of the invitation to interview letters and emailed them to Karen for printing out. Three candidates selected from all the applicants didn't seem like a lot, but Ed had been thorough. On paper, they all looked good. The final decision would be up to Blake who was due back at Trinity within the next week or so. Ed smiled to himself. Judging from the latest phone conversation, his boss was really torn between his company and his new life. It seemed Blake and Will were loving their lives as fathers, although Lizzie was apparently on the receiving end of quite a few phone calls, seeking advice.

That's one thing little Sophie's gonna miss out on—dotin' grandparents.

Will's parents had been absent since they threw him out when he was fifteen, upon discovering he was gay, and Will had no wish to seek them out. Blake's mother had died when he was very young, leaving his father Justin to bring him up. Sadly, Justin had died just over a year ago. Ed knew how close Blake and his father had become since his marriage to Will.

But what little Sophie lacks in relatives, she'll surely make up for in dotin' 'aunts' and 'uncles'—there was a whole *team* of them right here, all eager to meet Blake and Will's beautiful little daughter.

Ed leaned back into his chair and let out a happy sigh.

I seem to be doin' a lot of that lately.

It seemed as if he couldn't keep all his happiness inside. It wanted to burst out of him. And of course, everyone had noticed. He'd received comments from Beth and Peter, who'd both informed him he had this whole 'inner glow' thing going on. *Yeah, right.*

Karen stuck her head around his door. "Those letters are all printed for you, Ed. If you sign them now, I can have them in this morning's post."

Ed broke into a wide smile. "Bloody 'ell, that was fast, woman!"

Karen beamed and approached his desk, letters in hand. "Efficient, that's me." She handed then over.

Beth popped her head around the open door. "Sorry to disturb you, Ed, but I've had one of our authors raise some issues about an edit." She spotted Karen. "I can come back later, if you're busy."

Ed waved her in. "Nah, jus' signing some letters, thass' all." He signed his name and handed the letters to Karen. "Thanks for that, darlin'," he said with a wink.

Karen chuckled. "Well, I don't know who this mystery woman of yours is, but what a difference she's made."

Ed felt the heat rise in his cheeks.

"I was thinking the same thing," Beth said with a cheeky smile. "Gonna share details, Ed?"

"Nope," he said emphatically. "An' now you can clear out of me office and let me do me work, yeah?" He gave them a good-natured smile.

Beth pulled a face. "Aw, *you're* no fun." Then she grinned. "It *is* good to see you so happy, Ed. Good luck to you."

Ed smiled. "Okay, yeah.... Now what did you want to talk to me about?" They discussed the problem one of their authors seemed to be having with an editor. Ed put forward a few suggestions and Beth nodded in agreement while Karen hovered by his desk.

"Now remember—happy is good, yeah?" Beth winked and then exited the room.

Karen was still there. "Sure you don't want to tell *me* anything?" she asked hopefully.

Ed guffawed. "Get out of 'ere, you nosy wench."

Karen shrugged. "Oh well, it was worth a try." Then she chuckled. "Beth's right, though. Happy is a good look on you." With that, she walked out of his office, humming quietly.

Ed waited for a moment and then got out his phone. He scrolled through his messages from Colin. During the past two weeks he'd accumulated quite a few. It had gotten so that whenever his phone chimed, Ed reached for it eagerly, to see if it was from Colin. More often than not, it was just a short message about what was going on in his day. Now and again, however, the message was entirely different. Ed's cheeks flamed at the thought of some of them.

His phone chimed.

Just slipped out of my meeting to go to the bathroom. Was thinking of you.... See?

Ed drew in a sharp breath as an image appeared on his phone. It was of Colin's pants, open and pulled apart, his hand pulling his briefs away from his body to reveal Colin's hard cock, not all of it, but just enough to get Ed's heart racing. He loved the sandy-blond fuzz above Colin's dick. He closed his eyes and recalled Colin's scent, heady and overpowering, as Ed buried his nose in that pubic hair, face wet with tears as he strained to deep-throat Colin's thick, eight inches. That had been a damn good lesson.

"Oh my God, what *are* you looking at?"

Rick's voice shattered the moment. Ed jerked his head up to see Rick standing just inside his office, eyes wide, lips twitching.

Ed hastily dropped his phone face-down onto the desk. "Nothin," he growled. "An' since when 'ave you stopped knockin' before you come in 'ere?"

Rick guffawed. "Well, that just shows how engrossed you were. I did knock—twice, as a matter of fact." His eyes sparkled as he approached Ed's desk. "So, don't I get to see?"

"No, you bloody don't!"

Rick chuckled and sat down in the chair facing Ed. He leaned back and laced his hands behind his head. "I was curious as to how many nights you'd got to sleep alone during this last week, that was all." That cheeky grin spread across his face.

Ed gave it up. It was obvious Rick had no intention of leaving until he'd caught up on the situation. "If you must know, we've only 'ad one night apart during that time."

Rick bit back a giggle. "Well, at least you got *some* time to yourself."

Ed shook his head. "Yeah, you'd think that, but you know what? I missed 'im."

Rick snorted. "With the amount of sex you're having, I'm surprised you can still walk."

Ed became still. "That's the weird thing. It's not just the sex. I like being with 'im." Colin was a great guy to be around. Ed hadn't known what to expect, spending so many of his evenings with a guy who wasn't only his lover, but also a good mate. He'd thought that the sex might have made things awkward, but no, far from it. Colin was still...Colin—thank God. The last thing he wanted was to ruin their friendship.

He met Rick's gaze. "This is so weird, mate. I'm fuckin' a guy, sleepin' with a guy, an' far from freakin' me out, it just feels...right."

Rick's expression softened. "Then just go with it," he advised. "It was obviously meant to be, so enjoy it." He tilted his head to one side. "Did you expect to feel different?"

Ed smiled. "Yeah, exactly. I thought I'd feel more...you know, *gay*." Except he wasn't, was he? He was bi.

Rick barked out a laugh. "And what the fuck is that? Look at Blake, at Will, at me, Angelo...we're all different, right? No two gay men are the same. When you come out, they don't rubber-stamp you 'GAY' and you change personality overnight, okay? You're still Ed Fellows, except that now you've discovered a piece of you that you probably never knew was missing." He stretched across the desk and tapped Ed on the chest. "*This* is the Ed Fellows you were meant to be."

It was probably the most profound thing Rick had ever said to him. And it made Ed glow inside.

His phone rang. Ed turned it over to see Trevor Maitland's name.

Since when does Trevor ring me during the day?

Rick grinned. "Is that him?"

Ed shook his head. "Nah, it's the captain of the rugby team. I'd better see what he wants."

Rick rose to his feet and walked toward the door. "In which case, I'll leave you to it." He gave Ed one final cheeky smile and then exited the office, closing the door behind him.

Ed connected the call. "Trev! What can I do for ya?" He could make out a lot of background noise. Trevor was clearly phoning from work. He heard a door closing and then the noise level dimmed.

"Ed, sorry to disturb you at work, but there's something going on that you need to know about."

Ed frowned. "Go on."

"I had an email from Doug Evans, the captain of Southend Rugby club. You remember, we're playing them in a couple weeks' time, yeah?"

"Sure."

Ed heard Trevor sigh. "Okay, there's no easy way to say this. It seems Doug received a call from someone, asking how he felt about playing a team with, and I quote, 'a couple of fags in its ranks.'"

"What the fuck?" Ed sat bolt upright.

"And it gets worse. It seems every member of Doug's team got the same phone call."

Ed took a deep breath in an effort to stay calm. It was bloody hard work.

"Doesn't take much to work out who called them, does it?" Trevor said glumly.

Ed snorted. It had Murphy's fingerprints all over it.

"Maybe you two should sit out this next match."

Ed almost choked. "What? You're fuckin' 'avin' me on. What does this Doug say about it all?" He was so pissed, if Murphy had been within his grasp at that moment, he'd have choked the little shit.

"He thinks his guys will be okay about it." Trevor paused for a moment. "I was thinking of your safety, you and Colin."

Ed laughed, a harsh sound that burst out of him. "What, you think we can't take care of ourselves?"

He heard Trevor's sharp intake of breath. "No, no, that's not what I mean."

Ed breathed more easily. "Good, 'cause we're playin'."

"Do you want me to call Colin?"

Ed sighed. "Nah, Trev, I'll take care of it. But thanks for lettin' me know, yeah?" He disconnected the call and then sat back, struggling to keep a lid on his anger. *That fuckin' little....*

He waited for a moment before ringing Colin.

"Hey, this is nice. I'm just on a break." Ed loved the note of pleasure in Colin's voice. Quickly he relayed Trevor's call. He heard Colin expel his breath. "Okay, so Murphy's a prick. Tell me something I didn't know." Colin's voice dropped. "Look, I don't have a problem with playing. The question is, do you?"

Ed thought about it for a minute. Yeah, he was pissed off, but what surprised him most was that his overriding concern had been to protect Colin.

"I suppose if you're not worried, then neither am I," he conceded.

"Good," Colin said warmly. "Because I have something much better to discuss than Murphy's homophobia. We don't have a match on Saturday, but there's early practice at the rugby ground, right?" Ed confirmed it. "Okay, then how about you and I do something different this weekend?"

"What did you 'ave in mind?"

"How about right after practice, we get on your Harley and ride down to the south coast? I was thinking about booking us into a hotel in Brighton for the night. We could come back Sunday evening." There was a pause. "What do you think?"

Ed's heart pounded. The idea excited him, but set his stomach rolling at the same time. *A night away in a hotel?* All of a sudden, Ed got hard.

"Yeah, okay," he said quickly, before he lost his nerve and changed his mind.

"Fantastic." Colin sounded delighted. "I'll go ahead and book us into somewhere really nice. Just leave it to me. All you have to do is get us there."

"Sure, that sounds like fun." Ed's *cock* liked the sound of it, *that* was for sure. He arranged to meet at Colin's place that night, and then hung up.

Ed left his chair and went over to the window. He rested his hand against the glass and stared out at the London skyline. He really liked the way things were going with Colin. And as for Brighton? Saturday seemed *way* too far off right now.

The desk phone rang and Karen's extension winked its light at him. Ed picked up the handset.

"Karen, what can I do for ya?"

"Ed, I have someone in reception who has come about the PA position."

Ed huffed. "Then tell 'em the deadline for applications passed last week," he said, a little impatiently. *Why the 'ell is she even* botherin' *me with this crap?* Karen knew better.

There was a moment's silence. "I think you might want to speak to this applicant in person."

Ed paused. The cautious note in Karen's voice piqued his interest. "Fine. Bring 'em to me office." He put down the phone, straightened his desk and then stared at the door. When it opened, his mouth fell open. Melissa Richards stood in the doorway.

Ed stood stock still. He stared at her, goggle-eyed. "Oh, you 'ave got to be fuckin' *kiddin'* me, lady!"

Melissa regarded him haughtily. "Well, if *that's* how you're going to be, I may as well leave right now." She turned as if to go.

"Nah, 'old yer 'orses," Ed burst out. This he *had* to hear. "You made it this far, didn'tcha?" He gestured to the chair in front of his desk. "Take a seat, Miss Richards. I assume it *is* still *Miss* Richards? Unless you got wed in some secret ceremony that never made it to the society pages?" He chuckled. He'd seen nothing of Melissa in the six years since she'd walked—or rather, had been *marched*—out of Blake's life, after trying her hand at a little blackmail.

Melissa crossed the room and sat daintily in the chair. Ed took a long look at her. Gone were the designer clothes, the coiffured hair. Melissa appeared well dressed, but her clothing looked as if they'd be at home in any clothing store on the high street. She regarded him with a neutral expression. She clutched her handbag in her lap.

"Okay, Melissa, what are you *really* doin' 'ere?" he demanded. "'Cause I'm not buyin' this job-huntin' crap for a second." He folded his arms and stared at her, unblinking.

Melissa's cheeks were flushed. "Is this how you speak to all your applicants?" she sneered. Then she straightened her face quickly, but it was too late. The mask had slipped.

Ed regarded her coldly. "Nah, only manipulative bitches who try to blackmail me boss." He watched the colour drain from her face. "So tell me, why are you 'ere?"

Melissa shifted in her chair. "I...I need a job."

Ed gazed at her incredulously. "Pull the other one."

She nodded. "No, really. I do need a job. I thought six years was plenty of time for Blake to have got over my, er, past mistakes. I'm just the kind of person he needs as an assistant."

Ed didn't know what to make of it all.

And then the penny dropped.

He started to laugh. And the more he laughed, the more indignant and angry Melissa became—not that Ed gave a shit. There was no way this bitch would be working for Blake. He'd see to that.

Ed grinned. "Oh, I get it now. Daddy really *did* cut off 'is little girl's allowance, didn't he? Well, well, well. Good for 'im." He speared Melissa with an intense stare. "Go on, then—tell me 'ow many jobs you've 'ad since dear Daddy disinherited ya." He waited, still grinning.

"I've had a few, all right?" she gritted out through clenched teeth.

Ed chortled. "You're really scrapin' the bottom of the barrel if you're 'ere looking for a job."

Melissa lifted her chin. "I believe the position is as Personal Assistant to Blake. I'd like to speak with him, not his lackey," she said, eyes gleaming with spite.

Yeah, there's the Melissa I remember. Leopards really didn't change their spots, after all.

Ed smiled. "Well, sorry to disappoint ya, but Blake's not 'ere at the moment. He's on paternity leave." He watched her expression as she digested that piece of information.

Her eyes went wide. "P-paternity leave?"

Ed nodded. "He and Will 'ave a baby girl." Her lips narrowed, and Ed couldn't resist. "By the way, in case you were wonderin', he an' Will are very 'appy. Will's perfect for 'im."

A brief flair of disgust swept across her face, but she straightened it pretty quickly.

Okay, that's it. "Look, this 'as gone on long enough. There is no way on this earth that Blake would employ a poisonous bitch like you, so sling yer 'ook." She gasped but he wasn't finished. "Don't think I didn't notice your face when I mentioned the baby. Didn't like that, did ya? You're prob'ly one of these people who think gays shouldn't even 'ave kids, right?"

Her face tightened, and Ed caught it. His words had hit the mark.

Melissa quirked her eyebrows. "And since when did *you* become a gay supporter?" That sneer was back. "Or are you in love with him too?" Her eyes burned with spite. "Am I right? Has Blake infected you, too?"

Ed stood very still. For a moment he said nothing. Melissa stared back at him, her pretty face twisted with hatred.

"The door is that way, Miss Richards. I suggest you use it." Then he sat down at his desk and gazed at the computer monitor, as if she wasn't there. He heard her breathing, harsh and uneven, and then the scrape of her chair as she got up to leave. Ed kept his eyes on the screen until he heard the door slam. He waited for a few seconds and then sagged into his chair. The whole situation felt...surreal. He still couldn't believe she'd had the nerve to show up like that.

The door was flung open and Karen appeared.

"Are you okay? I heard raised voices."

Ed waved his hand. "S'okay, Karen, everythin's all right now."

Karen gave him a doubtful look. "You sure, Ed? Do you need anything? You look like you could use a coffee right now."

Ed smiled at her. "Actually, thass' a great idea. I'd love one." He waited until she'd left the room and then he pushed out his breath in one long sigh.

God, there's never a dull moment in this job. Then he grinned. He couldn't wait to see Blake's face when Ed told him about *this*. Then his grin faded.

He had something else to tell Blake, too.

CHAPTER TEN

"You ready for this?" Colin asked Ed as they entered the rugby club, kit bags slung over their shoulders.

Ed shrugged. "Look, if Murphy's gonna be a dickhead about this, it's not like we can stop 'im, right? We just 'ave to put up with the jerk." His face was glum.

Colin's heart went out to him. He'd put up with homophobia for a good deal longer than Ed had, but it saddened him that less than a fortnight into his new life, Ed was already experiencing hatred. He longed to grasp Ed's hand and squeeze it tight in reassurance, but this wasn't the place.

The locker room was surprisingly empty. Ed frowned. "Where is everyone?"

Colin spotted a sheet of paper taped to the back of the door. "Apparently in the social room. There's a meeting before practice." He glanced at his watch. "Which begins in about three minutes." He glanced at Ed and arched his eyebrows. "Strange that we should be late when the alarm clock went off in plenty of time this morning." Colin smirked as they turned around to exit the locker room.

Ed stared at him open-mouthed. "Oh, so it's *my* fault we're late?" he exclaimed.

Colin held open the door to the social room and leaned close to whisper in Ed's ear. "I have one word to say to you—shower."

Ed's mouth snapped shut and suddenly the tips of his ears burned bright red.

"Nice of you both to join us," Phil Maddox said with a grin. There were whistles and cheers from several of the players. Ed's cheeks matched his ears. Colin merely grinned and stuck up two fingers at Phil.

"Okay, that's enough," Trevor called out from the front of the room where he was sat on a table, clipboard in hand. "Grab a seat, you two, and we'll get started."

Colin and Ed found two empty chairs and sat down hurriedly. The noise died down to a low level. Colin looked around at the twenty or so men sprawled on plastic chairs, all watching Trevor. Well, nearly all—Murphy was staring at him, lip curled. Colin sighed and looked away.

"Okay, lads. Sorry to take time away from our practice with this impromptu meeting, but something came up." Trevor put down his clipboard and gazed around the room at the players, his expression serious. Now there was silence.

"As you know, we're due to play against Southend in a week or so. Well, it seems someone from our team contacted all their players, with the express purpose of outing Colin and Ed. And from the sound of it, this person tried to stir up, shall we say, ill feeling toward them."

Jeff Farrowday, one of the team's wingers, bounced to his feet in an instant. At six-four, Jeff was the tallest player among them. He pointed directly at Murphy and scowled. "You bastard. That was you, wasn't it?"

Murphy twisted around in his seat to face Jeff. "So? What of it? I don't want to play on a team with fags. And I think they had a right to know." His words were greeted with jeers and boos. Trevor's face fell as voices were raised, growing steadily more agitated. One of the flankers, Harrison Lloyd, stood up, his expression grave.

"Sorry, Trev, but I'm gonna speak my mind here. I think it's high time Murphy was kicked off the team."

Murphy snarled at him, but Trevor held up a hand, his eyes troubled. "For outing Colin and Ed? Isn't that a bit drastic?"

Harrison shook his head vigorously. "No, not just for that, though I have to ask myself, if he was prepared to call another team about our players, what else has he said?" There were rumblings of agreement from around him. "Let's face it, Trev, he's not a good player. Frankly,

I'm amazed he's still with us after the last few games." More murmuring broke out. Harrison retook his seat, and was patted on the back and shoulders by those around him.

"An' we should be supportin' each other, not letting 'im stab two of our best players in the back." This came from Pete Shorcross, the number eight. There were more calls for Trevor to do something. Colin didn't envy the captain. It was rare for the players to be so vociferous. They were generally an easy-going lot.

Murphy bounced to his feet and swung round to face his team-mates. His face was a contorted mask of fury. "You know what? I don't want to play with your stinking team anyway. Not if you're gonna stand by and let *those* queer bastards play." He grabbed hold of his jacket and kit bag. "So congratulations. You got your wish, 'cause I'm outta here. I'll go find a team who'll appreciate my skills." And with that he strode out of the room, slamming the door behind him.

"Good riddance!" someone called out after him, and there was a spattering of laughter. A ripple of half-hearted applause ran through the players.

Trevor held up his hands, shaking his head. "Enough of that." He waited until silence fell before speaking further. "Okay, this leaves us without a scrum half, so there's a change of plan for this morning. I'm going to be trying out some of our subs for the position. And before you subs all converge on me, eager beavers that you are, remember what makes for a good scrum half. I'm looking for someone who can pass accurately—"

"Yeah, 'cause Murphy never bleedin' managed *that*!" someone yelled.

"Someone who can pass accurately," Trevor repeated patiently, "has a great understanding of tactics, can run evasively and who thinks fast on their feet. If you think that describes you, I'll be down at the far end of the field. And I could use two or three players to help out with that."

He gazed firmly at the team. "As for the rest of you, I have only one word—defence."

A low murmuring started up, but Trevor waved his hand. "I want you in two groups, practicing rucks and mauls. You all know how it works. The quicker we can ruck or maul the ball back to our side, the more likely we are to create a penetrative attack. Phil, I'm putting you in charge of that, while I do the try-outs." He rubbed his hands together briskly. "Okay, lads, changed and out there in five minutes. We've wasted enough time this morning, and if we're going to beat Southend, we need every second we've got to make sure we're ready for them."

Everyone was on their feet and heading to the locker room within seconds. Colin clapped Ed on the back as they went to get changed.

Well, there's one *less thing to worry about,* Colin thought wryly. He wasn't sorry to see Murphy go.

For the next hour, Colin played part of the opposition, allowing the forwards to practice their defensive skills. It grew more interesting when he came up against Ed. God, the man was a battering ram. What delighted Colin most was that Ed didn't take it easy on him. In fact, watching Ed's raw energy out on the field only served to remind Colin of Ed's powerful thrusts of the night before. And just like that, he was hard and aching.

Thank God we're going to Brighton. Colin intended to spend a lot of his time away with Ed in bed. The thought of Ed bending him over and fucking the come out of him was enough to make his hole clench.

Practice over, the team piled into the locker room to shower. It was gratifying that players came up and patted them both on the back, calling out supportive comments. It got more personal in the showers.

"So, it's official, then? You two are definitely an item?" Dave asked with a cheeky grin as he stood under the forceful jets of hot water.

To Colin's surprise, Ed spoke up before he could comment. "Not that it's any of your business, but yeah, we are." Ed matched Dave's grin. "That's not a problem, is it?"

Bloody hell. It was the last thing Colin had expected him to say.

Dave held up his hands. "No, mate." Then he winked at the others. "Just needed to know if I should be careful bending over in the shower, that's all." Loud, raucous laughter followed.

Ed snorted. "I've seen your arse, Dave. Trust me—you're safe."

Colin almost doubled up laughing. Ed caught his eye and grinned. Colin shook his head, still laughing. He was overjoyed by the team's support, but Ed's reaction was nothing short of amazing.

He was still smiling as he dressed, Ed next to him. Colin tried not to stare at the naked form of his lover—*yeah, that would be a good way to freak out the straights*—but fuck, it was a difficult task. It wasn't long until they were the last two players left in the locker room.

Scrap that. Rod Bentnall was still there.

Colin liked Rod. He was in his late twenties, and really cute, not that Colin was about to admit that, especially to the man at his side. Colin looked up and smiled at Rod as he approached them. "I hear congratulations are in order."

Rod's smile lit up his whole face. "Yeah, I was flabbergasted when Trev told me I was the new scrum half. I'll do a good job," he said earnestly.

"I'm sure you will," Colin said in a reassuring tone. When Rod hovered, clearly unwilling to go, Colin cocked his head to one side. "Anything wrong?" Ed stopped pushing his damp towel into his kit bag and looked up.

Rod blushed. "Actually, I just wanted to say that the way you spoke to the team last week, Colin—when you told them you were gay—well, that was really inspiring."

Colin regarded him keenly. "Inspiring. Interesting choice of word." He bit back a smile. "Something you want to tell us?"

Rod's blush deepened. "Look, I'm not as brave as you, all right? I've only just come out to my family, and believe me, that was hard enough." He breathed deeply. "But it's nice to know I'm not the only one on the team."

Ed gave him a warm smile. "Welcome to the minority."

Colin's smile echoed Ed's. "And as for coming out to the team, that's up to you. You don't have to, you know. But if you ever need advice, at least you know where to come, right?"

Rod nodded gratefully and then left the room. Colin waited for a moment, and then walked up behind Ed as he zipped up his kit bag. Colin nuzzled Ed's neck, noting the shiver that rippled through him. He breathed in the scent of newly washed hair, body wash and the heady aroma of raw Ed.

"How about we drop off our bags at your place and then hit the road?" he suggested. He tugged at Ed's earlobe with his teeth, causing his lover to squirm. Colin grinned to himself as he moved to kiss and then suck at the fragrant skin of Ed's neck. Ed let out a groan and rolled his head back, leaning against him. Colin reached around to slide his hand down Ed's front, knowing exactly what he'd find. It really was playing dirty, going for his neck like that. After a week of fucking, Colin knew which buttons to press to get a reaction. Sure enough, Ed's dick was like a rock inside his jeans. Colin stroked his length through the denim, squeezing the thick shaft.

"If you keep on like that," Ed gritted out, "we're gonna be even later than we planned, 'cause I'm gonna throw you down on that bench over there and fuck you right now. Bloody 'ell, Col." His breathing was ragged.

Colin withdrew his hand slowly. "Let's save that for tonight, eh?" The catch in Ed's breathing told Colin his lover really liked that idea.

"We're leavin'—now." The hoarse quality in Ed's voice was gratifying. Colin grabbed his kit bag and followed Ed out of the locker room and the club, to where his Harley sat waiting.

A frisson of excitement skated down Colin's spine.

Oh, we're going to have some fun tonight.

He couldn't wait to see Ed's face.

Ed walked into their hotel room and stared in surprise. Large windows overlooked the seafront, and he could see the Brighton wheel and the famous pier. The bed was wide, with a fringed canopy above and deeply quilted bedspread over it, all done in gold. The bathroom was decadent, with a whirlpool bath and large walk-in shower.

"This is beautiful," Ed admitted after he'd finished admiring it.

Colin smiled, before dropping his overnight bag onto the floor and coming over to kiss Ed slowly and thoroughly. Ed sighed with pleasure. When Colin broke the kiss, he stepped back to look Ed in the eye. "Okay, tell me the truth. When was the last time you had a night away in a hotel?"

Ed thought about it for a moment. "Y'know, I can't remember." *An' 'ow sad is that?* He shook his head. "I know Blake 'ad to force me to take an 'oliday last year." He could still hear his boss yelling.

"Force you?" Colin repeated incredulously. He stared at Ed. "My God—I'm going out with a workaholic."

Ed scowled. "Look, I can't 'elp it if me life sucked so badly that I'd rather be in work, okay?"

Colin became very still. "I know so little about you," he said quietly.

Ed shrugged. "Not much to know, really." It wasn't as if they spent much time talking, when they were alone. Their evenings tended to follow a pattern. Ed would turn up at Colin's apartment, after both of them had eaten. A few hours of hot fucking later, they'd collapse in each other's arms and fall asleep, only waking in time for Ed to ride back to his flat in the morning to get showered and changed for work. It wasn't ideal, but it had worked.

Until now.

Colin gave him a speculative glance. "What say we grab a bottle of wine from the mini bar, stretch out on the bed and talk for a while? We've got plenty of time until dinner, and then we've got a club to go to."

Ed stared. "We're goin' to a club?" Then it came to him. "Is it a gay club?"

Colin chuckled. "Not only is it a gay club, it's in the basement of the hotel." He gave Ed an innocent look. "Oh, did I not mention that Legends is a gay hotel?"

Ed opened his eyes. "Er, no, you neglected to mention that." The idea of getting to know Colin a little better was appealing, however. "Okay, some wine and a chill-out on the bed sounds nice," he agreed.

Colin beamed. Ed clambered onto the bed and stretched out, sinking into the pile of pillows while Colin went to inspect the contents of the mini bar. He returned to the bed with a bottle of white wine and two glasses.

"So, who gets to start?" Colin asked as he poured out the wine.

Ed shrugged. "I guess I can go first." He clasped his hands together on his belly, trying to keep from fidgeting. It was clear, to him at least, that he and Colin came from very different backgrounds. He had only to listen to his voice. Colin sounded poised, self-assured, nothing like Ed.

Colin handed him a glass and after placing his own on the bedside table, he lay down beside Ed, head propped up on his hand. "Are you sure you don't mind this? Because right now, everything about you is telling me you're not comfortable."

Ed took a long drink of the delicious wine, letting it cool him. He put down the glass and stretched out once more on the bed. The hot July sunshine poured in through the opened windows, and noise from the promenade below filtered into the room.

"Look, I know that at work I kinda stand out from the rest of the team. I mean, they're from all over the country, different countries, even, whereas I'm from the East End of London."

Colin became still. "Are you embarrassed about your upbringing?" He shuffled closer. "You *do* know I think the way you talk is sexy as hell, right?"

Ed stared at him, aware of that fluttery feeling in his belly that so often occurred when he was around Colin. "Yeah?"

Colin nodded. "It's one of the things I've always liked about you. Whenever we'd go for drinks with the lads after a game, I loved listening to you talk. You don't mince your words. You say what's on your mind. God, that's so refreshing these days. With some of the people I come into contact with on a daily basis, you never know what they're really thinking. They hide behind this... facade, and I'm never completely sure who I'm talking to half the time." His eyes met Ed's. "With you, what you see is what you get, and I really, *really* like that."

The fluttery feeling eased. He rolled onto his side to face Colin, loving the way that Colin's leg hooked over his, connecting them.

"Me Mum an' Dad grew up in the East End, and they never moved out of it. Dad was a binman all 'is life, and Mum was a cleaner. Still is, as a matter of fact, though us kids would love 'er to quit." He smiled as he thought about her. Stubborn bloody woman.

"Didn't you mention that you went to university?" Colin asked.

Ed nodded.

Colin gazed at him, eyes gleaming. "That's pretty good for someone with your background, you know."

Ed chuckled. "Oh, I know. Mum tells me that when me teachers started tellin' 'em that I was a smart kid, that was when they started askin' for school to push me 'arder in me lessons. When I was eleven, they entered me for the entrance exams for the local grammar school."

"I take it you got in."

Ed grinned. "You should've seen their faces the day the letter arrived to say I'd got a full scholarship. God, me Dad was glowin' with pride." His face fell.

Colin laid a hand on his arm. "What is it?"

Ed sighed. "Dad died of an 'eart attack in 'is mid-fifties. Far too young."

Colin stroked his arm. "At least he got to see his son go to University. That must have made him even prouder."

Ed picked up his glass and took another drink. "Yeah, those were the days when students got grants if they came from a poor background." Just then his stomach rumbled.

Colin smirked. "I think I'd better feed you before we go any further. You're going to need your energy for tonight, anyway."

Ed downed the rest of his wine, ignoring the rolling sensation in his belly.

Going to a gay club. Fuck.

Ed was as nervous as a cat in a room full of rocking chairs.

CHAPTER ELEVEN

"What do you think?" Colin asked him as they stood next to the bar.

Ed didn't want to tell him what he *really* thought—that he felt out of place and uncomfortable as hell—so he pasted on a grin and gave him the thumbs up. He gazed at the dance floor where bodies gyrated under twirling lights, and where the average age looked to be in the late twenties. Okay, so he was only thirty-six, but watching the dancers made him feel every one of those years. Then there was the way they looked. None of the men he could see were even close to his build. He watched them dance together sinuously, their movements fluid and sensual, and then he looked down at his body, meaty thighs crammed into his tight black jeans, muscles straining against his black cotton shirt. Ed felt about as graceful as a pig on roller skates.

Colin cracked a smile. "I think the first order of the evening is a drink. Maybe a couple of them."

Ed thought that was a bloody good idea.

He stood and watched the floor show while Colin got the drinks. He gazed at the lean, young bodies, and for the first time since they'd got together, he wondered what Colin was doing with someone like him when he could have his pick of guys who looked like *that*.

"Here, drink this." Colin handed him a shot glass. Two pints of lager stood on the bar.

Ed regarded the tiny glass with suspicion. "Whass' this?"

Colin grinned. "Jägermeister, and trust me, you'll like it."

Ed raised his eyebrows, and then he lifted the glass to his lips and swallowed its contents. He let out a gasp. "That tastes strong," he croaked.

Colin gave a nonchalant shrug. "Only about 70% proof," he said lightly. Then he handed Ed the pint and raised his. "Cheers."

Ed clinked his pint glass and took a long drink. He leaned against the bar and drank some more. *Maybe I'll feel less conspicuous after a pint or two*. He had to admit, the shot produced a warming effect throughout his body. The music was heady, pulsing through him. Ed didn't even notice that Colin had moved from his side until there he was, proffering another shot glass.

Ed grinned. "You're tryin' to get me pissed." He leaned closer to speak into Colin's ear. "You don't 'ave to, right, 'cause you *know* you're gonna get lucky tonight." He winked salaciously and then tossed back the shot.

Colin chuckled. "Oh, I wasn't thinking about tonight." He took the empty glass from Ed, placed it on the bar and then took hold of his hand. "I wanted you nice and loose for this." And then he pulled Ed toward the dance floor.

Ed felt like resisting for all of five seconds, but then the alcohol got the better of him. Colin led him out into the middle of the floor and began to move to the rhythm, his eyes fixed on Ed as he got closer, their bodies almost touching. More guys joined them, and pretty soon Ed began to feel the heat as men pressed in close around him.

Colin leaned closer to speak. "Getting warmer, isn't it?" His eyes sparkled.

Ed nodded, and then the breath caught in his throat as Colin slowly unbuttoned his white silk shirt and slipped it seductively off his shoulders. Ed swallowed. The whole situation was getting him very hot, and not in a good way. He felt as though every eye in the room was trained on them. Colin tucked his shirt into the waistband at the back of his jeans. His movement grew more suggestive as he edged closer, undulating his body against Ed's. He began to slide his fingers under the fabric of Ed's shirt, undoing the buttons slowly.

Ed bit his lip. Colin's blue eyes were focused on him as he licked his lips. He paused and tilted his head ever so slightly, as though questioning if he should continue. Ed took a deep breath and then nodded. Colin grinned, a slow, sexy grin that made the muscles in Ed's abs go all quivery. Colin pushed the shirt off Ed's wide shoulders, moving his hands sensually over the bared skin. He pulled Ed closer and then reached around to tug the shirt out from his jeans. He removed it, taking his time. Their chests came into contact, and Ed bit back a moan as Colin brushed against him as he tucked Ed's shirt into his jeans.

And suddenly Ed was aware of what was going on around him.

Fuck. Are they starin' at me*?*

It seemed as though all the guys pressed around them were eyeing him up, and from what he could see, a couple of them looked like they wanted to *eat* him up. *Talk about 'ot glances.* Ed didn't know how to react to all the attention.

And then Colin put his hands on either side of Ed's head, drew him close and kissed him, slowly, thoroughly. And *oh my God,* it was no chaste kiss. Colin took possession, pure and simple. He pushed his tongue between Ed's lips, thrusting inside, fucking his mouth right there on the dance floor. And it was hot as hell.

When Colin broke the lip-lock and stepped back, grinning, Ed struggled to catch his breath.

"For fuck's sake, Col, we're in public 'ere." Ed's voice shook.

Colin leaned in. "Let's call it me staking my claim."

Ed stared at him for a moment and then burst out laughing. "Bloody 'ell, you don't do things by 'alves, do ya?" A feeling of well-being flowed through him, and he pushed aside his nerves and just let go.

From that point, things just got better. They danced, they drank some more, and Ed finally loosened up enough to enjoy himself. Loose enough that he noticed one of the guys dancing a little way away from them and couldn't keep his eyes off him. The guy wasn't that dissimilar from Colin—really toned, nice arms, a flat stomach. He caught Ed looking and winked at him. Ed grinned.

They went to the bar for another drink and Ed stood watching the guy.

"Thass' a nice-lookin' bloke there."

Colin raised his eyebrows. "Should I be worried here?" His lips twitched.

Ed felt the flush that rose up his chest, reaching his cheeks. "I've never looked at a guy like that before. This is so...new."

Colin stared at him. Ed noted his pupils, so large and black.

"Do you know how much I want you right now?" Colin growled. He grabbed Ed's hand and pulled it around him, moulding it around his arse. Then he slid his hand down to Ed's crotch, squeezing his length. His voice dropped lower. "How much I want this inside me?"

God, if he thought he'd been hard before....

Colin spoke into his ear, his breath warm on Ed's neck.

"Upstairs. Now."

Anything Ed had been about to say died in his throat. He nodded, and Colin put down his glass and led him by the hand out of the club into the elevator. Neither of them spoke as they walked along the corridor to their suite. Colin opened the door and pushed him inside. When it closed, Ed grunted as Colin shoved him up against it, lips locked on his, fingers fumbling with Ed's jeans. The kiss was brutal, demanding...and exactly what Ed wanted.

He groaned when Colin dropped to his knees and yanked his jeans down, before freeing his stony length from the tight briefs that imprisoned it. Colin gazed up at him, a predatory smile on his lips, before grasping Ed's dick around the base and sucking him deep. He reached up and tweaked Ed's nipple hard.

"Fuck." The word was torn out of him as Colin went to work on his cock, hungrily pulling him deeper. And all Ed wanted to do was fuck that luscious mouth. He grabbed hold of Colin's head and held him steady as he thrust deep, rocking his hips. The loud groan that escaped from Colin told Ed all he needed to know. Colin clutched at his arse, squeezing. Ed grunted as he fucked Colin's face, and then let out a guttural moan as Colin took his length deep into his throat. *Shit, that feels fantastic.* It took his past blowjobs and left them lying in the dust as Colin knelt there and just *took* it all, throat exquisitely tight around his dick.

Too tight. Too damn good.

Ed eased himself free of Colin's mouth and grabbed under his arms to yank him up. He propelled him across the room to where that wide bed awaited them, and then pushed him face-down over it. Colin's shirt sailed across the bed. Ed's fingers had trouble co-operating as he struggled with the button and zip, but at last he gripped Colin's jeans and dragged them down over that firm arse.

Ed bent over him and ground his cock against Colin's arse, sliding it between his cheeks. He bit at Colin's neck, causing him to cry out. Ed growled into his ear.

"Gonna fuck you 'ard."

Colin raised his head from the bed and twisted to stare at him. "Yeah. Hard as you can."

Ed opened the drawer where he'd left the condoms, pulled one out and tore open the foil with his teeth. He rolled the latex over his aching dick and went to pick up the lube, but Colin grabbed his thigh.

"No lube. Want to feel it. Get me wet with your tongue," he gritted out.

Oh fuck. Ed hadn't known it possible to be this hard.

He grasped Colin's hips, tilted his arse higher, and then spread him, licking his own lips at the sight of that pink hole, just waiting for him. With a groan he dove in, sucking and licking, pushing his tongue against the tight muscle that resisted him but not for long. He pressed further, loosening Colin up, tongue pointed as he rimmed him relentlessly.

"Oh, you fucking tease. *Fuck* me!"

Ed grinned and pushed Colin onto the bed, then knelt behind him and shoved his dick all the way inside in one long thrust. Colin howled and grabbed the bedspread. Ed pulled virtually all the way and then did it again. And again. And again. His body sang as he thrust into Colin's hot, tight hole, groaning at the way Colin's body wrapped around his cock.

"Oh God, just like that. You can go harder." Colin gasped out.

"If you...can talk," Ed grunted out, punctuating his thrusts, "then I'm not...doing me fuckin'... *job* right!" He shoved hard into Colin, loving the way he moaned as Ed filled him. Ed pushed Colin between his shoulder blades, forcing him down onto the bed and raising his arse higher.

Ed slid hard into him and Colin cried out. "Oh fuck, right there."

Ed laughed, a sound of sheer joy that tumbled out of him. He'd never felt so... *alive*. It all felt so fucking *good*. The feel of Colin's body beneath him, all firm flesh and muscles. The noises Colin made as Ed penetrated him, dick sinking into that heat. The smell of sex, raw and elemental, combined with Colin's musk.

Yeah. Too fucking good. Ed was about to come.

He reached under Colin to tug at his cock, and then pushed a finger into his channel, alongside his dick. Colin's wordless groan of pleasure sent him soaring, and Colin's body tightened around him, gripping his shaft. "Thass' it, I can feel ya. Come on. Fuckin' *come* for me!"

Colin stiffened and suddenly hot come coated Ed's hand. Ed let out a harsh cry as he felt Colin's orgasm all the way along his cock, milking his own climax from him. Ed thrust deep, grabbing Colin around the chest as he covered him with his body, pumping his spunk into the condom. He shuddered, his body pressed up against Colin as his dick continued to pulse inside him.

"Fuckin' love this," he whispered breathlessly into Colin's ear.

Colin turned his head and their lips met in a searing kiss, both of them moaning low. Colin murmured into his mouth. "Me too."

Ed lay there, cock deep inside Colin, unwillingly to move, not wanting to break the spell. Because in that moment, everything just felt...perfect.

Ed lay on his back, Colin's head on his chest, his hand resting on Ed's belly. Even though it was in stark contrast to the forcefulness of their coupling, having Colin lying in his arms like this felt...right. Ed had never minded post-coital snuggling, but he'd assumed guys didn't snuggle. He smiled to himself. Colin had dispelled that myth the first night they'd slept together. And far from feeling wrong to hold a guy in his arms, enjoying the languid warmth after sex, it felt—there was that word again—right.

"What are you thinking?" Colin murmured against his chest.

Ed smiled. "That this feels bloody good," he admitted.

Colin propped up his head on his hand, elbow resting on Ed's belly. "Can I ask you about something?"

"Sure." The way Ed was feeling, Colin could ask him anything.

"That guy you were looking at on the dance floor..."

Ed sighed. "Maybe I've been foolin' meself an' those feelings 'ave always been there. I dunno, maybe I've repressed 'em. But yeah, he looked good, in a way that I've never noticed a bloke before."

Colin chuckled. "It *is* okay to look, you know." He reached up and cupped Ed's face. "Did you have a good time tonight?"

Ed smiled broadly. "Yeah, although it took me a while to get used to the idea. Never 'ad guys look at me like that." He loved the feel of Colin's hand on his face, gentle and tender.

Colin laughed. "Oh, I'll bet *plenty* of guys have looked at you like that before tonight—you just didn't notice." He let out a yawn.

Ed snickered. "Aw, did I wear you out?"

Colin grinned. "I think you wore my *arse* out." He rolled onto his side and looked back at Ed. "You ready for sleep?" Ed nodded. "Then come on. You know how I like to sleep when you're sharing my bed."

Ed knew. He curled up to Colin and draped an arm across him, Colin's arse warm against his groin. Ed nuzzled into the fragrant skin of Colin's neck. *God, I love that smell.* Colin sighed, a sound full of contentment as he pushed back, snuggling against Ed's body.

Ed closed his eyes and let himself drift, his thoughts random. He pulled Colin closer and settled against him, body warm and sated. The last thing to cross his mind before sleep overcame him was the memory of Colin as Ed fucked him. It had been rough, almost primeval, but Colin had obviously loved every minute of it.

Does having someone inside you feel that good? he thought sleepily.

One thing was certain—Colin obviously thought felt it did.

CHAPTER TWELVE

"I didn't hear you get out of bed."

Ed turned toward the bathroom door where Colin stood, naked. He opened the shower door and stuck his head out. "Wanna join me?"

Colin's wide smile answered *that* question.

Ed waited until Colin was under the jets and then put his arms around him, pulling him close. "Good mornin'," he said quietly. He ran his hands over Colin's broad shoulders, loving the way the water beaded on his skin.

Colin kissed his cheek. "Morning." He cocked his head to one side. "What on earth were you thinking about just then? You were miles away." He soaped up his hands and then ran them over Ed's chest.

Ed stopped him, hand around Colin's wrist. "If I ask you somethin', will you give me an honest answer?"

Colin became equally still. "Of course."

Ed let out a sigh. "I was lookin' at all those blokes downstairs last night. Let's face it, there were some gorgeous men on that dance floor."

Colin's eyes twinkled. "Says Ed with his new Gay specs."

Ed laughed. "Yeah, okay, so I'm noticin' guys now." He paused. "Col, the way you look, you could 'ave an absolutely stunnin' bloke for a boyfriend. So I 'ave to ask meself...what are you doin' with a guy like me?" He fell silent, his eyes trained on Colin's face.

Colin stared at him. "My God, you're serious," he said softly. Ed opened his mouth to speak but Colin stopped him with a finger to his lips. "Wait. You asked me for an honest answer and I'm going to give you one, all right?" Ed nodded and Colin took away his hand. He trailed soapy fingers over Ed's biceps. "I love this," he said quietly. "All this muscle, this...power. It was one of the first things that attracted me to you—your size. I used to fantasize about you fucking me, your weight pressing me into the mattress, holding me down..."

Ed's cheeks were on fire.

"I like big guys," Colin continued, "but finding a guy built like you who's also into guys?" He snorted. "When I first laid eyes on you, I thought Christmas had come early." Ed chuckled. "When I got to know you, and it seemed clear you were straight, I had to content myself with watching you in the shower, on the field, anywhere I could look at you and not make it too obvious." He stroked Ed's chest, making him shiver. "But make no mistake, Mr. Fellows." He ran his hands over Ed's shoulders. "This? Is fucking sexy."

He ran his fingers through the hair on Ed's chest, twisting, pulling gently. Ed moaned.

Colin grinned. "And as for all this gorgeous body hair? Oh God, don't get me started." He pressed up against Ed, rolling his hips slowly. Ed closed his eyes and shuddered as Colin's heavy cock brushed against his. Colin moved his hands to stroke up and down his back, and then Ed caught his breath as Colin slid a single finger down his crease, rubbing gently over his hole. Ed opened his eyes to find Colin staring at him intently.

"Col," he began, voice cracking as that finger brushed over his pucker, slowly and deliberately. "I know you like big blokes, but..." He faltered, uncertain of how to phrase what was on his mind. Colin didn't break eye contact. Ed breathed in deeply. "Would...would it feel weird if you were to fuck a guy who was bigger than ya?" He swallowed.

Colin was so still. "What are you saying?" His finger paused in its sensual task.

Ed's throat was tight. He met Colin's intent gaze head on. "I'm sayin' I want to try somethin'. Somethin' we 'aven't done yet."

Oh, the look in Colin's eyes....

Colin reached down to cup Ed's arse, pulling him tight against that deliciously hard body. His breathing was harsh in Ed's ear as he leaned in to whisper. "You want me to fuck you?"

Ed nodded, unable to speak.

"You sure about that?" Colin asked. "Because there's nothing that says you have to, right? I'm more than happy to carry on the way we are." He waited, focused on Ed, as he resumed washing him.

Ed let out a sigh. It felt so good, having Colin run his hands over Ed's body, the water cascading down over them, plastering his hair flat against his chest. "I watched you last night when we were fuckin'. You looked like you were really enjoyin' it."

Colin grinned. "Well, that might be because I was. I love having you inside me." He kissed Ed's chest, paying special attention to his nipples. Ed hissed as Colin sucked the tiny nub of taut flesh, biting it gently.

"God, if you'd ever told me that 'avin' a bloke bite me nipples would make me as 'ard as a fuckin' rock...." Ed moaned and then grabbed hold of Colin's hair. He tugged him upright and then seized Colin's mouth in a bruising kiss, thrusting his tongue inside. Colin groaned and reached down to work Ed's dick, tugging it, sliding the foreskin back, making Ed whimper into his mouth.

Ed trembled. He broke away from Colin with a loud groan. "Please, Col..."

Colin held him, panting. "What? Tell me what you want." He wrapped a hand around both their lengths, squeezing, rubbing them together.

Ed felt as though he was about to combust. "Oh God, Col, take me to bed and fuck me."

Colin stared at him in silence for a moment, and then he released his dick and poured body wash into his cupped hand. He reached around Ed to squeeze his arse and spread his cheeks with one hand, while he slid a single soapy finger over his hole. Ed caught his breath as Colin slowly pushed inside him.

"Fuck." Colin was in virgin territory.

Colin's eyes gleamed. "You want me in there? Want my cock inside you?" That finger slid out, only to push back inside, deeper this time.

Ed groaned. "Oh my fuckin' God, that feels..."

It felt good. Bloody good. And Ed wanted more.

Colin slid in and out, moving faster. And *FUCK* there was another finger inside him now.

"Col, please," Ed begged. His legs shook. His heart pounded. He didn't want to wait another second. And then Colin was moving his fingers inside Ed, stretching him, turning them. It burned a little, and Ed heard a whimper resound around the shower enclosure. Then he realized it came from him.

"Need to get you ready for me," Colin whispered. He pushed deeper and Ed gasped at the sensation. Colin paused, fingers wedged inside Ed's hole. "Listen, you have to know, the first time isn't always the best, right? It *does* get better, though."

Ed was struck by the surreal situation. He stared at Colin in disbelief. "Col, your fingers are fuckin' me arse, an' *now* you tell me?" He laughed. "I 'ave fucked a few virgins in me time, mate. An' yeah, I'm talkin' anal, too. I kinda expect it to 'urt, okay?"

Colin slowly slid free of his body and Ed winced. Colin looked him in the eye. "I am going to take care of you, right? I am going to make this as pleasurable for you as I can."

A rush of warmth flooded through him at Colin's words. "Yeah, I 'ear ya," he said softly. He kissed Colin on the lips. "Now what say we go back to bed, and you show me 'ow good it can feel."

Colin flipped off the water and opened the shower door. He grabbed a towel and handed it to Ed, who dried himself quickly while Colin did the same. Ed tried to ignore the rolling in his belly. Something nagged at him.

"What is it?" Colin dropped his towel and came closer. He put his arms around Ed. "Your lips may be saying 'fuck me' but your body language is saying something else. Come on, talk to me." Ed dropped his chin toward his chest, but Colin was clearly having none of it. He cupped Ed's chin and lifted it. "Ed." The word was an entreaty.

Ed breathed deeply. "Look, just 'cause I want you to...you don't... you don't see me as..." He couldn't get the words out.

Colin's brow cleared. "Ed, do you think me any less of a man because I like being fucked?"

Ed widened his eyes. "Fuck, no!"

Colin smiled knowingly. "Then you're no less a man for wanting to experience the same thing. Okay?" He kissed him. "I like being fucked. I love how it feels when a lover is balls-deep inside me, filling me." His smile widened. "I'm not going to lie to you. It feels amazing. That's why I'm versatile. I get the best of both worlds." Another slow, lingering kiss. "And if you decide afterward that you prefer topping, that's okay." He locked eyes with Ed. "Really."

His words eased something inside Ed. "Thank you," he said at last.

Colin tilted his head. "But if you have doubts, then we don't take this any—"

Ed stopped his words with a kiss, taking his time. He brought his lips to Colin's ear. "Fuck me." His voice was rough with desire.

Without a word Colin led him by the hand into the bedroom. Ed lay down on the bed and then held out his arms to Colin, who stretched out beside him. Colin's lips grazed his, and Ed responded with a new hunger. He couldn't get enough of Colin's kisses.

God, he could kiss me for hours *an' I'd still come back for more.*

Colin broke the embrace and Ed let out a groan of disappointment, which changed in nature when Colin spread his legs wide and dove down to lick at his hole. "God, yeah, love it when you do that."

Colin's warm breath tickled his balls. "I know." And then that agile tongue was back, licking around the rim, pushing inside him. Ed reached down and grasped Colin's hair, holding him there. Colin chuckled, and it tickled his hole. "I get it, okay? More rimming. Fuck, talk about pushy." And then he was back at it, making Ed tremble, making him hot.

Except now Colin was sliding a finger inside him.

"Oh yeah, yeah..." Ed bit his lip as Colin wrapped a hand around the base of his dick and sucked him deep, while moving that finger slowly in and out of his arse. Ed didn't know which sensation felt better. And then Colin upped the ante by bobbing up and down on his cock, hand working it as he slid the foreskin back and forth, and all the while that finger pushed farther into him.

Ed writhed on the bed, rocking up with his hips to force more of his dick into Colin's hot, waiting mouth, and then back onto Colin's finger—which suddenly became two. Ed hissed out a breath.

"That...that feels...oh *shit*...feels full."

Colin pulled free of his glistening cock and looked at Ed. "You want me to stop?"

"No," Ed gasped out, "don't you fuckin' *dare*."

Colin grinned. He reached under the pillow for the lube, slicked up his fingers and then slid right back into him. That gorgeous mouth was back around Ed's dick.

Ed arched his back up off the bed. "Oh fuck...." But it felt better, and then it felt pretty fucking good—and he was ready for more. He couldn't lie still. Ed pushed down on Colin's fingers, chasing them. "Col.... for fuck's sake...." He didn't care that the words came out in a whine.

Colin eased out of him and then crawled up his body to look into his eyes. "Ready?"

Ed groaned. "God, yes."

Colin grabbed hold of him and rolled them until he lay pinned under Ed. "Condoms are in the drawer.

Ed scrambled up and opened the drawer to remove a foil square. His fingers trembled as he tore open the wrapper and eased out the rolled latex. Colin held his cock steady around the base, and Ed gloved up the solid shaft. He gazed at it, hole clenching, until Colin pulled him down into a slow, searing-hot kiss. Ed lost himself in the sensual onslaught, his momentary panic forgotten. Colin broke the kiss and gazed up at him, eyes shining.

"It's going to fit, I promise you."

Ed shivered. He spread his legs wide and positioned himself above the long, thick dick, feeling it press against his hole. Colin grasped his hand and laced their fingers together as Ed pushed against the blunt, wide head. He felt the muscle resist. In spite of his experience, he felt a brief moment of illogical panic.

"It's not gonna go, Col, I—"

He was robbed of words as his hole finally gave up and Colin eased into him, barely moving, but *fuck*, he felt it. Ed expelled his breath in a long stream and arched his back. Colin held still, allowing him to get his breath back.

Fuck, Colin felt *huge* inside him. And God, it hurt.

Ed shuddered at the alien sensation.

Colin stared up at him, eyes never leaving him. "Breathe. Just breathe. Try to relax. Take all the time you need," he said softly. He took Ed's cock in his hand and stroked it, working it slowly while still holding onto Ed's hand.

Ed drew in several long breaths, willing himself to relax. He concentrated on the way Colin was touching him, their joined hands. Then he pushed with his hips, aware that the burn was... less, somehow. In fact, it was melting away with every glide of Colin's hand on his shaft. And what had hurt him now started to feel...good.

Colin smiled at him. "That's it, yeah."

Ed began to move, slowly raising himself up, letting that thick dick ease out of him, and then sinking back onto it. Colin held himself immobile, letting Ed take things at his own pace.

Ed tightened his grip on Colin's hand and started to ride, rocking on his cock and sliding his dick through Colin's fist. Colin filled him to the hilt, making Ed cry out each time he sank down on that gloriously wide shaft. Colin stared up at him, eyes wide, lips parted, and totally focused on *him*.

Oh fuck, that feels good.

He rolled his hips, riding Colin harder now, but it wasn't enough. "Oh, God, Col, fuck me." The words were torn from his lips in a breathless prayer.

Colin let go of his hand and dick. He took hold of Ed's waist, dragging him down hard onto his cock. "Like that?" Colin gasped out.

Ed howled. "Oh fuck, yeah. Harder." The air was punched from his lungs as Colin tightened his hold on Ed's body, grabbing his arse and pulling his cheeks apart. Colin no longer lay passively but fucked him, pushing—no, *shoving*—hard into his channel. "Fuck, yeah!"

Colin pulled him down to kiss him, tongue and lips claiming him, fucking *owning* him. Ed moaned into his mouth as Colin ploughed into him, balls slapping against his arse, the sound loud and so fucking *sexy*. Colin squeezed his shaft, hand moving faster now.

And there it was—that electricity, tingling in his balls, heralding his imminent climax.

Ed straightened, hands on Colin's chest, and stared down at him. "Fuck, Col... gonna come." Fuck, he couldn't stop moving on that rigid length which filled him completely.

Colin's eyes sparkled. "Then come. Come on my cock. Let me feel it." He thrust up, hips bucking, his breathing ragged. "Oh yeah. That's it. Your arse is gripping me so tightly. Can you feel that?"

Feel it? Ed felt as though his whole world had narrowed down to nothing but that thick shaft in his arse, splitting him in two, making him come.

"Fuck, you feel so good. Come on, baby. Come for me." It was a command Ed's body couldn't ignore.

And Ed came with a roar.

A violent shudder rippled through his whole body as his cock erupted, thin ribbons patterning Colin's chest, reaching as far as his chin. Colin let out a harsh cry and slammed into him, stiffening.

Oh *God*. Ed could *feel* him coming. He leaned over to kiss Colin, desperate to deepen the connection. He felt the pulse of Colin's dick inside him, the warmth which spread through Ed's body like ripples in a pond, reaching every inch of him. The kiss was slow, all hunger extinguished as they explored each other leisurely, hands stroking over damp skin. There were still remnants of that electricity, sending jolts through him, making him shiver.

Colin held him, their bodies pressed together, Colin's cock still buried deep within him. He stroked Ed's cheek softly, and Ed closed his eyes, focusing on the sensations. Colin shifted beneath him and Ed felt his now-softened dick slip from the confines of Ed's body. And fuck, it felt like he'd lost something vital, something...

Colin rolled Ed onto his back and then snuggled up close against him, his cock limp, still encased in its condom with the evidence of his climax. He ran his hand over Ed's damp chest.

"So...how was it?" His eyes scanned Ed's face. "How do you feel?"

Warmth flowed through Ed.

The first thing he thinks of—how I am. The thought made him feel damn good.

Ed smiled at Colin. "You were right. It felt amazin.'" He cupped Colin's head and drew him close to kiss him, their lips soft against each other's. He drew back with a contented sigh. "An' yeah, I want to do that again."

Colin's face lit up. "Really?"

Ed chortled. "Oh God, yeah. 'avin' you inside me was..." He didn't have the words to describe it adequately. His voice softened. "I loved it, okay?"

The look on Colin's face made his heart soar.

Then Colin's words came back to him and he couldn't resist. He deliberately straightened his face. "Y'know, ever since we started fuckin', I've been waitin' to find *somethin'* about gay sex that turned me off. I mean, it seemed like *everything* we did felt bloody fantastic."

Colin raised his eyebrows. "And that's supposed to be a bad thing?" His eyes danced with amusement.

Ed chuckled. "Don't get me wrong. I love it when we fuck. It's fast, 'ard, downright dirty at times.... I just couldn't believe it felt so...so *right* to 'ave sex with a bloke. An' I kept thinkin' that there 'ad to be somethin' waitin' for me just around the corner, somethin' that would be a real turn-off."

Colin's brow furrowed. "And...?"

Ed sighed. "And it finally 'appened."

The concern in Colin's eyes was touching. "Tell me. Was it something I did?" Ed nodded, his expression grave. "Then what was it?"

Ed cupped Colin's face. His lips twitched. "Don't call me baby, all right?" He lasted about four seconds before erupting into a peal of laughter.

Colin's expression was priceless.

And then Ed found out he was ticklish in places he never knew about.

CHAPTER THIRTEEN

Colin saved the last changes to his design and closed the file. He leaned back and heaved a contented sigh.

Only another hour or two and I can see him.

Ed had been in his thoughts all day.

Colin had to face facts. What had started as a healthy case of falling in lust was developing into something else, and he wasn't sure how he felt about that right now. Walking along Brighton beach on Sunday afternoon, things had seemed much clearer. He and Ed had gone for a walk after lunch, and it had been great. The hot August sun beating down on their bare chests, the surf lapping around their ankles as they strolled along the shoreline, the smell of the sea air, salty and fresh... At one point Colin had wanted so badly to take hold of Ed's hand, but at the last moment had shied away from the idea.

Not sure how he'd feel about that.

He was pretty sure that as far as Ed was concerned, it was all about the sex. Colin didn't expect anything more. But that didn't mean he wasn't hoping.

Colin closed his eyes. He could still see Ed above him, riding him hard, the look of ecstasy on Ed's face as his orgasm exploded within him. But hell, the feel of Ed's body wrapped around his cock...

Colin gave himself a little mental shake. Yes, the sex was good. Then he laughed out loud.

Who am I kidding? The sex was phenomenal.

It had been a while since he'd dated, and the last few dates had been nothing special. That aspect of his life had taken a back seat lately as his job with Wilson & Beckett had started to take off. But certainly there'd been nothing like his time with Matthew. Until now.

Colin's laissez-faire philosophy was taking a battering. For the first time in a long while, he was thinking about a guy in terms of a relationship. Only, he didn't know how the guy in question would react.

He's only just discovering he likes dick. I can't ask him for any more than that.

Colin shook his head. That didn't stop him from wishing, though.

His phone rang, startling him. Colin smiled. He'd missed Ed in his bed last night. He went to answer it and then paused, eyes fixed on the screen. *Matthew.*

Colin frowned. It had been almost a year since he'd last spoken with his ex. The last he'd heard, Matthew had moved to Leeds when his company had transferred him.

"Hey, Matthew."

That husky voice hadn't changed. "Hi, Colin. How are you?"

"Fine, thanks. To what do I owe the pleasure?"

"I'm back in London, as of last week. Apparently the company couldn't function without me."

Colin snorted. "Delusions of grandeur, maybe? You're an accountant, Matt. I'm pretty sure they coped fine without you."

Matt chuckled. "Okay, so I lied. I couldn't stand it in Leeds a second longer. I *begged* them to transfer me back to London."

Colin laughed. "Ah, that sounds more like it. So you've moved back?"

"Uh-huh, which is sort of why I'm calling. Is there any chance we can meet up for a drink this evening?"

Colin hesitated. He'd planned to have dinner with Ed after work. "Tonight?"

"Oh. You've got plans."

He could hear the disappointment in Matt's voice. "Is it that important?" Colin asked him. He had no qualms about meeting Matt. What burned him was the idea of letting Ed down.

"Look, it's okay if you can't. It can wait." But something in Matt's voice was saying the opposite.

Colin came to a quick decision. "Listen, it's fine, okay? I'll meet you at that little pub in Soho where we used to go, remember? The one next door to the Gay Hussar restaurant?"

"Yeah, I remember." Colin couldn't miss the grateful note in his tone. "Thanks, Colin. I really appreciate this. What time?"

"About six-thirty? I'll come there straight from work."

Matt whistled. "Ooh, Colin in his suit. Aren't *I* the lucky boy." He chuckled.

Colin snickered. "Enough, you. I'll see you there at six-thirty." He hung up.

Now for the hard part.

Colin felt like a complete arse. If truth be told, he'd prefer to spend the evening with Ed, but Matt had sounded so down when Colin had hesitated.

Must be something important.

He speed-dialled Ed. After several rings it connected.

"Hey!" Ed sounded delighted to hear him. "Couldn't stay away, huh? D'ya miss me last night?" Ed chuckled.

Colin knew he was joking, but it didn't stop the thought flashing through his head.

God, yes.

"'Course I did," Colin replied, keeping the tone light. "Listen, I'm really sorry. The reason I'm ringing is that I'll have to skip dinner tonight. Something's come up."

"Aw, you're kiddin'. An' I was lookin' forward to that." Colin heard the sincerity in his words. Ed sighed down the phone. "Okay, fine. It's prob'ly for the best. The way things are goin' round 'ere, I might be workin' late meself. Problems with the printers." He made a sound that was sheer exasperation. "You gonna ring me tonight?"

"Yes," Colin responded promptly. "And I'll make it up to you, I promise."

Ed chuckled once more. "Like I'd let you forget it." Colin heard voices in the background. "All right, gotta go. I'll talk to you later, yeah?"

Colin assured him that would be fine and hung up. His chest tightened at the thought of Ed assuming it was a work issue—and Colin not disillusioning him of that supposition.

Why didn't you tell him about Matt?

Colin wasn't sure himself. It wasn't as if he had anything to hide. But part of him wondered how Ed would feel, knowing he was meeting up with an ex.

Then he sighed.

Ed probably wouldn't care less. It's not as if we're dating.

Then why was Colin's heart aching?

Colin sat at a corner table, from where he could see the door to the pub. The large bi-fold windows which overlooked the busy street were drawn back to allow air into the warm interior. August was shaping up to be the hottest on record. Colin's jacket lay over the back of his chair, his tie already folded up in its pocket and his shirt unbuttoned. Thank God his office had air conditioning.

He looked up as the door opened and Matt entered. He had to admit, the younger man was looking good. Colin did a rough calculation in his head. Matt had to be in his late twenties by now, and it had been two years since they'd dated. His gaze took in the crisp, white shirt and then drifted south to the tight, black leather pants and black boots.

Always was a stylish dresser.

Matt spotted him and his face broke into a wide smile. Colin stood to greet him and was surprised when Matt kissed him on the mouth, taking his time.

Colin jerked his head back and stared incredulously. "Er, excuse me?"

Matt grinned. "Aw, come on. We *were* lovers, right?"

Colin locked eyes with him. "Emphasis on the 'were' part. Right?" he mimicked.

Matt gave a shrug. "Sorry, I got carried away." His eyes gleamed. "I blame you. I can't help myself when you look so—"

"And you can stop right there," Colin said with determination. "What do you want to drink?"

"Medium white wine, please." Matt took a seat and stretched out those long, slim legs, encased in tight leather. Colin was disconcerted to find his gaze falling on Matt's crotch.

Do not even go there.

What made it worse was that Matt noticed. He gave Colin a cocky grin.

Colin made his escape to the bar. While he waited for the barman to get to him, he watched Matt surreptitiously. Matt hadn't taken his eyes off Colin, and seemed to be going out of his way to be provocative. He leaned back into his chair, one arm on the table, his hand resting on his thigh but slowly moving higher, just skirting his groin where the outline of his hard cock was unmissable. Colin shook himself. It had been a long time since he'd thought about Matt in those terms, and if he were honest, he didn't like the way Matt was regarding him. There was something almost...predatory in his expression. And that business with his hand? It felt as though Matt was trying to draw Colin's attention .

Well, he certainly succeeded, didn't he?

Colin was beginning to get a bad feeling about this get-together.

He went back to their table and handed Matt a glass of chilled white wine and then sat down to reclaim his pint. Matt took a sip and made a soft noise of approval before turning in his seat to give Colin his full attention.

"You're looking good there, Colin," he said with a smile. "How's the job working out?"

"It's fine." Colin tilted his head. "Was it the job you didn't like, or Leeds in general?" He couldn't help smirking. He imagined Matt had found Leeds stifling after living most of his life in London.

Matt groaned. "Oh God, don't get me started." He ran his hand carefully through his short layers of dark brown hair. "Okay, so there's a thriving gay community in Leeds, but I really missed London. Leeds felt so...small."

Colin laughed. "Needed more space, did you?" He gave Matt a keen glance. "Have you been single since you left London?"

There was that nonchalant shrug again. "I've been dating, sure, even had the odd boyfriend or two."

Colin was pleased. "Well, that's good, surely."

Matt grimaced. "It was, until the last guy. Then things got a bit...rocky." He lowered his chin to his chest and then looked at Colin through those long, dark lashes. It was an expression Colin remembered well. This was Matt trying to be alluring.

It used to work too, he thought with an internal smile. *Not anymore, though.*

Colin decided it was time to be blunt.

"Matt, why am I here?"

Matt's eyes grew large and round. "Because...because I wanted to see you," he said falteringly. "I thought it would be nice to get together and—"

"Matt, this is me you're talking to. We were together three years, so give me some credit for knowing when you're not being entirely honest with me." Colin folded his arms across his chest and waited.

Matt opened his mouth and then snapped it shut. His cheeks grew pink. "Look, there have been a few guys, okay? They've come and gone—well, they come and then they're gone, if you get my meaning," he said with a grin. "But I keep coming back to you." He held his hand up. "Yeah, I know we're very different. I know our friends didn't mesh—"

"At all," Colin interjected with a grin.

Matt nodded. "Yeah, yeah, I know. But lately I've been thinking that I want to give us another go." Another direct glance. "I think you're the one, Colin."

Colin let out a patient sigh. *Oh fuck.* He lowered his voice. "Matt, you've just said exactly why things didn't work out between us. It took us three years together to work out that we were too different. And you're right about our friends not gelling." He gave Matt a fond look. "It was fine for a while, but nothing's changed since we split. It wouldn't work."

"But I've grown since then," Matt protested. "You're older too. I think we can make this work." His face took on that stubborn expression Colin recalled so clearly.

Tell him.

Colin smiled. "Matt, I'm seeing someone."

Matt's face registered shock for all of a few seconds before he straightened it. "Since when?"

"A couple of weeks."

Matt huffed. "Well, it's not like you're engaged or something."

It was then that Colin had definitely had enough.

"One thing you may have forgotten about me," he said, getting to his feet. Matt stared up at him, mouth open. "When I'm in a relationship? I give it one hundred percent. And the one thing I certainly don't do is play around." He picked up his pint glass and drained the remainder of his lager. After placing the glass on the table, he smiled politely. "And now we're done. It was nice seeing you again, Matt. Enjoy being back in London. I don't expect our paths will cross much." Colin picked up his jacket and strode toward the door.

Matt reached out a hand to stop him. "Look, this didn't go like I'd intended."

Colin shrugged. "Doesn't matter. It's done now. Bye, Matt."

And with that he walked out onto the street without a single backward glance. The one thought in his head was that this shit had lost him an evening with Ed.

Ed was channel-hopping in the hope of finding something, *anything*, to arouse his interest, but so far, zilch. It wasn't as if he wanted to watch TV in the first place, but it was better than staring at his four walls and wishing he was with Col.

That was when it hit him.

Just what is Colin to me?

Colin had gone from being a mate, to them being mates who fucked, to...something else.

But what, exactly?

There was no getting away from one thing—the sex was amazing. Their appetites seemed to be in synch. *Or is this just how gay guys are?* All Ed knew was, if he was at Colin's and he wanted to fuck, chances were Colin was up for it. Every fucking time. And Colin's stamina matched his own. They usually fucked for *hours*.

Ed smiled to himself. *Are there* any *downsides to fuckin' a guy?*

If there were, he had yet to find them. But it still left him with that burning question—just what was Colin to him? He knew when the thought had first occurred to him—Sunday afternoon when they'd gone for a walk on the beach. Fair enough, it had been a gorgeous day for a stroll. But walking along a beach with a guy had this whole...romantic edge to it in Ed's mind.

That gave him pause for thought. *Romantic?*

Ed wasn't romantic. He just *wasn't*.

But was Colin? Ed didn't have a clue. And that was another thing—what was he to Colin?

An' do I wanna know this?

Now there was something that got his heart racing.

The phone rang, and he almost jumped out of his skin. When he saw Trevor's name, his heart sank. *Oh fuck, what now?*

"Trev, whass' up?"

"Listen, Ed, I need you to do me a favour, if you can."

Ed straightened up on the sofa. "Go for it."

"You know I made Rod scrum-half, to replace Murphy? Well, it seems he's not feeling very confident about his passing abilities. So I wondered, seeing as we don't have practice on Saturday, if you could meet up with him at the club and do a little practice? Maybe work on his passes, really put him through his paces?"

Ed considered the request. If he arranged to meet Rod early enough, he'd still have the rest of the weekend with Colin—provided that Col wanted to spend some time with him, of course.

"Yeah, sure," he said after a moment. "Text me 'is number an' I'll give 'im a call to set it up."

"Aw, thanks, Ed, I appreciate this." Trevor hung up.

Ed smiled to himself. Rod seemed like a good kid, really keen and with the makings of a damn good player. And if working out with him helped the team to win more games, then it would be a good use of his time.

He glanced at his watch and decided to see if Colin was finished with work.

"Hi." Ed loved the warm tone of Colin's voice, like he was really pleased to hear him. "You home?"

"Yeah." Ed sprawled out on the sofa, making himself comfortable. "You all done with work now?"

"Yes. Just walked through the door, actually." Ed heard the sound of Colin's keys as he dropped them onto the glass-topped table in his hallway. There was a moment's pause. "I missed you tonight."

Colin's words created a feeling of well-being inside him. "Yeah, missed you too." Ed cleared his throat. It felt awkward to voice his feelings outright. "Listen, I know there's no club practice on Saturday, but I'm hopin' to meet up with Rod for some extra practice, yeah?"

Another pause. "Oh?" Ed couldn't gauge Colin's reaction. His tone gave nothing away.

"Yeah, seems like Rod's feelin' a bit nervous 'bout takin' over Murphy's spot, so I'm gonna work with 'im on 'is passes." He waited, but nothing else was forthcoming from Colin. "We can still meet up afterwards, if you like?"

A second or two later Colin responded. "Yeah, that would be good. Hey, I've got an idea. Would you like to go out to dinner on Saturday night? Just a bite to eat, nothing like the last place, honest." He chuckled.

Ed groaned. "Oh God. Was it *that* obvious that I felt bloody awkward bein' there?" *An' there was me thinkin' I'd done so well, too.*

"Oh, not that much." There was something in Colin's voice that told Ed he was smiling as he said it. Ed could picture that smile, those bright eyes. "So we on then?"

"Sure." Ed liked the sound of that.

"And after dinner maybe you could come back to my place."

Ed cackled. "Ooh, would that be where I get me dessert?" His dick stiffened at the thought of the two of them getting down 'n' dirty in Colin's bed.

Colin laughed. "Oh, count on it."

Ed grinned. Oh, he was up for that.

CHAPTER FOURTEEN

"Well, that was great." Ed rubbed his belly, a contented smile on his face as they exited the pub.

Colin had to laugh. "Now, why do I get the feeling you were much happier having steak and chips in a pub than dining out in a fancy restaurant?" They walked at a leisurely pace along the street, heading back to the car park where Ed had left the Harley locked up.

Ed guffawed. "'Cause you know me too well, mate, thass' why." He grinned. "So we still on for dessert at yours, then?" There was a wicked gleam in his eye.

Colin lifted his eyebrows and moved closer, his voice dropping low. "If 'dessert' is a euphemism for several hours of hot sex, then yes." Ed's eyes lit up and Colin grinned. God, he wanted Ed in the worst way.

It's no use. I have to face facts. I am addicted to Ed Fellows.

And the remedy? Yeah, Colin knew what *that* was—and he intended to take his medicine tonight and most of Sunday. Since their stay in Brighton, Ed was happy to take it in turns bottoming, and Colin was delighted to oblige.

Right now Saturday morning felt like a lifetime ago, since he'd walked out onto the club rugby field to find Ed—and had seen him throw his arm around Rod's shoulders as they'd walked off the field together. He couldn't account for the surge of panic which had set his heart pounding. Okay, so Rod was young and sexy as fuck. That didn't mean Ed would be interested in him—right?

Colin had to keep reminding himself that Ed was on a voyage of discovery, as far as his sexuality was concerned. Maybe he'd already given some thought to experimenting with others, which might include a younger, handsome, virile guy like Rod.

And didn't *that* thought send Colin into a tailspin?

He gave himself a mental swift kick up the backside. Ed had shown no inclination to do any such thing, of course. It was just Colin's imagination working overtime—he hoped.

As they neared the car park, Ed's phone rang. His face registered surprise.

"Rod, whassup, mate?"

Colin stiffened. Why on earth would Rod be calling? He'd been with Ed that morning. He watched Ed's expression carefully.

"What—now? Really?" Ed screwed up his face. "Now's not so good, to be honest. Could it wait 'til—" His words trailed off as he listened intently. His expression grew concerned. "Oh, I see." He sighed. "Okay, well, 'ang on a minute." He pressed the phone against his chest and gazed at Colin, brow furrowed. "Rod wants to meet up for a chat with me."

Colin came to a halt. "Now?" *Oh, you have* got *to be kidding. Talking to Rod—instead of fucking?*

"Yeah." Give him his due, Ed looked really contrite about it. "Look, would you mind if we 'ad a change of plan? It sounds like it's important." Ed met his gaze. "Yeah, I know, I know, it's bloody awful timin'. I'll try to come round your place when we're finished, yeah?"

He sounded so apologetic that Colin felt bad for thinking badly of him. "That's fine. You go meet with Rod. I'll see you whenever you can get to the apartment, okay?"

Ed gave him a grateful smile. "Thanks, mate. Listen, you okay gettin' 'ome? Or shall I drop you off first?"

Colin waved his hand. "No, you go see Rod. Besides, the sooner you guys finish up talking, the quicker you'll be with me, right?" He pasted on a bright, cheerful smile.

"Right." Ed squeezed his arm briefly and then spoke into the phone. "I'm comin' round, okay, mate? Be there as soon as I can." Ed pocketed his phone, nodded toward Colin and then took off, heading toward where the Harley was stowed. Colin watched him clamber aboard the bike, helmet secured. Ed gave him a cheery wave as he rode out of the car park and along the street. Colin walked slowly to the nearest taxi rank and got in a black cab.

All the way back to the apartment, his mind could only focus on one thing.

Will Ed want to explore his sexuality? Or would I be enough for him?

He thought of Ed meeting up with Rod—and he didn't like the answer.

It was nearly eight o'clock when he walked into the hallway of his apartment building. The night doorman got up to greet him.

"Mr. Reynolds, there's been a delivery for you." The glint in Ian's eye was intriguing.

"Oh?" Colin wasn't expecting anything. He stared, wide-eyed, as Ian went behind the desk and brought out a huge bouquet of red roses. What the.....

"Aww, someone loves you," Ian said with a goofy grin.

Colin took the flowers and thanked Ian. Once inside the elevator, he picked out the small white envelope from amid the beautiful blooms and took out the stiff card. He let out a groan when he read the wording on it.

I meant every word. Please think about it.

I love you, always.

Matt.

Colin scowled. *Fuck—that's all I need right now.*

He let himself into the apartment, dropped the flowers onto the coffee table and went into his bedroom to change into his sweats and a T-shirt. When he came back into the lounge, he regarded the roses with a sigh, before taking them into the kitchen to find a vase.

"It's not *your* fault the guy who sent you is a conniving little shit," he told the flowers as he arranged them in water. Then he burst out laughing. "That's it. I've finally flipped. I'm talking to roses."

Still smiling, he walked back into the lounge and placed them on the coffee table. The card lay with its envelope on the floor where it had fallen, and Colin picked it up and placed it face down next to the vase.

He stretched out on the sofa and aimed the remote at the TV. No sooner had the picture appeared than his phone chimed. He smiled when he saw Ed's name.

"Don't tell me you're finished already," he said, nestling back into the plump cushions. He couldn't help feeling relieved. Ed had only been away from him for about an hour. Definitely not long enough to get up to anything. Then he berated himself for even thinking like that.

"Col, can I ask you a favour?" Ed spoke rapidly.

"Sure."

"Can I bring Rod over to your place? We need to talk to you."

Colin's mouth was suddenly bone dry. "What about?"

"Look, it'll be easier if I explain when I get there, okay?"

Colin's heart raced. All of a sudden he had a terrible idea he knew where Ed was going with this. *Oh God, please let me be wrong.* But he couldn't refuse him.

"That's okay. Come round, both of you." He did his best to keep his voice from cracking.

"Aw, thanks. You're a real mate," Ed said warmly. "Be there as fast as we can." And then he was gone.

Colin dropped the phone as if it burned his fingers. In his befuddled brain it all made sense.

Ed's getting to see what's it's like to have guys want him. Rod clearly wants him. He's approached Ed with the idea. And now Ed wants more. God, he might want a threesome.

The thought of sharing Ed made him feel sick.

I don't think I can do that. In fact, I'm bloody sure I can't.

Colin did. Not. Share. Never had. It just wasn't in him.

He switched off the TV and sat there, staring at the rug. He'd know soon enough.

About thirty minutes later the intercom buzzed, and Colin roused himself to get up and let them in. He opened the door and listened as the elevator whirred quietly. Ed was first out, followed by Rod who looked distinctly nervous.

"Come on in." Colin ushered them through into the lounge and gestured for Rod to take off his denim jacket.

Rod glanced at his surroundings, gaze darting everywhere.

"Sit down, please," Colin told him.

Rod gave him a grateful look and sat on the sofa, perched awkwardly on the edge of the seat cushion. Ed gave Colin a smile, which faltered when he caught sight of the roses. Ed said nothing, but he pressed his lips together and then sat next to Rod, patting his knee.

Colin took the armchair. "Okay, so what's so important that you couldn't tell me over the phone?" He tried to ignore the lump in his throat, not to mention the rolling in the pit of his stomach.

Ed gave Rod a glance, and Rod nodded. His pale face seemed strained.

Ed sighed. "Rod came to ask me advice, an' I didn't think I could 'elp 'him. I think he assumed I 'ad a lot more experience. And then I thought of you." His eyes met Colin's. "See, Rod's only just out at 'ome, and today he got a bit upset. He 'ad this massive row with 'is brother about 'im comin' out, and Rod didn't know 'ow to 'andle it."

"I'm sorry for disturbing you both like this," Rod interjected, "but I didn't have anyone else I could turn to. I don't know any gay guys, apart from you two." He looked absolutely miserable.

Two emotions warred inside Colin. His heart went out to the young man. Colin remembered only too well those first days when he'd finally plucked up the courage to tell someone about his sexuality.

And Colin's face tingled as he recalled his assumptions. *What an idiot I was to even* entertain *thoughts like that about Ed.* The memory of his foolish suppositions made his cheeks burn hotter.

He put aside his feelings of self-disgust and turned his attention to Rod.

"I know it feels difficult right now," he said soothingly, "but it *will* get better, honest." He smiled at Rod. "And although it was clearly a shock to your brother, he'll come around. Are the two of you close?"

Rod nodded. "I couldn't believe it when he reacted like that."

Colin got up from his armchair. "I think I'll make us some coffee—which will make *one* of us *very* happy"—he caught Ed's eye and gave a half-grin—"and then we can have a chat about it."

Rod let out a relieved sigh. "Thanks."

Colin went into the kitchen and partially closed the door behind him. He placed his hands flat on the kitchen table and took a long, steadying breath.

How could I doubt Ed? Don't I know him by now?

The incident had left him shaken. Ed had done nothing to warrant Colin's mistrust. It was his own lack of faith in Ed that had set the ball rolling. Colin straightened and caught sight of himself in the small mirror on the windowsill.

If you're serious about wanting a relationship with him, then you'd better start believing in him, he told himself sternly.

When he felt calmer, he put the coffee on and when it was ready, took it through to his guests. The three men chatted for about an hour, and Colin was gratified to see that Rod calmed down a lot. Finally, Rod stood up to leave.

"Thank you so much, both of you," he said with a gentle smile. "I really appreciate you taking time away from your evening together to give me some advice."

"You sure I can't give you a lift to your place?" Ed asked.

Colin had to smile. His Ed was a big-hearted teddy-bear.

Then he stopped. *His* Ed?

Rod shook his head. "Thanks, but there's a tube station just up the road. Besides, I've taken up enough of your time."

Colin showed him to the door and gave him a quick hug. "If you need to ask about *anything*, you know where to find me now."

Rod's face glowed. "You two are the nicest guys I've ever met." He smiled and then went for the elevator.

And didn't *that* heap coals onto Colin's guilty conscience?

He closed the front door and went through into the lounge—and stopped dead.

Ed was reading the card.

He jerked his head up as Colin entered the room. For a moment he said nothing. Then his eyes met Colin's. "Nice flowers," he commented. Then he fell silent.

Well, fuck.

Colin bit his lip. "I was going to tell you."

Ed's eyebrows arched and Colin's stomach rolled over. "It's okay, you don't 'ave to tell me." His tone was cool.

Fuckfuckfuckfuckfuck....

"No, really," Colin began, "let me—"

"I think I'm gonna go back to my place tonight, if thass' all right." Ed didn't look him in the eye.

Colin's heart was beating so fast, he thought it would explode. "Please, Ed, stay. It's—"

"I said it was okay, right?" There was an edge to his voice. Ed began to walk toward the door.

"They're from my ex," Colin blurted out.

Ed stopped. "Okay, they're from your ex," he said, smiling. A faker smiler Colin had never seen. "But I'm still goin' 'ome." He paused at the front door. "I'll call you, yeah?"

Oh, why don't I believe that?

"Look, you're not going and leaving things like this," Colin protested. "Can't you at least sit down and listen to me for a minute?"

Ed stood stock-still. "What is there to listen to?" he demanded. "You said they're from your ex? Fine. End of conversation." His eyes glinted. "*Now* can I go 'ome?"

"Okay, sure," Colin said at last. He watched Ed go out the door, shoulders hunched.

That's it? For God's sake, go after him, a voice screamed inside his head.

He hurried to the front door in time to see Ed about to step into the elevator. He called out Ed's name.

Ed turned. "Col, just go back inside. I'll talk to you tomorrow."

"And if I want to talk now? What about that?"

Ed stared at him. "But I don't, all right? It can wait 'til tomorrow."

And with that he was gone.

Colin stood staring at the closed elevator door, listening as it hummed during its descent, taking Ed farther and farther away from him. He could just about hear the sound of the doors opening on the ground floor.

His chest aching, limbs heavy, Colin went back into the apartment and closed the door, shutting out the world.

Right now, Colin wanted nothing to do with the world outside his apartment.

This is payback, he thought incoherently. *That's what it is—payback for not trusting Ed in the first place.*

And payback hurt like hell.

CHAPTER FIFTEEN

Ed *hated* having a hangover. Especially the one he got from whiskey.

Well, it's your own stupid fault. You shouldn't've drunk so much of it, should ya?

He'd started on the whiskey on Saturday night. When Sunday had rolled around, he hadn't felt like stopping. And why? All because of Matt, whoever he was.

Well, whoever he is, I can't compete. I don't even know *how to compete.*

All the doubt and insecurity that had surfaced at the club was back with a vengeance. It didn't matter that Ed felt connected to Colin, that something good had been developing between them. All of that faded into the background. It had only taken a few words on a little card and a vase full of beautiful red roses to make him doubt *everything*.

So Matt loves Colin. Fine. At least he knew. No more wondering what Ed meant to Colin, because apparently, he meant nothing.

You don't know that for certain, he argued with himself. But then those four little words on that card were suddenly there in his mind, burning into his brain.

I love you, always.

See? he told himself. *Why should Colin bother with a guy like me, when there's a bloke sendin' 'im bleedin' bouquets and tellin' 'im he loves 'im?*

In Ed's tortured, sleep-deprived brain, it made perfect sense. Colin didn't need him. Colin had Matt.

Is he fucking Matt, too? It was a question that had still bothered Ed in the early hours of Sunday morning, when he yearned for the soft oblivion of sleep, but was denied. He didn't know why it should bother him, but it did.

When Monday morning came, Ed had awoken to face it with an aching head and a heavy heart. And if it hadn't been for the fact that

Blake was due back at work on Tuesday, Ed would have stayed in bed. So he got up, took two aspirin and made it into work with five minutes to spare.

Rick was in the office kitchen, having already set up the coffee machines, bless him. Ed poured himself the largest mug he could find and tried to reach the safe haven of his office to get his head in gear before the team meeting. No such luck—Rick had no intentions of letting him escape.

"You look awful." Rick spoke in a low voice, for which Ed was profoundly grateful. Noise was the last thing he needed. Rick poured himself a mug.

Ed sighed. "Blame it on Johnnie Walker." He took a sip of coffee and closed his eyes at that first jolt of caffeine. *Nectar.*

Rick frowned. "Want to come to my office for a minute?"

Ed gave him a baleful stare. "Not really, but you're not gonna accept that as an excuse, are ya?" Rick shook his head. Ed was touched by the look of concern in his eyes. He huffed. "Go on, then." He followed Rick down the corridor and into his cozy little office.

Rick shut the door after them and then leaned against his desk. "Okay, what gives?"

For a second or two, Ed debated fobbing him off. Then he realized that he needed to talk to someone. He sat down, took another long drink of coffee and then poured his heart out. Just *telling* it hurt. Through it all Rick watched him in silence sipping his coffee. When he'd finished, Ed sat back, momentarily wiped out.

Rick regarded him, his expression neutral. Then he rolled his eyes. "God, Ed, you are so dense."

Ed's mouth dropped open. "What?"

Rick lifted his eyebrows. "You didn't give Colin the chance to explain or anything, did you?"

Ed thought about that. With a guilty start he realized Rick was correct.

Rick was nodding. "If you really want this, then for God's sake, *fight* for him." He tilted his head. "Did Colin actually *say* he didn't want you there?"

Ed's face fell. "No, he asked me to stay." He could still see the look on Colin's face.

Rick's face lit up with a triumphant expression. "And there you have it. You want to know what I think?"

Ed regarded him wearily. "I'm sure you're gonna tell me whether I want to or not, so just get it over with, yeah?"

Rick folded his arms across his chest. "I think this is all in your head." His brow furrowed. "What did you mean, you couldn't compete?"

Ed gestured to his body. "C'mon, Rick, *look* at me. I 'ave no idea what this Matt looks like, but I'll bet ya anythin' you like that it's nothin' like me." He gazed into his coffee mug. He'd thought long and hard about this. "I'm obviously not gay enough for Colin."

What sounded like Rick trying not to choke had Ed looking up in a hurry. Rick stared at him, eyes wide.

"Well, now I've heard everything." Rick looked like he was trying not to laugh. "Not gay enough? There's no *scale of gay*, all right?" He shook his head. "I thought you said Colin liked the way you look."

"Yeah, well," Ed began, suddenly feeling less sure of himself. "That's what he said, but—"

"What would you do if Colin had been a *woman* and you thought maybe someone else was in the picture?" Rick demanded.

No hesitation. "I'd go after her."

There was a gleam in Rick's eyes. "So why is this any different?" His jaw set. "You need to get your phone out *right this minute* and call Colin. Take the morning off if you have to, but sort this out. I can hold the fort here."

God, it was tempting. Could it be *that* simple?

Rick's gaze met his. "Ed, it's clear to me just from listening to you that however this started between you and Colin, it's progressed beyond two guys meeting up for sex. How much further it goes from this point on is up to you." Then a gentle smile spread across his face. "But you want to be with this guy, don't you?"

God help him, he did.

Ed reached into his pocket for his phone, just as it vibrated under his fingertips. He took it out and stared at the screen. Colin.

Rick let out a soft chuckle. "I'll leave you to it. Stay here. I'll come back in a little while." He exited the office, leaving Ed gazing at the phone, his mind racing. The ringing persisted.

He's not giving up, is he?

With a sigh, Ed connected the call. "Hi."

He heard Colin expel his breath at the other end. "Good morning." He fell silent.

Ed waited anxiously for him to speak. As the silence continued, he realized it was down to him to make the first move. "D'you think you could meet me for a coffee this mornin'? Someplace between our buildings?"

Colin's reaction was immediate. "There's a coffee shop opposite King's Cross Station. Do you know it? I'll meet you there in half an hour."

Relief flooded through Ed. "Okay. See you then." They hung up.

Ed held his phone against his chest, breathing deeply.

Okay, now to let Rick have his office back—*and* let him know Ed was taking him up on his offer. Rick could run the team meeting. Ed had somewhere important to be.

Colin checked his watch for what had to be the fifth time.

He'll be here. Patience.

Colin still couldn't believe Ed had agreed so readily. Since Ed had walked out of his apartment on Saturday night, Colin had all but convinced himself that he'd screwed it up for good. And when Ed hadn't called like he'd said the following day, that seemed like a confirmation. A day later and Colin felt like crap. He'd hardly slept and it showed.

The coffee shop door opened and Ed entered, biker jacket slung over his shoulder. He spotted Colin straight away and walked over to his table.

Christ, he looks as bad as I feel. Colin's next thought was more pleasant. *But at least he's here.*

"I waited until you got here to order. Americano?" Colin knew Ed's taste in coffee by now.

Ed nodded. "Yeah, and make it a large one, eh?" He rubbed his hand across a stubbled cheek.

Colin smiled. "Yeah, having one of those mornings myself." He left Ed to sit and went over to get the coffees. When he returned to the table, Ed was leaning back against the cushions of the comfy sofa. He looked shattered. Colin placed the large cups on the table and then sat beside him.

"You all right taking time out of work like this?" Colin knew Ed was in charge until Blake returned from paternity leave.

"Yeah. Rick's dealin' with it for me." Ed took a long sip of coffee and smiled. "God, that tastes good."

Colin drank some of his black coffee, loving the bitter aroma. For a moment neither of them spoke.

There was an empty feeling in the pit of his stomach as he waited for Ed to say something, *anything,* that would give him a clue to what was going on in Ed's head. 'Cause this waiting was driving him—

"I'm sorry I left, okay?"

Colin jerked his head up to look into Ed's eyes.

"Yeah, I know, I was an idiot," Ed went on to say. "That's already been pointed out to me once today."

"I wouldn't say you were an idiot," Colin said quietly. "It was as much my fault as yours. I should have told you about meeting with Matt." He sighed. "Matt wants me back." He knew it was best to be honest. *'Cause look where hiding shit got me?*

Ed swallowed, his Adam's apple bobbing. "Oh."

"Look, he can want all he likes," Colin hastened to add. "It's not going to happen, though. I don't want him back."

Ed's eyes widened. "You sure? I thought maybe..." His words trailed off.

"What? What did you think?" Colin wanted to know. He couldn't take his eyes off Ed.

Ed pushed out a long sigh. "I thought maybe you'd found someone who was more... you know..." His chin dipped briefly and Colin was just about able to catch the next word. "Gay."

Colin stared. What the...?

Ed looked up and smiled. "It's okay. Rick already clued me in. Now you know why he called me an idiot."

Colin liked Rick more and more.

He leaned forward. "I repeat: you're not an idiot. And for the record? I like you just as you are."

Ed's cheeks flushed pink.

Colin placed his hand on the table next to Ed's. He stroked the side of Ed's hand with his little finger. *Moment of truth.*

"I don't want Matt back. Been there, done that, and it didn't work out. But I *do* want to see where this goes with you." His eyes met Ed's. "I want that very much."

Ed gazed back at him, mouth slightly open, brow creased. He blinked rapidly, giving Colin every indication of being unsure how to react to Colin's words.

Colin let escape a patient sigh. "Ed, I've loved what we've shared so far. The sex is...fantastic, and I really enjoy your company. But I need to be honest with you. I want more."

Those clear green eyes widened.

Colin leaned back. "Look. Don't say anything now, okay? Maybe you need to think about this." He got to his feet. "So I'm going to go back to work and let you do just that. And when you're ready to tell me how you feel, then call me, all right?"

Ed finally found his voice. "All right," he acknowledged.

Colin smiled. "Thank you." He badly wanted to kiss the man, badly enough that he ached to hold him, but this wasn't the place. "I'll see you soon, I hope." He picked up his suit jacket from over the back of a chair and gave Ed one last nod, before exiting the coffee shop.

Once outside, Colin sucked in a deep breath.

I really hope I've done the right thing.

And he just *knew* he wouldn't be able to relax until Ed got back to him. He sent out a silent plea to the man he'd left sitting in the coffee shop.

Please, Ed, don't rush this. Think about it.

Ed got out his keys to open the glass door to Trinity's suite of offices, and then stopped when he realized they were already open.

Of course. Blake's back.

Ordinarily, he would have been pleased as Punch to see his boss, but after spending yet another night without a decent amount of sleep, Ed wasn't thinking clearly. For one thing, it had completely slipped his mind that Blake was going to be there.

An' 'ow could I forget that?

Blake, who knew Ed better than anyone—and who seemed to possess the ability to read Ed's mind. Logically, he knew this wasn't possible, but God, the man had an uncanny knack of seeing right through him.

An' right now? That's the last thing I want.

Blake, who was walking toward him at that very moment. His boss looked like he could use a whole week of sleep, but he still wore a grin.

"Nice to see you're still an early bird."

Ed snorted. "You've only been gone, what, five weeks, Boss? Did ya think I'd let the place go to rack an' ruin while you were away?" *An' let's 'ope no one mentions yesterday's little lapse....*

Blake merely arched his eyebrows. Then he grinned. "Coffee?"

Ed matched his grin. "God, it's good to 'ave you back, boss." Then he remembered. "An' you're not gonna believe who turned up 'ere wanting a job." He couldn't wait to see Blake's face.

Blake turned to go to the kitchen and beckoned Ed to follow. "Well, that can wait 'til I've had a coffee. I didn't have one this morning."

The aroma of freshly brewed coffee filled the small kitchen, and Ed sniffed the air appreciatively. Blake's words suddenly registered.

"Is that 'usband of yours not lookin' after ya?" Ed asked with a chuckle.

Blake laughed. "I didn't have a coffee because I overslept. Sophie's not sleeping through the night yet, and we're taking it in turns to feed her. I was so tired last night, Will said he'd do the feedings. And by the time I woke up, Will hadn't made coffee because he'd fallen asleep on the spare bed in Sophie's room. When I went in, she was lying there next to him, laughing and gurgling."

Ed loved the expression on Blake's face. It was plain Blake was besotted with his little girl. "'ow is she?" Sophie had been born three weeks' premature.

Blake's face glowed. "She's fine. She's a really healthy weight, and usually she sleeps well between feeds. Just not last night."

Ed smiled. "You were prob'ly feeling bad 'bout leavin' 'er an' Will to come back to work and she picked up on it. Babies are sensitive like that." Blake's eyebrows shot skyward and Ed's face heated up. "So I've 'eard," he added hastily.

Blake shook his head, eyes wide. "Well, well, well. This is a side to you I've never seen before. Who are you, and what have you done with my brash, speak-before-you-think office manager?" He chuckled.

Ed blinked.

Oh, you 'aven't 'eard the 'alf of it yet.

Blake leaned against the worktop. "So you were telling me about someone who came for a job?" He took a long drink of coffee and sighed happily.

"Oh, yeah." Ed waited until Blake has another mouthful of coffee, timing his words just right. "Melissa Richards."

The coffee ended up all over the Blake's suit, not to mention the carpet. Ed let out an evil little cackle.

When he'd finished choking, Blake stared at Ed in disbelief. "You *are* kidding, right?" He grabbed a cloth and began wiping up coffee. He stared down at his no longer clean shirt in disgust.

Ed snickered. "Like I'd make *that* up." He filled Blake in on the conversation, Blake listening with wide eyes and slack jaw.

"Well, I hope you sent her away with a flea in her ear," Blake said when Ed had finished.

Ed nodded.

Shane appeared in the doorway, his face breaking into a wide grin when he caught sight of Blake. "Welcome back, boss." He blinked when he spotted the coffee stains on Blake's shirt. "And did we have a slight accident? Miss our mouth? Hmmm?"

Blake smiled. "Morning. And are we any nearer to finding your replacement?" His eyes held a wicked gleam.

Shane sighed dramatically. "I see. Work for a man for six years and he can't wait to get rid of you."

"Interviews are all set up for the end of the week," Ed added. "An' be nice to the lad. We 'aven't got 'im for much longer."

Blake's expression grew glum. "Don't remind me. I really thought I'd cracked it when I took you on." He gave Shane a mock glare. "I hope Laura knows what a good deal she's getting. Have you two set a date yet?"

Shane nodded. "We've found a house, too—well, our friend Lauren who lives in Sydney has found us a house—and the move is all set for three months' time. The wedding will be just before we leave, and we'll be having a honeymoon over there."

"Nice," Blake remarked. "Well, shall you and I go and sort through the pile of work you so kindly left on my desk?"

Ed chuckled. "I'll let you both get on with it." He walked out of the kitchen and along the corridor into his office. He closed the door and then leaned against it. The less time he spent around Blake, the better. Blake could be far too intuitive at times.

For the rest of the morning, Ed threw himself into his work. It was the only thing that seemed to combat the thoughts colliding around inside his head. He could still see Colin's face, that look in his eyes when he said it...

An' if I want more? What does that say 'bout me?

That was the part Ed didn't want to think about.

He was ready for his lunch when the door opened and Blake entered, eyes twinkling with good humour. He pulled out the chair facing Ed and sat down, arms folded.

"So.... Is there something you want to tell me?"

Oh... fuck.

CHAPTER SIXTEEN

"Excuse me?" Ed swallowed. His heart pounded so loudly, he swore Blake could hear it.

Blake wagged a finger. "Did you think you could keep it a secret? The whole team is talking about it."

Ohfuckohfuckohfuckohfuckohfuckohfuck...

Ed couldn't speak. His throat seized up.

"So, what's her name?"

Wait.... Go back a minute...

Ed cocked his head to one side. "Whose name?" This was getting weird.

Blake grinned. "This mystery woman who's had you smiling at everyone for the past couple of weeks. It's all I've been hearing all day. 'Ed's loved up.'" He waggled his eyebrows. "So? Gonna tell me who she is, then?"

There was no way Ed could lie, not to Blake.

"Listen. I need to talk to you, right?" Ed looked his boss in the eye. "But not 'ere."

God, talk about déjà vu....

Blake regarded him carefully. Then he got out his phone and hit a key. He gazed at Ed as he spoke. "Hi, babe. Listen, I don't know what you have planned for dinner tonight, but there'll be an extra mouth to feed." He paused. "Ed's coming round." Blake smiled. "Yeah, that sounds great. I'll see you tonight." Another pause. "Love you too. Kiss Sophie for me."

Blake put his phone away and gave Ed an inquiring look. "Good enough?"

Ed puffed out a sigh of relief. "Yeah, perfect."

Blake nodded. "Then I'll let you get on with it. Just as long as you know, you really have me intrigued. I can't wait to hear this."

Ed snickered. "Well, tough. Get your arse back into that office, Mr. Davis. Now that we've got you back 'ere, we'd better get some work out of ya, yeah?"

Blake opened the door to leave but gave Ed a mock glare before he exited.

Ed sagged into his chair. He had a lot to tell his mate, and he wasn't sure where to start.

Well, let's see... 'So I was just givin' Colin a blowjob...'

Ed snorted. Blake was going to have a field day with this.

"Damn, Will, you can cook." Ed leaned back against the seat cushions and rubbed his belly appreciatively. "Nice to see you're spendin' your days doin' somethin' productive like learnin' to cook." He winked at Blake. "'Cause everyone *knows* all writers do is sit around on their arses all day, drinkin' coffee and chattin' on Facebook."

Blake hooted. "God, you do like living dangerously, don't you?" He turned to his husband beside him and kissed Will tenderly. "And don't listen to the evil little troll over there," he told Will with a grin. "I know how you spend your days, babe."

Will snuggled up closer, his head on Blake's chest. "Thank you." He stuck his tongue out at Ed, who laughed.

Ed patted the arm of the sofa where he was sitting. "Did you always 'ave two sofas, or is this one new?"

Blake arched his eyebrows. "One, yes, it's new, and two, why don't you tell us whatever it was that you *couldn't* tell me at work? Because I'm pretty sure you didn't come round to discuss interior decorating."

"Yeah, not unless you've suddenly gone gay since we last saw you," Will added with a cackle.

Fuck. For a moment, Ed was lost for words—and panicking.

Blake became very still. "Ed? You okay?" Will sat up straight and gazed at him, his brow creased in a frown.

Oh well, no time like the present...

"Look, I've met someone," Ed began, fiddling with the red velvet cushion which he'd pulled onto his lap.

"Well, duh." Will snickered. "That much I already knew from Blake."

Ed shook his head. "Yeah, but..." Fuck, he'd talked about this with Rick, so why did this feel so much more difficult?

Because that's one of your closest friends sat over there, that's why.

Ed drew in a deep breath. "Thing is.... it's a guy." He held his breath.

Blake stared at him. Just...stared. And then a slow grin spread across his face. "Well, bugger me."

Ed recovered some of his composure. "If it's all the same to you, I'd rather not...I think your 'usband might not approve," he said with a snort.

Will cracked up. He hugged his middle and laughed until tears rolled down his cheeks. Blake nudged him with his elbow. "Quiet, you'll wake Sophie."

That shut him up fast. Will got it together and wiped his eyes.

Blake gave him a fond glance before focusing his attention on Ed. His eyes sparkled. "Well, that was all very Tom Daley-like." He smirked. "This I've gotta hear. But my first question has to be...who?"

Will gave Ed a triumphant smile. "It's that rugby mate of yours, Colin."

What the fuck? Ed gawked at him, mouth slackened. "'ow the 'ell did you know that?"

Will buffed his fingernails on his shirt. "'Cause my gaydar is *amazing*, that's why." Then he smiled. "It was just something I picked up on when I met him in the hospital. It was obvious *you* didn't see it, though."

Blake got up, walked into the kitchen and returned with three squat tumblers and a bottle of whiskey. He placed them on the table and poured out three glasses. He handed one each to Will and Ed, and then sat back down, his arm going around Will, drawing him closer. "Okay, let's start at the beginning, shall we?"

Ed sighed. He took a sip of the whiskey, relishing its burn on his throat and then began. The couple listened mostly in silence, each asking the odd question here and there. When he'd finished, Ed sagged back into the cushions. "There...now you both know everythin'."

"But it's not everything, is it?" Blake said, a knowing look on his face. "There's something bothering you. I can see it in your eyes." He gave Ed an affectionate glance. "Come on, mate, we've known each other too long to hide shit. What is it?"

Ed took another slurp of his whiskey. "I'm just tryin' to figure out where this leaves me."

Blake looked puzzled. "What do you mean?"

Ed did his best to put his feelings into words. "I like bein' with Col. I love the sex—God, the sex is *amazin'*"—both Blake and Will chuckled, and Ed's cheeks heated up—"an' we 'ave a really good time. So... does that make me gay? I mean, I've 'ad girlfriends, yeah? So am I gay, bi....?"

Blake smiled. "Why do you need a label? Let it be what it is. Don't try to dissect it, or try to put it in a nice, tidy box. Just roll with it."

Ed considered his words. That felt...right.

"I'm more interested in what happens next," Will said, his eyes fixed on Ed. "Colin's told you he wants more—how do you feel about that?"

Ed stared into his whiskey. "Scared shitless, if you must know."

"That's understandable," Will said quietly. "But from what I can see, you're coping really well."

Ed raised his head. "Yeah?" Will nodded. "Thanks, mate." He swirled the amber fluid around in its glass. "Yeah, if I'm honest...I want more, too. Only thing is, I'm not ready to go singin' it from the rooftops just now. I mean, me rugby mates know, an' they seem okay with it—an' at least we've lost that arsehole Murphy—and there's you two, an' Rick an' Angelo, but I don't want anyone else knowin' just yet." He gazed at the couple. "Is that okay?"

Blake smiled. "Ed, it's your life, mate. You decide who you come out to, yeah? Though if you *are* serious about being with Colin, at some point you're gonna have to tell your mum."

That made him stop and think. "God, me mum... I 'aven't got a clue 'ow she'll take this."

"There's no hurry," Will assured him. "Just take your time, yeah? It's still early days. Let's see where this takes the two of you before you decide to tell her anything."

Ed regarded them in silence for a moment. Then he grinned. "What with you two, an' Rick an' Angelo, I'm not short of guys to go to if I need advice." It was a comforting thought.

Blake gazed at him warmly. "Anytime, mate. Anytime." Then his face lit up. "Wanna go look at a little girl who's sleeping right now?"

"I thought you'd never ask." Ed smirked. "I bet you two thought I'd come over 'ere to see *you*, didn't ya?"

They all laughed at that. Ed rose from the sofa to follow Blake and Will to their daughter's bedroom. He peered around the slightly ajar door and gazed at the little girl lying on her back in her cot, tiny fist clenched, mouth open.

"God, she's so small," Ed whispered. "But she's beautiful. Guys, she's adorable."

Blake and Will stood next to him, their arms around each other, gazing adoringly at their daughter. They pulled him away by the arm and then closed the door, leaving a gap. As they walked back into the lounge, Will chuckled.

"We'll see if you're still saying that when it's your turn to babysit."

Colin switched off the TV and dropped the remote onto the seat cushion beside him. It wasn't as if he'd been paying attention anyway. His mind was on other things—well, one thing, really.

He couldn't believe it had only been five weeks since that night in the hospital. Because it felt like much, much longer. He hadn't heard from Ed since their coffee the day before, and he kept telling himself that no news was good news.

What if I've scared him off? What if all Ed wants is a fuck buddy, no strings attached?

It wasn't as if Colin hadn't had his fair share of casual sex. He'd been more than happy to go with the flow. But Ed? Ed was different.

The intercom buzzed, startling him from his reveries. He glanced at his watch, surprised that it was already past ten o'clock. Colin padded barefoot to the front door and pressed the speaker button. "Hello?"

"Col, sorry to stop by unannounced."

Colin's heartbeat picked up at the sound of Ed's voice. "Come on up," he said, pressing the door release button. He opened the door and glanced down the corridor toward the elevator, his mind in a whirl as he tried to second-guess the motive behind Ed's visit. The elevator hummed to a halt and Ed appeared, smiling when he spotted Colin waiting in the open doorway.

"This is a nice surprise," Colin said as they passed through the hallway into the lounge. "I didn't expect to see you so soon."

Ed stood there, hands stuffed into the pockets of his jeans. "I've just been to see Blake an' Will."

"Oh? How's the baby?" Colin took a seat on the sofa and gestured for Ed to join him.

"God, Col, she's gorgeous." Ed gave a broad smile. "An' she looks really well."

"I was just thinking about that night." Colin leaned back. "It seems so longer ago now."

"An' a lot's 'appened since," Ed added, his voice lowering. He hunched forward, hands laced, elbows resting on his knees. For a moment neither of them spoke.

"Would you like a drink?" Colin asked him.

Ed shook his head. "Nah, there's somethin' I gotta say."

Colin's heart pounded. He couldn't bring himself to say anything. He just...waited.

Ed stared at the rug for a minute before raising his head to look directly at Colin. "Look, I'm not about to go wavin' rainbow flags an' mincin' along the street in a Pride parade—"

Colin guffawed. He couldn't stop himself. Ed's eyes widened and Colin waved a hand. "God, I'm sorry. That was so rude of me. It's just that I couldn't imagine you *mincing* anywhere."

Ed cracked a smile. "Yeah, doesn't bear thinkin' about, right?" His expression became more serious. "But like I was sayin'... I want to see where this goes. Us, I mean."

Colin stared. "You mean that?"

Ed nodded, his gaze focused on Colin. "Yeah, I do." He swallowed. "If you still want that, too." He licked his lips.

Colin was seized by an urge which swept through him, flooding him with warmth. "God, I want to kiss you so badly right now."

Ed groaned. "Oh, for God's sake, Col, don't tell me that, just fuckin' *kiss* me."

Colin pushed Ed down onto the sofa, stretched out on top of that glorious body and attacked that mouth which was begging to be devoured, in an all-consuming kiss. Their tongues collided, hands roaming over each other's bodies, both making urgent noises of sheer need as they got into it.

"Fuck," Ed panted, breaking the kiss to draw breath.

"Good idea," Colin said with a grin. "Here? Or in bed?"

Ed's eyes gleamed. "Why not both?"

Colin laughed. "Oh, I like the way you think."

And that brought an end to all conversation for the next hour or two.

⁂

"So, what was your impression of the candidates?" Ed asked Karen. The last one had just gone in and he wanted Karen's opinion. She was a good judge of character.

Karen pursed her lips. "I liked that Tom, if Blake wants to carry on the tradition of a male PA. He was very personable, if a little shy." She sipped the tea Ed had brought her. Tea was only an excuse, of course—picking Karen's brains had always been on Ed's agenda.

"Don't let that count against 'im," Ed said with a grin. "Look at Shane. He wouldn't say boo to a goose when he first got 'ere, an' now look at 'im." He chuckled. "I heard 'im givin' Blake lip the other day." Ed put his hand over his heart. "I was *so* proud of 'im." They both laughed.

"Roberta seemed very capable," Karen announced. "Of the three of them, I think she's the best one for the job. She seems really keen and very friendly."

"Maybe," Ed said with a shrug. "Although on paper the best one 'as to be Samantha." She was the final candidate to be interviewed.

Karen pinched her lips together but said nothing.

Ed frowned. "What? What is it?"

Karen shrugged. "Oh, it's probably just me, but...."

"But?" Ed perched on the edge of Karen's desk. "Come on, babe. It's not like you to 'old back." He gave her shoulder a playful shove. It was no secret around Trinity that Karen had a soft spot for him.

Karen took another sip of tea before answering. "Okay, in her favour? She's older. That's good—Blake always scared off the younger ones." Ed snorted. "She has a ton of experience in the publishing world."

"Agreed." Ed folded his arms across his chest.

"She acts very professional, and she's attractive."

Ed said nothing but waited for the punch line.

"It's just that..." Karen scowled. "There's something about her that I don't like. Something not right there, and I'll be damned if I can put my finger on it." She drummed her manicured fingers on the desk.

Ed stood up when he heard Blake's voice along the corridor. Blake rounded the corner, accompanied by Samantha who was dressed immaculately in a grey suit. They shook hands.

"Thanks for attending today," Blake said with a wide smile. "I'll be making my decision shortly and you'll be informed, whatever the outcome. It was a pleasure meeting you, Samantha."

"Likewise," she said with an equally wide smile, "and it's Sam, please."

"Sam," Blake echoed. "Goodbye and thank you again."

Ed watched Sam give a cheery wave as she exited the reception area. He turned to Blake and quirked his eyebrows. "Well?"

Blake gave a happy grin. "Oh, no question. She gets the job. She came across as very confident, she's perfectly qualified, and I can't see her complaining that I'm a tyrant, so she might even outlast Shane." He turned to Karen. "Draw up a confirmation letter, would you, Karen? And then make sure it catches today's post." He swung around and walked off toward his office, whistling.

Karen's expression grew tight.

Ed squeezed her shoulder. "Maybe your woman's intuition is way off, ever thought about that?"

She huffed. "Maybe."

Ed gave her a warm smile and headed back to his office. As he walked away, he heard her mutter under her breath.

"And then again, maybe not."

CHAPTER SEVENTEEN

"You feeling nervous?" Ed asked Rod as they got changed for the game. The locker room was noisy, everyone eager to play.

"A little," Rod admitted with a shy smile. "But less than I was a couple of weeks ago, that's for sure. You really helped."

Ed huffed, and Colin patted his back. "That's our Ed," he said with a grin. "Helpful little soul."

"Little? Ed?" Harrison snorted. He winked at the players who were changing around him. "I think Colin needs some glasses." There were snickers at this.

"Why?" Pete asked, his eyes gleaming. "Is Ed's dick too small to see without 'em?" Guffaws echoed around the tiled room.

Colin held up his hand. "One, I don't need glasses, and two, Pete obviously hasn't been paying attention in the shower if he thinks that *baseball bat* Ed has between his legs is small." He winked.

"Yeah, but does he know 'ow to use it?" someone called out. Hoots and expletives resounded.

"Okay, now we're *definitely* strayin' into the realms of too much fuckin' information," Jeff said with a groan. He covered his ears. "La la la la la la la...."

Loud raucous laughter rebounded off the tiles.

Colin gave Ed a sheepish look. "Sorry, you know how they get."

Ed gave him a look. "You an' I will discuss this later, right?" His grin belied any real threat.

"Woo hoo! Looks like Colin's gettin' some tonight, lads!"

"Okay, that's enough of that." Trevor shook his head. "I swear, you lot keep getting worse."

There was a loud knock at the door. Jeff strolled over to open it. To Colin's surprise, about five or six of Southend's players entered the room. Ed's team all stood up, every eye on the intruders.

"So who are the gay guys?" asked the tallest player. He scanned the locker room. His teammates stood behind him.

There was no mistaking the reaction of the players. Everyone froze.

"Well?" the Southend player demanded. "We all got a call, so a few of us thought we'd come check out these famous 'fags' we've heard so much about." He grinned.

Colin saw the tension on his teammates' faces as they moved slowly toward the opposition. Trevor stepped in front of them.

"Are we going to have a problem here?"

The ringleader's face fell. "Oh God, no, mate! You got us all wrong."

"Yeah." Another Southend player inched forward. "'aven't you guys met Derek Miles, our number eight? He's as queer as a nine pound note."

Colin's teammates looked at each other in surprise.

"Then why are you 'ere?" demanded Pete.

The ringleader smiled. "We all wanted you to know that we didn't pay any mind to the evil little bastard who made those calls. Derek would be the first to tell you he puts up with a lot of stick from us, sure, but we support our own. There'll be no funny business out there today, lads. Count on it."

Colin could almost see the tension seeping away, as stiff backs and squared shoulders relaxed.

Jeff pointed to Colin and Ed. "Those two are our little gay mascots," he said with a cheeky grin.

The ringleader followed his pointing finger and gaped. "Little? *That* one's built like a brick shit-house!" More raucous laughter followed and the atmosphere returned to its prior state. The look on Ed's face was adorable. It was a mixture of pink-cheeked embarrassment and open-mouthed shock, not to mention a glimmer of pride.

"All right, lads. Back to your changing room." Trevor took control. "We've only got about five minutes left. See you out there." He gave them a friendly nod. The players grinned at the home team and exited.

Trevor stared at his team-mates. "And if you prima donnas are ready, we've got a game to win." He winked.

Colin pulled on his red and black jersey, ready to do battle.

Rod approached them. "Derek Miles is gay?" he said in an awed voice.

Ed's eyes rounded. "Got a thing for Derek, 'ave we?" He waggled his eyebrows.

Rod's blush crept up his neck, staining his cheeks. He coughed, and Ed and Colin laughed. Rod sidled up to Colin. "So Colin, *does* Ed know how to use it?" he asked with a sly grin.

Colin burst out laughing. "It's none of your business." Then he leaned closer and lowered his voice to a stage whisper. "Bloody hell, you bet he does." He caught Ed's gasp and chuckled.

Ed glared at him. "When you've quite finished corruptin' young Rod 'ere...."

Colin was still chuckling when he, Ed and Rod joined their team-mates to jog out onto the playing field. Everyone seemed to be in a great mood.

"Bleedin' fags! It's a fuckin' disgrace, letting queers play!"

Colin stared, open-mouthed. *What the fuck?*

Harrison ran up to him, scowling. "Is someone heckling out there already? We haven't even started playing yet."

Colin straightened and cocked his head. "It's coming from over there."

A sizable crowd had already gathered. Kensington was a popular rugby team and they always had a good following.

"Send the queers off!"

Colin scanned the crowd. "Can you see who's doing it?"

Harrison was joined by Phil and Jeff. They peered into the waiting spectators.

"*Co-lin Rey-nolds takes it up the arse.*" A chant began, men's voices rising above the crowd. Cold spread throughout Colin's body.

Suddenly Phil stiffened. "Oh, that fucking little *shit*!"

Ed appeared at Colin's side. His face was pale. "I heard it. Who is it, Phil? Do you know any of them?"

Colin could hear murmuring from people in the crowd as they took issue with the hecklers.

Phil nodded slowly. "Oh yeah. Three of them play for Maida Vale, and they're nasty little fuckers, dirty players every one of them." He scowled. "But it's who's with them that's *really* pissing me off." He turned to face his teammates. "Murphy."

And now the chant changed.

"*Ed Fel-lows, Ed Fel-lows, pokes the arse of GAY fel-lows.*" Voices rose as more people demanded for them to be quiet.

Colin whipped around to look at Ed. His face was white.

"Don't think much of their lyrics," he quipped, his voice faltering. Colin could see Ed was shaking.

Players from the opposition jogged over to join the little group. Among them was Southend's number eight, Derek. He grimaced. "I think I'm gonna go over there and teach them a lesson." He clenched his huge fists.

Harrison grabbed his arm. "I'm coming with you."

Derek frowned. "This isn't your fight."

Harrison clenched his jaw. "And it's yours because you're gay and I'm not? Fuck that." His eyes were cold. "I may not be gay, but two of my team-mates *are*, and I say, let's go teach those *arseholes* over there that they can't do this."

Derek nodded. "Let's do it." His voice was tight.

The two huge men stride across the field to where Murphy stood, three jeering men flanking him. Murphy's face was a mask of hate.

Colin couldn't pick out the words as the six men confronted each other, but their faces told the story.

Derek reached into the crowd and hauled two of the men toward him and pummelled both of them. Harrison laid into Murphy, fists flying. The third man took one look at the proceedings and took off, the crowd jeering him as he fled.

And then the referee was there, followed by Trevor and Doug, Southend's captain. The three men pulled the brawlers apart, holding them around the arms.

"Oh God," Phil said with a loud groan. "The ref is gonna pull Derek and Harrison from the game."

"What?" Ed's jaw dropped. "But they didn't start this!"

"Doesn't matter," Phil said gloomily. "Just listen to that commotion."

Trevor and Doug sent Murphy and his two friends packing. The crowd around the three men booed them as they slunk away.

Derek brushed himself off, took a step toward Harrison and enveloped him in a huge hug. The crowd erupted, cheering as the two men embraced before they were ordered off the field by the ref.

Colin turned to Ed. "You okay?" he asked his lover.

Ed breathed deeply. "I will be. Right now I'm so fuckin' mad I could spit." He met Colin's concerned gaze. "Let's play, eh?" He squared those wide shoulders.

"Great idea," Phil murmured, and there were nods of assent from both teams.

As they ran over to get the match going, Colin struggled to control the anger that surged through him.

When will there be an end to all this hatred?

"Fantastic game, lads!" Trevor sounded jubilant as he came out of the locker room and waded through his team members who stood around laughing and chatting. He clapped them on the back as he passed each player. "And what a score!" It had been close, but Kensington had beaten Southend by five points. Players from both teams stood outside the club, making plans to get together for a drink.

"We going to the pub?" Colin asked Ed as he squeezed his kit bag into the luggage compartment of the Harley.

Ed's face lit up. "Course!" His mood had improved since the start of the game. But that was Ed. Colin loved how he threw himself wholeheartedly into everything he did. There were no half measures with Ed Fellows.

Colin looked around. "Have you seen Rod? I wanted to congratulate him. Talk about lightning reactions—that lad was a marvel out there."

A wicked smile stole over Ed's face. "Rod's, er...busy," he said, cheeks pinking up.

"Busy with what?"

"That." Ed nodded to something over Colin's shoulder. He turned—and stared.

"Well I never."

Rod ambled out of the club house, engaged in a clearly engrossing conversation with Derek Miles. What made it even more interesting was the way Derek was looking at Rod.

"Are you thinkin' what I'm thinkin'?" Ed asked Colin with a grin.

Colin met his gaze. "Oh yeah." He held out his hand. "Now give me a helmet and let's stop staring at him. We'll make him nervous at this rate."

Ed snuck another glance in their direction. "Aw, I think it's really sweet."

"Helmet—now."

Ed raised his eyebrows. "Get you. Maybe I need to remind you who's top dog in this relationship." His eyes twinkled.

Colin moved closer to him. "So...we're definitely in a relationship?" He smiled.

Ed's voice became husky. "To quote you? 'Oh yeah.'"

Colin edged closer, pulled by the lure of Ed's soft lips—until someone threw a kit bag at him, hitting him in the middle of his back.

"Get a room."

"Are you *tryin'* to make us heave?"

"Take a cold shower, mate!"

Colin whirled around to find his teammates standing around with huge grins. "You sods."

Ed thrust the helmet against his chest. "Come on, you, I can 'ear a pint or three callin' me from 'ere."

Amid guffaws and chuckles, Colin climbed onto the back of the Harley behind Ed.

"'old on tight," Ed called back to him, "an' no playin' with the merchandise."

Colin put his arms around Ed's waist and tightened them, loving the feel of the strong, firm body in front of him. He rested his chin on Ed's shoulder.

"Spoilsport."

He could feel Ed's laughter reverberate through him.

"Oh bloody 'ell, it's catchin'," Pete groaned.

Ed followed Pete's line of sight and had to smile. The two teams had crammed into the Elephant & Castle about two hours ago, taking up most of the tables. Players perched on stools around tables or squeezed up together on the padded seats, numerous pint glasses on the tables with varying levels of liquid in them.

Tucked away in the corner, Derek Miles was leaning in to talk in a low voice with Rod. The slighter built young man was gazing at Derek with wide eyes, an expression of rapt attention on his face. What was very noticeable was Derek's hand, casually stroking Rod's thigh. And Rod looked like he was all but melting under that touch.

"Somethin' you wanna tell us, Rod?" Jeff called out. There were snickers and smothered chuckles from around him.

Derek's hand tightened around Rod's thigh, but he glanced up at Derek and smiled. Rod caught Ed's eye and then drew in a deep breath.

"No," he said with a smirk. Then he winked. "I should have thought it was perfectly obvious." And then he went back to talking with Derek.

Jeff's mouth fell open. "Oh my God. Another one." He stared at his teammates with wide eyes. "Are there gonna be any *more* of us turnin' gay?" Laughter broke out.

Ed couldn't resist. "'Aven't you 'eard? We've got a plan. We're aimin' to take over the world." He winked at Colin. "This time next year? It'll be the Kensington Gay Rugby club."

"Oh fucking hell." Phil shook his head. "God, it's like buses. Not a gay player in sight, and then three come along at once."

There was a moment of silence before the bar erupted into laughter.

"Hey, Harrison!" Derek called out. Harrison glanced across at the player, and Derek raised his pint glass to him in a salute. "You were great today, mate. We showed 'em, yeah?" His white teeth gleamed in a broad smile.

Harrison raised his own glass. "That we did. And any time, Derek." He gave the number eight a firm nod. Derek grinned and then turned his attention back to Rod.

Phil whistled. "I'd say you were in there, mate, but I think that's spot's already been taken." He leered at Harrison. "Unless Derek over there is into threesomes?"

Colin burst into a peal of laughter, and several players around him joined in. "Oh God, you guys crack me up."

Ed watched the proceedings, his mind elsewhere.

Colin nudged his knee. "Where are you? And what are you thinking right now?"

Ed let out a sigh. "I was jus' thinkin' 'bout today. That on the one 'and you could 'ave fuckers like Murphy, all twisted up with 'atred, and on the other?" He glanced around him at the laughing players. "You could 'ave guys like this lot, who just accept ya an' get on with it." His gaze travelled over to where Rod and Derek were deep in conversation. "I mean, look at Rod. We both know he was nervous about tellin' the guys, yeah? An' yet he just took the plunge an' did it." He grinned. "An' this bunch just rolled with it."

Colin beamed at him. "Maybe Rod found it easier after he saw the team's reactions today. Maybe it gave him a little courage." He peered around the pub and gestured to the players. "Make no mistake, though. This isn't typical. You're always going to have evil bastards like Murphy, ready to give you a hard time because you're gay. But then sometimes you meet people like this group, and it really gives you faith in mankind."

Ed studied Colin's face for a moment. "I think I'm playin' for the right team." He smiled.

"I think I could be a good gay," Tony Meadows announced to the assembled group. His words were greeted with guffaws and choking sounds from his teammates. He glanced around in surprise. "What? I would. I'm in touch with my feminine side."

Jeff spluttered beer. "I don't think bein' gay has anythin' to do with your feminine side, mate." He pointed toward Ed and Colin. "I mean, look at those two. And Derek. Those guys are mean-lookin' bruisers."

Phil barked out a laugh. "I think Ed and Col are having us on, you know, lads." There was a wicked gleam in his eyes. "I mean, they *say* they're gay, but have we seen any evidence of it? Nah."

Pete doubled up laughing. He wiped his eyes and shook his head at Phil. "So what do you want 'em to do? Fuck in front of you to prove it?" Ribald laughter echoed around the packed pub.

Phil choked on his pint. "Fuck no." His teammates chuckled. Then Phil gave Ed and Colin a sly grin. "But I'd pay good money to see 'em kiss." He winked at his mates. "Wouldn't you? These two big, hefty blokes in a lip-lock?"

Jeff shook his head. "I really worry about you sometimes, Phil."

Colin shook with laughter. Ed just stared at his teammates. The funny thing was, it wasn't scaring the shit out of him. In fact, the prospect of kissing Colin in front of an audience was a bit of a turn-on.

Colin's eyes met his. "Ready to step out of that closet and shut the door after you?" he said with a smile.

Ed's heart pounded. He met Colin's direct gaze head-on. "Why not?"

Colin turned to Phil. "Okay then, let's see your money."

Phil goggled "What?" His jaw dropped.

Colin's eyes sparkled. "You just said you'd pay good money to see me and Ed kiss, so... I want to see the money first or else we don't perform." Ed bit back a laugh at the look on Phil's face.

"He's right, pay up, Phil!" one of Southend's players called out. His demand was repeated by his team-mates.

Phil started to bluster. He reached into his jeans pocket and pulled out a scrunched-up five-pound note. He dropped it onto the table in front of Colin. "There." Phil sat back and folded his arms, face red.

Jeff peered at the bank note and laughed. "And what do you expect them to do for *that*?" He shook his head. "Cheapskate."

Phil appeared pained. "What, more?"

Pete guffawed. "Mate, you're askin' two great 'ulkin' rugby players to kiss each other in the middle of a pub, in front of a load of straight guys. You'd better make it worth their while." He winked at Ed and Colin. Colin grinned back at him.

Phil grumbled and dug deeper into his pocket. He pulled out a wad of notes and started to sort through them. Next to him, Harrison peered into his hand and reached over to grab a twenty-pound note. He flung it on top of the fiver. "Now *that's* more like it," he said with an evil grin.

Phil's mouth fell open. "Hey! That's my money you're being so generous with." He went to take it back but Harrison placed his hand on top of it.

"Uh-uh," he warned. He gazed at Ed and Colin. "That enough for ya?"

Colin gazed inquiringly at Ed, who shrugged. The whole situation was just surreal. "Sure."

It felt as if every guy in the pub was staring at them as Colin leaned in and began to kiss him, softly at first, but then growing more demanding. Ed had to bite back the groan that was just behind his lips. There was no way he was about to let his teammates know the effect Colin's kiss had on him. Colin's hands gripped his head as he devoured Ed's mouth. After a few seconds, Colin broke the kiss and sat back, eyes gleaming.

And Ed was as hard as a rock.

"Bloody 'ell," Pete said in a low voice. "That was... " His words trailed off.

"Fucking hot is what it was." Derek's voice pierced the fog of lust that enveloped Ed's brain. Derek began a slow handclap, and other players joined in. The applause grew louder.

Ed surfaced from the kiss and stared at the rugby players who regarded him with varied expressions. He cleared his throat, deliberately keeping his hands away from his crotch where he badly wanted to adjust his aching dick.

"An' now that you're all 'appy," he said as the applause died down, "I'm gonna leave ya to carry on gettin' pissed, while I take Colin 'ome." He got to his feet.

Whistles and hoots broke out among the players.

Colin gazed around the pub and winked. "I think my luck's in tonight, lads."

Ed growled and grabbing Colin's upper arm, he dragged him out of the pub amid cheers and laughter.

It was Monday before Ed saw the world outside Colin's apartment. And that was fine by him.

CHAPTER EIGHTEEN

"Oh, I could smack that woman sometimes!" Karen fumed as she helped herself to a coffee in the office kitchen.

Ed looked up from his lunch, surprised. It wasn't like the usually placid Karen to be so vocal. "Whass'up, babe?"

Karen let out a low growl. "I've been trying to talk to Blake about taking some time off. My cousin's getting married and I've been invited to the wedding, but it's in Germany, so I'd need at least three or four days off."

Ed frowned. "So what's the problem? Blake won't mind about stuff like that."

"The problem," Karen gritted out through clenched teeth, " is that I can't actually get to speak to Blake. Sam fields all his calls now, so you can't ring him directly."

Ed stared at her. "Then just go see 'im." It seemed perfectly obvious to him.

"Don't you think that thought hadn't occurred to me?" she groused. "But every time I go to his office, the door is shut and the sign says to see Sam. And *she* won't let me in to see him. He's always 'busy'"—she hooked her fingers in the air—"or 'on a conference call', or something." She huffed and then met Ed's gaze. "Well? When was the last time *you* spoke to Blake?"

Ed thought for a second. Now that she mentioned it... Ed no longer saw Blake first thing in the morning. By the time he got to work, Sam was already there, making coffee. Sure, Ed got emails, but that had been it. And yeah, he'd been seeing less and less of Blake in recent weeks.

"And then there are the team meetings," Karen continued. "Sam's formalized them. There's always a tight agenda. It's like she's micromanaging *everything*." Her face fell. "It just doesn't feel the same around here anymore."

Ed left his chair and put his arm around Karen, hugging her. She leaned against him. "Listen," he said quietly, "you send Blake an email about the time off, yeah? He'll see that. An' don't worry. Maybe Sam's just bein' a bit overzealous, you know, new job an' all." At least, he *hoped* that was all it was. He released Karen from the hug and she stepped back, blushing.

"Thanks, Ed, you're sweet."

Ed poured himself a coffee and gave her a last smile before leaving the kitchen to go to his office. He went over Karen's words in his head. Work had been fairly hectic the last few weeks. It seemed every day brought a new glut of submissions. Ed and the team had never been so busy.

Maybe that's why I 'aven't picked up on this, Ed thought. *Been too busy workin'.*

Then a guilty flush spread through him. It wasn't just work that had been occupying his time. There was also the matter of a certain gorgeous man who was taking up more of his evenings. Not to mention those odd moments of the day when the opportunity presented itself—like now....

He went into his office and closed the door. He might have finished his lunch, but his break wasn't over just yet. There was still time to make a call.

Ed sat down, propped his feet up on the desk and got out his phone. He knew Colin would answer within a few rings. This had become a regular occurrence.

"I was just about to call you," Colin said as they connected. "How's *your* morning going, because the less said about mine, the better."

"Whass' wrong?" Ed settled back to chat.

"Oh, nothing I'd want to bend your ear with," Colin replied. "You want to come round this evening for dinner?"

"Yeah, that sounds great." Ed smiled at the thought of dinner with his lover.

Me lover. Even the words made him glow inside and out.

"Where are you right now?" Colin asked.

"In me office. Why?"

"When's lunch over?"

Ed glanced at his watch. "You've got me for another fifteen minutes." There was a fluttery feeling in his belly. He knew what was coming.

"Go and lock your door."

The authoritative note in Colin's voice had the same effect it always did—Ed's dick suddenly started to pay attention. Ed lurched from his chair across the room, locked the door and was back at his desk in a matter of seconds. He pulled out a set of earbuds from his drawer and attached them to his phone, grinning the whole time.

"You ready?"

Ed popped the button on his waistband, unzipped his pants and slipped his hand into his briefs. "Oh yeah." He palmed his stiffening shaft. "You got your cock out too?" He pictured Colin sitting at his desk, sliding his long, thick dick through his fist.

"To quote you, 'oh yeah.'"

Ed chuckled. "You make me do wicked things, ya know? Phone sex during office hours? Tut-tut, Mr. Reynolds."

Colin's voice was quiet. "It's all your fault." His breathing picked up speed. "I just get to thinking about you in my bed, all stretched out, naked, your dick standing to attention. Ready for me to ride it."

"Oh fuck," Ed said softly.

"Which is exactly what I intend doing to you tonight after dinner."

The breath caught in Ed's throat. "You gonna fuck me?"

"Oh baby, I am *sooo* going to fuck that sweet arse of yours." Colin's voice was husky, and sexy as hell.

"What did I say," Ed gasped, his hand sliding faster as he worked his dick, "about you callin' me baby?" Colin laughed. In Ed's mind he was already on his hands and knees, Colin pounding his hole from behind.

He loved it when Colin just *took* him. His pucker clenched as he recalled the feel of Colin's cock deep in his arse, filling him completely.

"You want that, don't you?" Colin panted. "You love it when I fuck you, hard and fast."

"Fuck, yeah." God, he was already so close.

"One of these days you and I are going to get tested."

"Tested?" Ed's hand stuttered on his dick.

"God, yes. I want to slide bare into you, feel your heat all around my shaft."

Fuuuuuuuuuccccckkkkkkkk....

"You want that?" Colin demanded. "Want to feel my bare cock inside you? Feel my hot load pump into you?"

And suddenly it was all too much for Ed. He grunted as his balls rode up and he quickly grabbed a tissue from his desk to catch the hot spunk which erupted from his dick. He opened his mouth wide, no sounding coming out as he arched his back, body trembling.

"Oh fuck, you sound so hot when you come." And then Ed could hear Colin's soft cry, followed by harsh breathing.

Ed sagged back into his chair, panting, tissues clutched around his softening cock. "God, I swear you bring me off faster every time we do this," he said breathlessly.

"You think I could get you to come within five minutes?"

Ed chuckled. "Probably, the rate you're goin', but where would be the fun in that?" He wiped himself off and dropped the tissues into the wastepaper basket. "Now I'm gonna be thinkin' about you fuckin' me for the rest of today, you know that, right?"

Colin laughed. "Drat! You saw right through my evil plan." He cackled. "Have fun this afternoon."

Ed shook his head. "You're an evil sod, all right." He said goodbye and hung up. Once he was all tucked away and presentable again, he picked up his mug and grimaced at the taste of cold coffee.

Think a little flip-fuck is in order tonight, he thought. *Call it revenge for making me coffee go cold.*

Then Colin's words finally hit home. *Tested.*

The implications of that one word sent a surge of heat through him. *Fuck.*

Ed smiled.

"Ed, you got a minute?

Ed looked up from the figures he was perusing. Karen peered around his office door. "Sure, Karen. Whass'up?"

"Do you think you could come to Blake's office with me?"

Ed put his hand over his heart and gasped dramatically. "What—no pitbull today?" He chortled. *'Pitbull'* was Karen's not-so-nice nickname for Sam.

"She rang in this morning. Apparently she had to take her cat to the vet." Karen frowned. "So can you come to Blake's office? It's important."

"Sure." He got up and walked over to her. "But if Blake wants to know why the monthly stats are late gettin' to 'im, I'm blamin' you." He grinned but was surprised when Karen didn't react. He followed her to Blake's office where she knocked on his door and then entered, Ed right behind her.

Blake glanced away from his monitor and smiled. "We having a meeting I didn't know about?" He quirked his eyebrows. "Does Sam know about this?" Blake gestured toward his sofa, and Karen sat down. Ed leaned against Blake's desk. Blake gazed at Karen and his smile faded. "Okay, something's obviously wrong, because that didn't get a reaction." He swivelled his chair to face her, arms folded across his chest. "Out with it."

Karen studied her hands for a moment before speaking. "You both know I had an abusive boyfriend a few years back." Both Ed and Blake nodded. "Well, when I finally chucked the bastard, a friend suggested I get some counselling, and it was good advice. I learned a lot. Well, I've been watching Sam since she started working here, and I have to tell you, alarms bells started going off, and it was all to do with my counselling."

Ed didn't have a clue where this was going, and from the look on Blake's face, his boss was equally clueless. "I'm not followin' this at all."

Karen twisted her hands together. "Okay. My counsellor showed me how Tom had begun to alienate me from my friends and colleagues. He wouldn't let me see my friends, always insisting I stayed at home with him. If they rang the house, he answered. All my calls went through him. If friends wanted me to go out with them, they had to ask Tom first. And if they called me at work, I had to tell him about it when I got home. He'd tried to make me dependent on him alone. She told me it was classic battered spouse syndrome."

"Okay, now I'm really confused here," Blake said, frowning. Ed nodded. "What does this have to do with Sam?"

Karen's eyes went wide. "You don't think you're experiencing this?" she asked Blake.

Blake's eyes went blank, but all of a sudden Ed got a sinking feeling that he knew where Karen was headed with this.

"Spell it out for 'im," he suggested.

Karen gave him a grateful look and then turned to Blake, counting off on her fingers. "No one has 'access' to you anymore—we all have to go through Sam. All calls to you go through her. If we try to see you, we're told you're unavailable. She keeps everyone at arms' length from you. She's reorganized everything this way." She looked beseechingly at Blake. "Can't you see it? I recognize the signs, and I had to say something. This was the first chance I got."

Blake stared at her, a look of consternation across his face. "Karen, I'm gratified that you're concerned, but I think you're seeing stuff that isn't there. Sure, Sam has reorganized how I work, and I have to say, I get a lot more done these days."

"Let me guess—'cause you're spendin' more time workin' and less time socializin' over a coffee, right?"

Blake jerked his head to stare at Ed, which told him he'd scored a hit.

"Does that sound familiar? Like maybe somethin' Sam 'as said to ya?" Ed pinched his lips together. "Okay, maybe Karen's got it totally wrong, but I think it's somethin' ya need to bear in mind, yeah?"

Blake shrugged. "All I can say is thank you for coming forward, Karen."

Karen got to her feet. "I'll be getting back to my desk now." She hurried out of the office, giving Ed a quick smile as she passed him. Ed watched her exit.

"I think Karen's seeing things myself."

Ed turned to face his boss. "Yeah? Well, I'll give ya my view, shall I? I'm your office manager, your *second-in-command* as you've called me a few times. So technically, I rank above your PA. So why is it that even *I* 'aven't been able to get into this office durin' the last few weeks?" He shook his head, frowning. "I blame meself for not sayin' anythin' sooner. I've 'ad a lot going on in me own life and maybe I've let things slide when I shouldn't 'ave. I've left things alone 'cause I figured it'd pass, but after everythin' Karen's just said? I'm gonna be keepin' a very close eye on *Samantha*, you can bet on that."

He walked toward the door. "An' if you want *my* advice, you should, too."

And with that he went back to his office, heart pounding.

An' if he wants to talk about it, he knows where to find me.

Colin left things alone until dinner was finished, but the silence began to get to him.

"What's wrong?"

Ed looked up, his brow furrowed. "Wrong?" He'd been staring at his empty plate, tracing the pattern with his finger for the last five minutes.

Colin let out a patient sigh and moved Ed's plate out of reach. He took hold of Ed's hand and cupped it in his own. "There's obviously something bothering you tonight. You've hardly spoken a word since you got here."

Ed's gaze dropped to their clasped hands. A little smile crossed his lips. "Thass' nice."

"Yeah?" Colin rubbed his thumb in slow circles over the back of Ed's hand, exerting just enough pressure. Ed closed his eyes, as if he were losing himself in the intimacy of the moment. "Ed. Talk to me."

Ed huffed and opened his eyes. He raised his head and met Colin's gaze. "Just a few things on me mind, that's all. Nothin' to worry you about."

Colin released his hand and straightened. "And just who am I?"

Ed frowned. "Huh?"

Colin stared at him, unflinching. "I'm your lover. The man who shares his bed with you on a regular basis. You know, the guy you're in a relationship with?" He cupped Ed's chin and tilted his face. "And if all of that means you still can't share what's going on in your life, then we have a problem." He let go and collected the dishes to take into the kitchen. He placed them in the bowl and turned to put the coffee machine on, only to find his path blocked. Ed stood there, a pained expression on his face.

He grasped Colin's arm. "Look, I'm sorry, all right? This...this is difficult for me. I've never 'ad a relationship where I talked about me feelins, yeah? I was the bloke, an' blokes didn't share stuff like that."

Colin raised his eyebrows. "Let me guess. All your past relationships were based on sex, right? Purely physical, no emotional connection?" He leaned into Ed, drawing their bodies closer. "We have so much more than that," he whispered. He felt the shiver that rippled through Ed. Slowly, so slowly, Colin kissed him, his lips brushing against Ed's in a touch as light as gossamer. He loved the feel of Ed's beard against his skin. He moved down Ed's neck, lips ghosting over the skin which carried Ed's scent, warm and fragrant. Colin loved to bury his face in Ed's pillow on those few nights when his lover slept in his own bed. He'd fall asleep surrounded by Ed.

Ed stood there, eyes closed, hands by his sides. Colin knew this wasn't the kind of kiss Ed was used to receiving from him. *Those* kisses would come later, in bed. Colin moved back to Ed's mouth, kissing him lightly, fleetingly, a whisper-light connection.

Ed opened his eyes. "That... that felt good."

Colin smiled. "I'm glad. I've wanted to kiss you like that for a while now." He took Ed's hand and led him back into the lounge. They sat down on the sofa.

"Okay, let's start again." Colin stretched out his body along the couch and put his head in Ed's lap, the muscled thighs providing a firm cushion. He stared up at Ed, who cracked a smile to see Colin lying like that. "I'm listening."

Ed smirked. "Comfy, are we?"

"Mmmm, very." Colin gave a little wriggle. He gave Ed a mock-glare. "Waiting here."

Ed sighed. "All right. Two things, really. The first is some developments at work. I might 'ave dropped the ball on somethin'." He told Colin about the fears of the office receptionist, Karen, with regards to Blake's new PA. "What amazes me is that Blake 'adn't noticed. An' neither 'ad I." His eyes were troubled.

"Okay, let's look at this for a moment. Karen might have it all wrong, for one. And Blake's probably been preoccupied these last weeks, what with coming back to work after spending so long with Will and baby Sophie. I'll bet that's where his mind has been." Colin reached up and chucked Ed under the chin. "Even *you've* let your attention wander at work recently."

"An' whose fault is *that*, I wonder? When this sexy-arsed guy rings me up an' gets me all 'ot an' bothered." He grinned at Colin and then tweaked his nose. It was an intimate little gesture that gladdened Colin's heart.

"Has Rick noticed anything?" he asked.

Ed thought about it for a moment. "If he 'as, he's not said anythin'." Then he grinned. "But then we're back to that 'ole *I've 'ad me mind on other things* situation again."

Colin chuckled and then folded his arms. "You said two things. What's the second?"

Ed brought his hand to rest on Colin's chest, stroking it. "Ah, that's a bit more...personal. I'm workin' up me courage for somethin'." Colin tilted his head to peer intently at him and Ed sighed. "I'm plannin' on seein' me mum this weekend. There's somethin' I 'ave to tell 'er."

Colin scrambled to an upright position in seconds. He knelt on the sofa beside Ed, gaze fixed on his face. "Yes?" he asked.

Ed gave a lovely, gentle smile. "Well, I figured it was about time she knew about the man in me life." He swallowed.

Colin drew in a long, slow breath. "God, Ed." His heart soared.

They regarded each other in silence for a moment, and then Ed did something very un-Ed-like. He stroked Colin's cheek, fingers moving over the cheekbones and into his hair.

"Let's go to bed."

"Yes." Colin's voice came out more gravelly than he'd intended.

"But...can I 'old you for a while? I mean, yeah, we can 'ave sex, but..." There was something in those green eyes, a look of need Colin hadn't seen there before. "Jus' wanna 'old ya."

Colin got to his feet and held out his hand. "I'd like that," he said quietly.

Ed rose up and Colin led him into the bedroom, shutting the door behind them. All Ed's concerns and fears could stay outside his bedroom door for one night.

CHAPTER NINETEEN

Ed stowed the Harley in the garage and locked it. He walked slowly to the back door. He knew Mum was home—he'd made sure of that before he left Colin's place. He paused at the door. Colin's last words were still in his head.

"She loves you, yeah? Then she's going to be okay about this. All right, it might be a shock at first, but she'll come round. And that's my opinion, based only on what you've told me about her. So have faith, baby."

Ed smiled to himself, despite his misgivings.

I am gonna cure 'im of usin' that word if it's the last thing I do.

The strange thing was, he was starting to like it.

He pushed open the door and entered the small kitchen. Mum was at the sink, washing up a few dishes. She spun around and her face lit up.

"What you doin' 'ere on a Saturday?" Her eyes twinkled. "An' didn't I just speak to you on the phone?" She wiped her hands on a tea towel and held her arms out. "Come 'ere, you. Got an' 'ug for your ol' mum?"

He smiled as he stepped up to her, wrapped his arms tight around her and hoisted her into the air, hugging her. Mum laughed and hit his shoulder. "Put me down, you soft git."

Ed let her gently down to the floor, all five feet nothing of her.

She stared up at him and rubbed a hand across his bearded cheek. "God, you get more 'n' more like yer Dad every day." He didn't miss the touch of sadness in her glance. Mum smoothed down her skirt and blouse, and then went to put on the kettle. "I take it you want a coffee?"

"That'd be great, Mum." Ed pulled out a chair and sat down at the wooden kitchen table that had seen so much over the years. The kitchen was where the family went to discuss important stuff over a cuppa, though never all of them at the same time. The small room couldn't hold everyone.

Mum glanced over her shoulder at him. "Oh, like *that*, is it?" His choice of location obviously wasn't lost on her. She turned back to her task. "Well, I figured it 'ad to be somethin' important to bring you over 'ere on a Saturday. No match today?" Ed listened to the noises of teaspoons in cups, jars being unscrewed, without really hearing them.

"Nah, not today. No practice either." Which had meant a leisurely morning in bed—that had become very *un*-leisurely when Colin had rolled onto his belly and presented Ed with his already lubed-up hole. Ed tried to suppress the shudder that ran through him at the memory of fucking his lover until both were hoarse from yelling out their pleasure at each other.

Talk about distractin'....

Mum placed a mug of instant coffee on the table in front of him and then sat opposite, tea in hand. She propped her elbows on the table and sipped her drink.

Ed studied her for a moment. Mum had always been a tough old bird. His Dad had once joked that she was never ill because no germ would have the nerve to invade *that* body. And there was his famous line that when the bomb went off, all that would survive would be the cockroaches and Mum.

Right now Mum looked tired. Like, *really* tired.

"You okay, Mum?" Ed couldn't help it, not that he expected her to reply. No one in the Fellows family ever whined about their health.

She arched his eyebrows at the question.

Ed shrugged. "You just seemed, I don't know, not yerself."

There was a moment's hesitation before she replied. "Nah, I'm fine." She looked closely at him. "Okay, out with it." She smirked.

God, the woman knows me way too well.

He drew in a deep breath. "Okay..."

Mum lost the smirk. A frown creased her forehead. "Oh God, this is bad, innit? You've not lost yer job, have yer?"

Ed shook his head. "Nah, nothin' like that, promise."

She sagged into her chair with a barely concealed air of relief. "All right, if it's not yer job, then what is it?"

Fuck, this is harder than I thought it would be.

"Mum," he began, eyes on his mug. "I've...I've met someone."

It was as if all sound in the kitchen had been sucked into a black hole.

He looked up sharply. Mum was beaming. In fact, she looked radiant.

"Oh Ed." Her voice was soft, and Ed's chest constricted at the love held there. "You're me oldest, so I worry 'bout you more than the others, I suppose, but I was startin' ta think you were gonna wind up on yer own, love."

Oh fuck.

He reached across the table to take her wrinkled hand in his. "The thing is..." He swallowed.

"What's 'er name?" Mum asked, her face still wreathed in a huge smile. She patted his hand fondly.

Ed straightened, Mum's small hand buried in his huge one. He met her gaze head-on. "Colin."

The black hole was back.

She cocked her head, skin crinkling around her eyes as she stared at him. Her hand came up to touch the base of her neck. Her eyebrows squished together. "I...I don't understand."

Ed sighed. He summoned up all his courage to say the words he'd not yet uttered to a soul. "I'm gay."

Mum pulled her hand free. She blinked, lowered her gaze to the table, then back up to his face. "Gay?"

"Well, gay, bi—the wordin' don't matter, Mum. The important part is that I'm with a guy, an' he makes me 'appy." He searched her face.

Mum picked up her mug and took a long drink from it. She studied the contents for a moment. With every second that passed, the lump in Ed's belly grew bigger, until it felt like there was a bowling ball in there.

"I don't know what to say," she said at last. "I mean, you've 'ad girlfriends—not that I ever *met* any of 'em, mind you, but I knew there were some lurkin' around somewhere." Her eyes narrowed. "You sure this is nothin' to do with that boss of yours? 'Cause I know *he's* gay, yeah?"

Ed had to smile at that. "Yeah, I'm sure. An' it's not like I 'aven't done things with a bloke before, Mum." He tried to swallow past the lump in his throat when her eyes widened. "It was a long time ago, but yeah, this isn't a new thing." He took a slurp of coffee. "An' you're right, there 'ave been girlfriends, an' the reason I've never brought any of 'em to meet ya is that they weren't important enough."

"And this Colin is?" she asked, head jerking up.

That gave him pause. "Yeah," he said with a slow nod. "Yeah, he is."

She nodded, as if it made perfect sense. Then she sighed.

"I think I'd like to be on me own right now, if you don't mind."

Shit. He gazed at her, heart racing. "Mum?"

She attempted a smile. "It's just a lot to get me 'ead round, to be honest." She got up and walked around to his side of the table. Her hand came out as if to touch him, but then she drew it back. "I just need a bit of time, all right?"

Ed tried to push down the panic that rose up his throat and made it difficult to breathe. Something must have shown in his face, because she cupped his cheek. "It'll be okay. Just let me deal with it in me own way, me own time, yeah?"

Ed nodded. "Yeah." The words came out as a croak. He stood up and grabbed his helmet from where he'd left it near the back door. A thought occurred to him. "Is Debs around?"

"She's gone shoppin' with 'er mates. She 'ad an interview yesterday, and it was a big deal, so she's lettin' off a little steam." She crooked her eyebrows. "I'll be fine, okay? You just leave me to it, yeah?"

Ed let out his tension in a shuddering long, drawn-out breath. "Yeah, okay." He walked to the door and paused. He turned to see her standing by the sink, looking out over the tiny back garden. "Bye, Mum."

She turned her head. There was that half-smile again. "Bye, son."

He walked out of the house and over to the garage to get the Harley, his head in a whirl.

God, I 'ope you're right, Col.

Monday's team meeting was nearly over when Rick piped up.

"Er, if I can just have everyone's attention for a sec?"

All eyes turned to look at him, including Sam's.

She stiffened. "I'm not sure we have time right now. We still have to go through—"

"I'm sure we 'ave time to 'ear whatever Rick 'as to say," Ed interjected, staring hard at her before cocking his head toward Blake. "Right, Boss?" He levelled a firm look in Blake's direction.

Blake smiled. "Of course we do. Besides, an agenda should be written on an Etch-a-Sketch, not in stone." He glanced at Sam and turned that smile of his up to full wattage. "Don't you think?"

Ed watched as several emotions played across Sam's face. He wondered with amusement which one would win.

She gave Blake a warm smile. "Of course." Then she turned to Rick. "Please, do go on."

Blake gave Ed a look that could only be interpreted as *I told you so.*

Ed wasn't convinced, but he pushed his doubts from his mind and turned his attention to Rick.

"Well, I know this is short notice, but Angelo and I would like to invite you to our flat for a party on Saturday night. You're all invited, and please feel free to bring husbands, wives, partners..." Ed didn't miss the quick flick of Rick's eyes toward him at that point. "We've been waiting until Blake had settled back into work. The party is to celebrate

Sophie's birth, and also a belated birthday party for Will, 'cause things got a little hairy back in June, what with them rushing off to the hospital and everything."

"It's not another themed party, is it?" Beth asked with a groan.

Rick chuckled. "No. Not that our *last* themed party wasn't great—Will's totally *awesome* Doctor Who party—but this will be your plain, come-casual, bring-a-bottle party."

Murmuring broke out among the team. Ed smiled. This lot loved *any* chance of a knees-up.

"Hey, are you going to bring your new lady friend, Ed?" Peter called out above the chatter.

Ed froze. *Oh fuck....* Then he thought about it. *What 'ave I got to be scared of? Next to me rugby team mates, this lot are a bunch of pussy-cats.* And maybe it was time to stop living a lie at work.

"Yeah, I'll see what I can do," he said after a moment.

Beth giggled gleefully. "Oh, roll on Saturday. It's going to be a fantastic party, I just know it."

Ed looked up to find both Rick *and* Blake regarding him with amusement.

Oh, you 'ave no *idea.*

Ed climbed out of the taxi and waited for Colin to emerge after him. He had a *serious* case of rampaging butterflies. By the time Colin had paid the cabbie, shut the door of the taxi and turned to face him, Ed was already breathing deeply.

Colin edged closer to him. "Easy now. It's going to be fine. You can do this. You've *already* done this, remember—twice. Third time *has* to be the easiest." He leaned forward and kissed Ed lightly on the lips.

Ed sighed. "Do that again. I need it."

Colin smiled. "With pleasure." He kissed him once more, this time lingering a little longer, his lips warm and soft against Ed's. Then he pulled back and regarded Ed intently. "Ready?"

Ed tightened his grip on the neck of the bottle of wine they'd brought and nodded. "Ready."

They walked to the door of Angelo's studio. Above them Ed could already hear music and animated voices. "Remind me again why we're arrivin' so late?"

Colin chuckled. "All the guests should be there by now. So when we walk in, everyone will see us. Get the shock over and done with in one fell swoop." He grinned. "Shall we?" He raised his hand and rang the doorbell. Ed breathed evenly. He knew *why* he felt so bloody nervous. He saw these people five days a week. They weren't just his colleagues—these were his friends—and he had no idea how they were going to react to such a change.

Rick opened the door and grinned. "Wanted to make an entrance, huh?" He stepped aside to let them in. "It's great to see you again, Colin."

Colin smiled. "You too. And thanks for inviting me."

Rick chuckled. "Oh, I wouldn't miss this for the *world*. Everyone's here, and Sam is already pissed." He shook his head. "That woman can't hold her booze." He led the way across the studio and up the staircase. At the top of the stairs he paused. "You guys ready?"

"Hang on a sec," Colin said quickly. He reached down and took Ed's hand. Raising it to his lips, he kissed Ed's fingers. The sweetness of the gesture filled Ed with warmth. Colin lowered their hands and tightened his grip around it. "Now we're ready."

Rick nodded in approval and pushed open the door to the apartment. "Hey, look who finally got here!" he called out as they entered.

Ed stepped into the apartment, Colin beside him and came face to face with all his colleagues, plus Will, Dave and Lizzie, Rick's family and Angelo's sister Maria. Everyone had turned to greet him. He could see the puzzled glances when they spotted Colin—and then watched as they looked down to where Colin held his hand.

Ed lifted his chin high. "Hi everyone. This is Colin."

Just then the music came to an end and the room fell into silence. Ed's heart hammered. He stopped counting how many jaws had dropped.

And then Beth's face broke into a huge grin. "You sneaky little bugger."

Ed went weak at the knees with relief. *Oh, thank fuck....*

It seemed as though Beth's words were the catalyst. Will came forward, hand outstretched.

"Pleased to meet you again, Colin."

Ed recovered quickly and nudged Colin. "'ere's yer chance...*babe.*" He smirked.

Colin gave him a look that told Ed in no uncertain terms he'd be in for it when they got back to Colin's apartment. Then Colin grasped Will's hand and shook it firmly. "I am so happy to meet you. I know you must hear this a lot, but I'm a huge fan." Will smiled broadly at him.

Then Dave and Lizzie approached them, smiling. "Didn't we meet you at the hospital?" they asked Colin.

Colin smiled. "That's right." He cast a glance in Ed's direction. "That was actually an important night for us, wasn't it, Ed?" His eyes sparkled. Colin was enjoying this—the sod.

Ed coughed. Rick caught his eye and pushed his tongue firmly into his cheek.

That little bastard....

Colin caught this, and Ed was convinced his lover was about to cough up a lung, he was laughing so hard. It seemed as if no one even batted an eyelid at the sight of Ed holding hands with a bloke. Well, *almost* no one—Sam didn't seem particularly enamoured. But then again, she hadn't known Ed as long as the others.

"So it's official?" Peter said with a grin. "You two are a couple?"

Ed reached for Colin's hand and raised it to his lips. He kissed it softly. "Yeah, we are."

Colin's eyes shone. He simply *beamed* at Ed.

Blake's face glowed with pride. "Congratulations, both of you."

And then *everyone* was saying it.

Ed's throat tightened as his colleagues surrounded them, glasses raised in the air as they joined in. Colin shook hands with every one of them.

Rick appeared at Ed's side. "Well done, mate. You've got a good one there."

Ed regarded his lover and smiled. "Don't I know it."

Colin glanced over at him, as though he'd heard Ed's words. His face was alight.

Somewhere inside Ed, warmth spread out, filling every little part of him, bringing something else with it—realization. For the first time in his life, Ed found himself on a completely unknown road.

He'd fallen for someone. And he couldn't wait to see where the road led next.

"So where's this baby of yours tonight?" Sam asked Will, swaying slightly. She seemed to have difficulty focusing on him.

Will gave her a polite smile, but Ed knew better. His former colleague was irritated. "She's with a babysitter."

"S'not right, y'know, two guys 'dopting a kid. Not when there are plenty of normal couples out there who are dying to get on the adoption bandwagon."

Oh fucking 'ell.

Seeing as this party was for Will and Blake, there was no *way* Ed was going to let the Pitbull wade in and get Will all riled up. Not while Ed was breathing, anyway.

Ed got close enough to be nearly flattened by the alcoholic fumes that rolled off Sam in waves.

"An' just what does that mean, *normal* couples?" Ed asked, frowning. Then he smiled as though a light bulb had just gone off. "*Ohhh*, I get it, you mean *straight* couples, yeah? Well, next time you decide to make a bigoted comment, better get your facts *straight* first—pun intended. Will an' Blake 'aven't adopted a kid—she's *their* daughter. They 'ad a surrogate."

Sam stared at him with wide eyes, her mouth falling open.

He felt Colin's hand on his arm and then Colin spoke quietly into his ear. "Leave it. One, she's drunk, which means two, she's probably not going to remember any of this come Monday morning. It's not worth it."

Ed breathed in, allowing Colin's calm to permeate him. He watched as Peter came up to speak to Sam, who looked puzzled by the stares she was receiving from the party goers. Peter led Sam toward the door.

"Peter's going to put Sam into a taxi," Beth explained to them. "I think he has the right idea."

"Sensible man," Colin commented. He leaned closer to Ed and tapped his empty glass with his index finger. "I'd love a glass of wine, if you're getting a refill." He gave Ed a smile.

Ed kissed him on the cheek. "Sure thing." As he walked away, Beth grabbed Colin and dragged him toward the sofa. "Come and talk to us now we've got rid of Ed. We'd *love* to get to know you better."

The last thing he saw was Colin mouthing *help*, his eyes huge. Then he grinned.

Shaking his head, Ed went into the kitchen to grab two glasses of wine. He smiled to himself as he listened to the chatter in the lounge.

Colin was proving very popular. He paused in the doorway and turned back to face his friends. He wagged his finger at them.

"An' don't think I don't know what you're all doin'. It's no good tryin' ta get me other 'alf to dish the goss on me, 'cause he knows what'll 'appen if he does." He gave Colin a mock-glare. "Don'tcha? Your privileges will be cut off." Ed waggled his eyebrows. There were gasps and smothered giggles at this.

Colin smirked. He glanced at the guests around him and shrugged. "You'll have to forgive my *other half*," he said with a sweet smile. "He's under the illusion that he wears the pants in this relationship." He met Ed's gaze and gave him an evil grin. "And we'll see whose privileges are cut off when he finds himself tied to the bed tonight." Colin's eyes glittered.

There was a momentary lapse into silence and then Ed's so-called friends collapsed laughing.

"Oh God, Ed, I think you've met your match at last," Will said, wiping his eyes.

Ed gave Colin one last stare and then went back to his hunt for alcohol, acutely aware of the hoots of laughter behind.

Looks like I'm gonna need it tonight.

Then he chuckled to himself. Who was he kidding? He was having fun.

As he entered the kitchen, he caught the tail-end of a conversation between Maria and Angelo.

"I tell you, I know a bitch when I see one. She's dangerous. Blake needs to be careful there."

Ed frowned. *Who the 'ell is she talkin' about?* Maria caught sight of him and stopped talking. Ed approached Angelo with a smile.

"I'm after two glasses of white wine, if there's any goin'."

Angelo bit his lip. "If you hold on for a moment, there'll be some handed round. There's something I have to do first." And with that he slipped out of the kitchen, leaving both Ed and Maria staring after him.

Maria frowned. "Something's going on tonight. My brother has been in a strange mood all day, as if he's on pins. I'd thought it was because of you and Colin, but now I'm not so sure."

Ed nodded toward the lounge. "Let's go see what's goin' on, yeah?"

They walked into the lounge and Ed joined Colin, standing behind him as he sat on the sofa, chatting with Rick, Will and Blake—well, more with Will. They were eagerly discussing one of Will's books. Blake caught Ed's eye and rolled his eyes. Ed smirked. He knew Blake got this every time they went to a book launch for Will's latest release. He must have been used to it after all this time.

Ed leaned on the back of the sofa and reached down to squeeze Colin's shoulder. Colin placed his hand over Ed's and left it there.

"If I could have your attention, please?"

Everyone turned to look at Angelo who stood by the fireplace. He ran his fingers through his dark, curly hair. He gazed around the room and beckoned for Rick to join him. Rick rolled his eyes. "Thank you time," he whispered to Ed. He got up and went over to stand beside Angelo.

Angelo smiled at him and then turned his attention back to the guests.

"Rick and I would like to thank you all for coming tonight. It's been good to celebrate Will's birthday, albeit belatedly, and to share their joy at the birth of Sophie."

There were murmurs of agreement from all around the room.

"And I'm sure you're all delighted to finally see Ed's mystery woman," Angelo continued with a grin. Chuckles and guffaws greeted this. Ed's face was suddenly very hot. Colin squeezed his hand tightly. "Although Colin might make a very *nice* woman, with the right clothing." He winked at his audience. "Of course, what they choose to wear in the privacy of their own bedroom is entirely up to them."

Ed almost choked on his glass of wine. He glared at Angelo who stared back at him, lips pinched together in a blatant effort not to smirk. The people around him had no such qualms. Everyone was laughing, some doubled over.

Wait 'til I get 'im alone.

Angelo held up a hand and waited for quiet to descend. He turned to face Rick and the look of love in those dark eyes was intense.

"But I have to confess, when I mentioned to Rick about throwing a party, I wasn't entirely truthful with him." Rick frowned and Angelo took his hands and held them. "Rick, we've been together for six years now, and I have loved every day that you have been in my life."

A soft chorus of *ahhs* broke out.

"However, since we got together, something has changed, something which matters very much to me." Angelo lowered his voice. "I'm a very traditional sort of man. You can't be brought up in an Italian family and *not* be." Maria snorted at that. Angelo grinned at her and then turned back to Rick. "So now that the law is finally changing in this country, I get to do this."

He dropped down onto one knee, amid stifled gasps. Angelo reached into his pants pocket and drew out a small black box. Rick's eyes widened and his mouth fell open.

Angelo gazed up at him, eyes fixed on Rick's face. "Rick Wentworth, you've made me the happiest man on earth these last six years. So will you make my joy complete by agreeing to be my husband?"

A hush fell over the whole room as Rick stared down at his lover.

Ed caught his breath as he awaited Rick's response. Colin gripped his hand.

Rick's face melted into a joyous grin. "Like I'm gonna say no."

Angelo burst into laughter and pushed the white gold band onto Rick's ring finger. Rick helped him to his feet and pulled him into a deep kiss, their arms entwining around each other.

And then the room erupted. Rick and Angelo were surrounded as everyone came forward to congratulate them. Rick's parents hugged

Angelo, and it was plain to Ed how much they cared for their soon-to-be son-in-law. Maria's face was wreathed in a gleeful smile as she hugged Rick. Blake and Will were at their side in an instant, their arms around Rick, and then Angelo was pulled into the hug.

Ed took advantage of the sudden availability of space on the sofa to sit next to his lover.

"Let's wait until all the commotion dies down before we give our congratulations, yeah?" Colin said quietly. Ed nodded, his gaze still trained on the beaming couple.

"God, they look so 'appy," he mused.

Colin nudged him with his shoulder. "People in love generally do," he said softly.

Ed glanced at Colin's face as he watched Rick and Angelo, a faraway look in his eyes.

People in love, he thought.

Then Colin turned to look at him, and Ed's breathing hitched.

God, 'ow he's lookin' at me right now....

Ed liked it. Liked it a lot.

CHAPTER TWENTY

"Sam, I need to talk to Blake." Ed put his hands flat on Sam's desk and leaned in. "An' *don't* tell me he's on a call. You've been feedin' me that line all mornin'."

Sam gave him a cool look. "And that's because he's *been* on calls—all morning." Her lips stretched into an insincere smile. "Right now he's busy finalizing details of our trip to Frankfurt." Suddenly her face took on a pinkish tinge.

Ed straightened. "If you're goin' to the Frankfurt bookfair with 'im, better stock up on energy drinks 'n' caffeine pills. Blake just doesn't stop when he's there."

Sam flushed. "I'm sure I'll be able to provide Blake with all he needs."

Then her words registered. "Er, 'our' trip to Frankfurt? You make it sound like he's takin' you away for an' 'oliday. You're gonna be knackered by the end of that week."

Just then the adjoining door to Blake's office opened and Blake stepped out. He smiled when he saw Ed. Sam was on her feet in an instant. "Can I get you anything?"

Blake gave her an amused glance. "No, thanks. I was just going to get a coffee."

"I can do that for you," Sam replied quickly.

Blake gave her that smile Ed knew so well. It was the one he wore when he was being very polite.

"That's fine, Sam, but I need a break. Besides, you have a lot to do organizing the Frankfurt trip. That's actually what I wanted to ask you about. Have you booked the hotel yet?"

"Yes, and I managed to get us adjoining rooms." There was that flush again.

"Good," Blake said absently. He looked at Ed. "Wanna grab a coffee with me?"

"Sure, Boss," Ed said with a wide grin, knowing full well it would piss Sam off. They exited Sam's office and went to the kitchen.

"You know, I swear I can feel her eyes boring into my back from here," Blake whispered once they were inside the kitchen. He let out a contented sigh when he spied the full coffee machine. "God, I need this." He went into the cupboard and rooted out the largest mug in there.

Ed chuckled. "God, so it seems. Is Sam not allowin' you your caffeine fix, then?"

Blake took a long drink of coffee and let out a low moan. "Oh, that's good." He met Ed's gaze. "Okay, maybe you and Karen might have a point. Since we talked that day, I'm noticing more and more. I get the impression Sam would be happier if she kept me in the office all day."

"On a leash," Ed added. Blake widened his eyes at that, and Ed laughed. "Oh, come on, Blake. If I didn't know you were gay, I'd swear she wants to keep you all to 'erself an' 'ave her wicked way with ya."

Blake paled. "Oh God, you're joking, right?"

Ed chuckled. "Adjoining rooms in the 'otel? Did you miss that part?"

Blake became very still. "Fuck." He stared into his coffee for a moment and then raised his head to stare at Ed. "But she knows I'm gay. Hell, she's met Will."

Ed gave a shrug. "Maybe she's one of them women who think a gay bloke is just one who 'asn't met the right woman yet." He couldn't resist. "Oh, maybe thass' the reason behind the rooms business. She's gonna try 'n' turn you back onto the right path." Ed loved winding Blake up, except this time he wasn't sure he was that far off the mark. Sam bothered him.

Blake snorted. "Yeah, right, I wish her luck with *that* plan." He sighed. "Maybe I should just take Will and Sophie instead." His eyes lit up. "Yeah, he could be my PA for the week."

Ed shook his head. "Ain't gonna work, Boss. Besides, he'd 'ave 'is 'ands full with Sophie. Nah, you're gonna 'ave ta suck it up and make the best of it." He winked. "Just remember to lock yer door at night, thass'all."

Blake glared at him. "Not funny, Ed." He let out another sigh.

Ed tilted his head to one side. "You okay, Blake?"

Blake regarded him in silence for a moment before speaking. "There are days when I don't know how Dad did it, you know. Run a business *and* have a family." Then he grimaced. "Oh yeah, I do. He ran the business and spent as little time with me as possible. The business always came first." Blake's chin dropped to his chest.

Ed was shocked into stillness. He hadn't heard Blake talk like this for nearly seven years. "You 'ad a great relationship with yer Dad," he said at last.

Blake jerked his head up. "You're right, I did—*after* he finally gave up the reins and let me take over the company. Those last five years he was a different man. Relaxed, happy...." He locked eyes with Ed. "I don't want a life like that, Ed. I'm thirty-seven in a few weeks' time. I have a husband that I absolutely adore, a baby daughter who I see in the evenings and on weekends. When she takes her first step, I probably won't be there to see it. When she says Dad for the first time, only one of her Dads will hear her."

Beth stepped into the kitchen at that moment and Blake clammed up.

"I'll be in my office if anyone wants me," he said, and then exited the kitchen.

Ed stared after him, aghast. Only a short conversation, but it shook him to the core.

"Is Blake okay?" Beth asked with a concerned expression.

Ed gave her a hopefully reassuring smile. "Yeah, think he's just tired, thass'all." He poured himself a coffee and went back to his office with a heavy heart. He sat behind his desk and took a sip of coffee, his mind faraway—well, in Hackney, to be accurate. Mum still hadn't rung him. It had been two weeks since their conversation and each day without word from her only increased his anxiety. Colin had said nothing, but Ed knew his lover had picked up on it. In spite of his worry, he smiled to himself. Not much got past Colin, where Ed was concerned.

His phone chimed, startling him. He stared at the screen in surprise. *Deb.*

Bloody 'ell, is there an x in the day? His sister wasn't one for phone calls.

"Hey, sis, this is a turn up for the books. Whass'up?"

"Ed, I need to talk to you. You got a minute?"

For one brief moment, his chest constricted at the thought that Mum had told her. Then he dismissed it. Mum wouldn't do that without talking to him first. "Go for it."

"I've got a job." He could hear her excitement down the phone. "I'm going to work for the World Health Organisation. I start work next month!"

"Oh Debs, that's fantastic!" Ed was overjoyed. "What did Mum say? I bet she was bowled over, yeah?"

"Oh God, she 'asn't stopped talkin' about it since she heard."

Ed snickered. He had no doubt that every firm Mum cleaned for would have heard about Deb's job by now. "So where will you be based? London?"

There was a pause. "See, that's the thing. It's gonna involve a lot of travellin'."

"Okay." Ed got a feeling something big was coming right at him. The pause that followed only confirmed his suspicions. "Deb, what is it?"

"Look, I don't think Mum should be on her own, yeah? She's not in the best of 'ealth to start with."

What the 'ell? "Whoa, back up there. Mum's not well? Since when?" He thought back to the last time he'd seen her. Sure, she'd looked tired, but surely she'd have said if there'd been something wrong with her. Then he grimaced. This was Mum he was talking about—of *course* she wouldn't.

Deb sighed. "I think she's worn 'erself out, personally. But at least while I've been livin' at 'ome, she's had less to do around the 'ouse. I do the shopping, keep the place tidy, you know, just generally try to take things off her 'ands." She paused. "Which is what I wanted to talk to you about."

Ed suddenly got that sinking feeling in his gut.

"I think you should move back in with 'er," Deb said emphatically.

The first thought that raced through Ed's brain was that living with his Mum would kill any chance he had of moving forward with Colin.

Fuck... livin' with yer mum ain't exactly good for the ol' love life.

Ed liked his life—hell, he loved it. Most nights he spent in Colin's apartment, plus every weekend. His flat was simply the place where he stored his clothes and belongings.

The second thought was that Mum clearly hadn't warmed to the idea of having a gay son. So living at home *and* carrying on a relationship with Colin would likely be a recipe for disaster.

And the third and final thought was that right now, he couldn't even tell Deb any of this.

"I know it's not an ideal situation," Deb said, "but right now it's all I can think of."

"Deb, I'm thirty-six. Thass' a bit long in the tooth to be livin' with me mum, don'tcha think?" His stomach rolled over at the thought. He knew it was selfish of him, but for the first time in his life, Ed had someone who meant a great deal to him—and he wanted to keep him.

"Well, 'ave you got a *better* idea?" his sister retorted.

Ed groaned. "Look, Deb, you're gonna 'ave ta leave this with me, all right? Let me 'ave a think about it. An' we should also think about getting the others involved too."

"Okay," she agreed, although he could hear the reluctance in her voice.

Yeah, it'd make life easier for yer if it got all sewn up, nice 'n' neat, eh?

No sooner had he thought it, Ed berated himself for thinking that way about his sister. Deb had worked bloody hard to pass her nursing exams. She deserved this chance.

"It'll all work out, Debs, you'll see," Ed reassured her with more confidence than he felt. They said their goodbyes and he disconnected the call.

Ed sat back in his chair and stared out of his window. He knew what he had to do next.

He had to talk to Colin.

"Look, you must do what you think is best," Colin said in as calm a voice as he could muster. Ed lay on his back next to him in bed, Colin stroking Ed's chest with slow, gentle movements.

Inside he didn't feel calm. Anything but.

He wanted to yell. Scream. Chain Ed to the bed and keep him there.

Okay, so that last thought was a bit drastic, but he didn't see how their relationship could survive if Ed moved back home. And especially if it turned out she wasn't receptive to having a gay son.

Yeah, that could be the kiss of death for them as a couple right there....

And he couldn't say *any* of this. It had to be Ed's decision.

Ed let out a sigh. "God, I 'ate this."

"I know," he said sympathetically. "Maybe talking it over with your brother and sisters is the only way forward." That was as far as he was willing to go, in terms of advice.

Ed stared at him for a moment, eyes so grave that they tore at Colin's heart. What came next out of Ed's lips sent that heart soaring.

"Make love to me."

Colin's breath caught in his throat. He gazed at this big, strong man who'd had no qualms about fucking a guy but who'd struggled with the notion that he could care for another man. Ed's words stirred something deep inside him—hope.

"Yes." It was all the reply that was needed.

Colin reached under his pillow for the lube he knew would be there, and then opened the drawer to take out a condom. All the while, Ed's gaze never moved away from him, his hand moving slowly over his stiffening cock. Colin slicked up two fingers and trailed them down over Ed's balls, loving the way Ed's erect dick twitched when Colin reached his hole. Colin bent down and took Ed's mouth in a sensual, slow kiss, while he pressed inside Ed's body, his fingers sucked in. Ed let out a low moan and slid his tongue into Colin's mouth, hips pushing up as he rode those fingers. When Colin couldn't wait a moment longer, he gloved up, ran a lube-slicked hand over his aching cock and then lifted Ed's legs to rest against his shoulders.

Colin kept his eyes fixed on Ed as he eased his length into hot, sweet heat. Ed's groan rolled out of him as Colin filled him to the hilt. He held onto the furred, muscled thighs and began to rock into Ed, hips rolling.

"Feels so good inside you," Colin said, the words a whispered confession in the quiet of his bedroom. He rotated his hips, loving the gasp that burst from Ed's lips. "Like that?"

"Fuck, yeah." Ed's breathing quickened. "Fuck, how that feels...."

"I know." God, he knew. Colin had never felt such a strong connection to a lover. Maybe it was because their relationship was already becoming more than physical.

Colin wasn't one to say *I love you* in the heat of sex. But right then, deep inside the man he had lusted after for so long, for the first time he ached to say the words.

"Col, go slow, okay?" Ed gasped out. "Make...make it last."

Colin moved Ed's legs to wrap around his waist and then lowered his body to cover Ed's, keeping the movement of his hips languid as he slid in and out of Ed's channel, the love-making slow, sweet and so very sensual. "How's that?"

"Oh God, that's perfect," Ed sighed, arms coming up to hold Colin, hands stroking up and down his back. His thighs tightened around Colin, heels pressing into his buttocks as Ed propelled Colin deeper into him. "Oh *fuuuuck......*"

Colin maintained the pace, hand slipping between their bodies to stroke Ed's cock which rubbed against his abs. There was no hurry, only a leisurely pace that kept them both on the edge without letting them tumble over it.

And when they finally fell, it was with soft cries and moans, clinging to each other as each man rode out his orgasm, breathless and ultimately sated.

CHAPTER TWENTY-ONE

"Will! What on earth are you doin' 'ere?" Ed stared in surprise to see Will standing beside Karen's desk while she cooed over Sophie, strapped to Will's front in a baby carrier.

"I've just taken Sophie to see our doctor," he explained, his hand cupping Sophie's head protectively as she snuggled against his chest, dozing. Ed smiled when he saw the baby grow covered with images of little teddy bears. Then the word *doctor* finally registered.

Ed was at his side in an instant, peering anxiously at Sophie. "Is she all right? What is it?"

Will caressed his daughter's head. "She's not been well for the last day or so. She started with a fever yesterday, and we thought it had broken. But once Blake had left this morning, it came back, only this time she was coughing and sounding really croaky." Will's brow furrowed. "It was when it seemed she had difficulty breathing that I really began to panic." He placed a gentle kiss on Sophie's head.

"An' what did the doc say?" Ed brushed the tiny hand that rested against Will's chest with his little finger.

Will gave a shaky laugh. "She said it was croup, and nothing to worry about. I can give Sophie children's paracetamol, and that will help lower her temperature. I'm glad I brought the baby carrier, because it's better if she's kept upright." He stroked her head so gently. "And we need to make sure she drinks enough, and comfort her if she becomes agitated."

"An' you want to tell Blake," Ed reasoned, "so he can stop worryin' too. I did wonder this mornin' if there was anythin' wrong."

Will smiled. "Neither of us got a lot of sleep, to be honest."

Ed patted his arm. "Go an' see your 'ubby. You'll 'ave to go through Sam's office, though—your old office, yeah? Just tell Sam you wanna see Blake right away."

"Ah." Will gave him a knowing glance. He lowered his voice. "The Pitbull."

Karen almost snorted out tea through her nose.

Ed let out an exaggerated gasp. "Don't let 'er 'ear you say that!" Then he grinned.

Will returned his grin and then walked off in the direction of Sam's office. Ed turned to look at Karen who was wiping up tea from her desk. He wagged his finger at her and grinned.

"Sophie's beautiful," Karen said with a sigh. "I was trying to work out which one of them she resembles, but I think it's too early to tell. She isn't even three months old yet."

Ed chuckled. "Oh come on, with those two for parents, it's a safe bet she's gonna be a stunner."

"Is that the opinion of Ed their friend, or Ed the newly-out gay man?" Karen teased.

Ed shook his head, laughing. "Ooh, watch it, you."

She giggled.

Will's raised voice drifted down the corridor.

"What the 'ell?" Ed ran toward Sam's office, Karen behind him. On arrival he found Will glaring at Sam, cheeks bright red, eyes narrowed. Sophie was awake and mewling, clearly agitated.

Sam stood behind her desk, lips pinched together.

"What's goin' on 'ere?" Ed demanded.

Will didn't take his eyes off Sam. "This...harridan won't let me in to see my husband."

Just then Blake's door was flung open. "Just what in hell is going on?" Blake's eyes opened wide when he spied Will and Sophie. His anger died away as fast as it had erupted. "What is it? Is Sophie worse? What's wrong?" He dashed forward and looked at her intently.

Will's anger had cooled too. He put out a hand to grasp Blake's arm. "It's okay, babe, She's going to be fine. It's just croup, the doctor said."

Blake sagged visibly with relief. "Oh, thank God. I've had my phone out all morning, waiting for you to call."

Will smiled. "I knew you'd be worried, and I thought you'd want to see her."

"Both of you," Blake corrected, and he leaned forward and kissed Will on the cheek. Then he straightened. "Now will someone please tell me why there was a shouting match taking place out here?" He kissed Sophie's head.

Will's expression grew cold as he turned to face Sam. "Perhaps your PA can explain why she refused to let me in to see you."

Blake stared at her. "Sam? What's the meaning of this?"

She swallowed. "You said you were busy. To hold all calls."

Blake's jaw set. "Obviously that does not include my husband and our daughter."

The skin around Sam's mouth tightened.

Blake wasn't finished. "Well?" he demanded.

Will approached her desk. "Exactly what do you have against me, Samantha?" His voice was low and menacing.

Sam's eyes grew cold. "I don't have a clue what you're talking about."

Will placed one hand on her desk and leaned toward her, the other on Sophie. "I'm talking about recalling some things you said during Rick's party a few weeks back. Some very revealing things. Now I'm remembering what you said and I'm putting two and two together." His voice dropped even lower. "And I don't like the answer I'm arriving at. So I suggest you start talking—right now."

And just like that, Ed saw the light.

He walked over to where Sam stood, her arms folded. "You're very fond of Blake, aren't ya, Sam?"

Sam jerked her head round to look at him so fast, he was surprised she didn't get whiplash. "What?" Her face paled.

Ed stared at her. "You know what I mean. I see the way you look at 'im. Such a shame he's gay, yeah?"

Oh yeah, there was no mistaking Sam's reaction. Her eyes glinted. "You shut up." Behind him, Ed caught Karen's quiet gasp.

Yeah, I've got ya now. "'Course, maybe he's not met the right woman yet. Maybe all Blake *really* needs is a woman who understands 'im."

"I said shut up." Spots of red coloured Sam's cheekbones.

"An' as for 'im being married, well, thass' just not right, is it? Guys marryin' guys, 'avin' kids..."

Will caught on. "So if the right woman comes along, what do you think Blake might do? Leave his husband? His daughter?" He gave her a thin smile. "For someone like you, maybe?"

Sam's eyes lit up. "Exactly," she said triumphantly. "Everyone knows you can't be born gay. It's a choice."

Ed went cold. "An' if someone 'appens to make the wrong choice..."

"Then it's the duty of right-minded people like me to show them where they went wrong, and help them back onto the right path." She smirked. "Not that I'd expect you to understand that. You're as confused as they are."

Blake snorted. "Ed, I take back everything I said. You too, Karen. The pair of you had her pegged weeks ago, and I should have listened."

Ed grinned. "Don't even think about it, Boss. Jus' glad to 'elp." He nodded toward Blake. "Your call."

Blake gave a slow nod before returning his attention to Sam. "Collect your things together and then leave. Your last payslip will be forwarded on to you." He gazed at her unblinking. "Now I'm going to go into my office with my husband, my daughter and my manager. When I come back out, I don't expect to find you here. Is that clear?"

"Perfectly," she spat out.

Blake smiled. "I'm so glad." He turned to Karen. "When Sam is ready, please escort her from the building, Karen. If she causes any trouble, don't hesitate to come get me."

Karen stood very straight, her gaze fixed on Sam. "Certainly, Blake." Her jaw was set.

Sam's eyes flashed. In grim silence she began to empty the drawer in her desk.

Blake watched her for a moment before giving the others his attention. "Will, Ed? My office, please." Blake led them into his office and closed the door behind them. Ed sank down into the sofa and shook his head, laughing quietly.

Blake leaned back against the door and sighed. "What is it about me that seems to bring out the crazies?"

Will chuckled as he undid the baby carrier from around Sophie, and then handed her to Blake. "Babe, I have no idea. But that's not going to be an issue anymore, is it?"

Ed frowned. "Eh? What does that mean?" He gave Blake a hard stare.

Blake looked from Will down at the baby in his arms and sighed. He bent down and kissed his little girl's cheek, and then joined Ed on the sofa. Will took Blake's office chair.

Blake looked Ed in the eye. "I'm sorry for doubting you. I should have known, I suppose. You're a damn good judge of character."

Ed chuffed. "God, Boss, you'll 'ave me blushin'." He stared glumly at the floor. "Well, I suppose I'd better starting advertisin' for a new PA for ya." He shook his head. "You don't 'ave a lot of luck with 'em, do ya?"

Blake smiled. "By all means, put an advert together. However, it won't be for a PA for me, but for you."

Ed cocked his head to one side. "I don't get it."

Blake leaned back into the sofa and cradled Sophie. "Remember you and I had a conversation a while ago? About how I didn't want a life like Dad's?"

Ed nodded, his throat suddenly tight.

Blake's eyes shone. "Well, I've come to a decision. I want to see my daughter grow up, maybe even provide her with a baby brother or sister. I want to spend more time with Will. So I'm handing over the reins.

Trinity Publishing will still be my company, but I'd like you to be its CEO."

"What?" Ed swallowed.

Blake smiled. "When I took over the company all those years ago, all I cared about was making Trinity successful. Well, I've done that. But I'm not that man anymore." He gazed directly at Ed. "You're the perfect choice. You ran the company while I spent time with Will and the baby when she came out of hospital. And you ran it brilliantly. So I'd like you to carry on doing a brilliant job. I'll still pop in from time to time—I've spent too long with this team to desert them completely—but unlike my father, I'll let you know when I'm due to visit." His eyes twinkled.

Ed sat there open-mouthed.

"Well?" Blake demanded, laughing. "Do I have a new CEO or don't I?"

Ed drew in a deep breath and then looked Blake in the eye. "You do."

Blake's face broke into a huge grin. "Oh, thank God for that. You had me worried for a minute."

Will got up, walked across to Ed and held out his hand. "Congratulations. Now all Blake's headaches have just become your headaches." He grinned.

Blake snorted. "Way to go, babe. Are you *trying* to get Ed to change his mind?"

Will shrugged. "Just trying to paint an accurate picture, that's all."

Ed huffed. "I 'ave enough 'eadaches of me own, thank you very much."

Will frowned. "What's wrong?"

Sighing, Ed told them about Deb's phone call. Blake and Will listened, their faces grave.

"Can I say something here?" Blake asked.

"Sure, go for it." Ed still had no idea which way to turn.

"If your mum decides she's not happy having a gay son, and then you are in the position of having to live with her, putting it bluntly, you're going to be fucking miserable."

Ed stared at his boss in surprise.

Blake continued. "I've been there, remember? I was going to marry Melissa, leave Will, yeah? You can't do it, Ed. Think about how you've felt these last few months." He stared at Ed. "Have you been happy?"

Ed didn't even hesitate. "'appier than I've ever been."

Blake nodded. "Then don't throw that away. Tell your brother and sisters that you've not a single man anymore, you're in a relationship—one which you hope will lead somewhere." He smiled. "Because that *is* what you hope, isn't it?"

Will cleared his throat. "Just *how* important is Colin to you, Ed?"

Ed sighed. "Enough for me to realize that I don't want to be without 'im."

Will smiled. "Then take it from there. Next stop—family meeting."

Blake nodded. "You're not the only one involved here—it should be the whole family's decision. But I would like to point out one thing. As CEO, you get a pay rise. Maybe you could hire a live-in housekeeper for your Mum? Carer? Companion? You have more options now."

The same thing had occurred to Ed. But at least his mind was made up on one thing—whatever his family decided, Ed's future included Colin.

The dishes were all washed, dried and put away. Everyone had a cup of tea or coffee.

It was time to get things moving.

Mum sat in her recliner near the fire, and the rest of the family took up space on the two sofas or on the floor. Ed glanced at his siblings. At least they'd all agreed to come. Despite their differing ages and occupations, the Fellows siblings got on okay with each other. When their Dad died, Ed had thought it would bring them all closer, but the opposite had been true. It was as if Dad had been the glue that held them all together.

Ed knew if anything was to be decided, it was up to him to get the ball rolling—and to be truthful with his family. For a moment his thoughts went to Colin, waiting for him at his apartment. He'd told Colin about the meeting. He could only imagine what was going through Colin's mind right now.

He's prob'ly just as nervous as I am.

He cleared his throat. "I'm glad we're all 'ere, cos there's somethin' we need to discuss."

Mum stiffened. "This is to do with Debs movin' out, innit?" Silence met her words. She gazed at her family and scowled. "Great. Now me kids see me as a flippin' burden."

"God, Mum," Yvonne began, "no one's said that, have they?" She glared at her mum. "Well, have they?"

"No," Mum admitted, grudgingly. She lifted her chin and glanced around at them all. "But I'm sure some of you are thinkin' it."

Tracy sighed patiently. "Mum, we're here because we love you, okay? And if you were honest, you'd admit that you don't find things as easy as you used to." She met her mother's stare. "Well?"

Mum huffed. "Maybe."

Ed laughed. *Typical bloody Mum.* Phil and Tracy joined in with him. Yvonne's husband Dan had come along, too. Ed could understand why. He and Mum got on like a house on fire. But Ed knew he had to say something.

"Listen, a while ago now, I shared somethin' with Mum. Now, I *know* she 'asn't said anythin' to any of ya, 'cause believe me, if she 'ad, one or more of you would be talkin' about it."

Phil frowned. "Is everything all right, Ed?"

Ed nodded. "Yeah, but thanks for askin'." He gave his younger brother a fond smile, and then gazed around at his siblings. "Look, I've met someone."

Ed loved the smiles that broke out on their faces, every last one of them.

"Aw, way to go, big brother!" Debs looked so happy for him.

"Sounds like it's serious," Yvonne said with a grin. "About time, too."

"Yeah, it *is* serious," Ed admitted. "An' it's precisely *because* it's that serious that I 'ave to share it with you all."

The room fell silent.

Ed was conscious of his Mum's gaze. He wished he know how she felt before he broke the news, but it was too late now.

"'is name's Colin." He looked around the room as smiles faltered and foreheads creased. Ed nodded. "Thass' right—your big brother is bi." They stared at him, stunned. Ed pressed on. "I suppose it's early days for us, but I've come to realize just 'ow important he is to me. Too important to want to give 'im up, for a start."

He glanced at his Mum. To his surprise, she was staring at him with tears in her eyes.

"What I must 'ave put you through all this time," she said softly, "makin' you wait while I tried to get me 'ead round it." She gave a half-smile. "You must really care for this bloke."

"I do, Mum," Ed replied earnestly. "An' it's *because* I care for 'im that I'm not gonna be movin' back 'ome."

Mum straightened in her chair. "Nor would I want you to. You 'ave yer own life to lead now. You can't start off with this bloke while you're livin' with yer old mum." She snickered. "Talk about crampin' yer style." There were chuckles at this. "I don't think I ever told any of you, but when me an' yer Dad first got married, we were livin' with 'is mum." She chuckled. "God, it was bleedin' awful. I think he really struggled with who he should be loyal to—me, or 'is mother. When yer Dad stood up to 'er and said we was movin' out, it was the best decision he ever made, he said afterward. It actually brought 'em closer together." She stared at Ed. "I'd 'ate for you to think I'd come between you and this...."

"Colin?" Ed offered.

Her face cleared. "Yeah, this Colin."

Ed rose from the sofa, walked across to where his Mum sat and bent down to envelop her in a tight hug. She pressed her cheek against his and whispered in his ear. "Like I said, you're *so* like yer Dad." She chuckled. "Except yer beard isn't as scratchy as 'is used to be."

He laughed quietly, kissed her cheek and then returned to his seat. To his relief the shocked expressions had morphed into bemused glances.

"Well, don't just stop there!" Phil demanded. "How long have you been seeing him? Are you moving in together? Are wedding bells in the offing? Details, bro, details!" He grinned.

"Whoa, 'old yer 'orses," Ed said, holding up his hands. "Talk about jumpin' the bleedin' gun. I'll tell you everythin' later, yeah? But Phil..."—he gave his brother a stern glance—"*weddin' bells*? Bloody 'ell!" He couldn't help laughing. God, he loved his family. "Right now we 'ave somethin' more important to discuss, an' that's Mum."

"An' there ya go again, thinkin' of me as some kinda flippin' burden," Mum grumbled.

"And like we said before, as if we'd ever think of you like that!" Yvonne looked shocked.

Dan nudged her, smiling. "Go on, tell them."

Yvonne beamed at her husband. Ed loved the way her whole face just...glowed when she looked at him. She glanced around at her family. "We were pleased to get to see you all like this because Dan and I have news. He's been offered a new job, in Kent. It's a fantastic opportunity. And... I'm going to have a baby."

There were loud exclamations as Tracy and Debs launched themselves at her and hugged her. Ed was so happy. He knew they'd been trying for a while.

"And the rest," Dan said with a grin.

Yvonne extricated herself from the group hug. "The thing is, we've just bought a house. It's a lovely, big place in the countryside, perfect for a family. And..." She gazed at Mum, eyes shining. "There's a separate annex, Mum. It's in the grounds of the house, and it's self-contained. And we'd love you to come and live in it."

Mum's eyes widened, and Dan rushed to speak. "It's perfect. You'd still have your independence, but we'd only be a few feet away if you needed us. Plus, you'd be there to see your grandchild grow up. Yvonne would love that. I would, too." He smiled. "Please, say you'll think about it?"

"An' while you're at it, think about givin' up work," Debs said with a frown. "Come on, Mum. You don't need to work anymore. We all earn enough to make sure of that. And before you say it again, this does *not* make you a burden, yeah?" Her frown faded. "You've looked after us your 'ole life. You 'n' Dad brought up five kids on two small wage packets, and from what I can see 'ere, you both did a bloody good job. So let us take care of *you* now."

Mum cleared her throat. "Kent's a long way away. When would I get to see the rest of me kids?"

Ed laughed. "You daft ol' bird. We'd come visit ya. An' Kent ain't exactly the ends of the earth, yeah? Besides," he said with a wink, "think 'ow nice it'll be to come stay with your kids whenever you feel like it. I won't always 'ave me poky little flat, y'know."

When Mum's face finally broke into a smile, Ed felt as though a huge weight had been lifted off his shoulders. He gazed at his family and grinned, anticipating the grilling he was sure was about to take place. But in his mind there was only one thought—to put Colin out of his misery.

He's prob'ly goin' spare right now.

CHAPTER TWENTY-TWO

What on earth can be taking so long?

Colin was trying his best to remain calm, but his nerves frayed a little more with each passing minute. It was the *not knowing* part that was killing him.

He wasn't worried about Ed coming out to his family. From the sound of it, they were a solid bunch, and even Ed admitted he wasn't that worried.

No, what concerned him most was the direction Ed chose to take next.

What if he moves back home? What then?

Colin stopped pacing long enough to go into the kitchen and pour himself a coffee. He leaned against the fridge and stared out of the window.

Not sure which direction Hackney is in from here, but I'm sending you positive vibes. He could only guess at what was going on in Ed's head. They hadn't talked much about previous relationships, beyond him and Matt, but Colin got the impression that Ed hadn't had many lasting ones. And yet here *he* was, expecting Ed to choose between looking after his mother and committing to a long-term relationship with Colin.

His biggest fear was that Ed would choose his mother.

And it *was* fear, no mistake about that.

I should have told him, Colin thought with a pang of regret. *I should have let him know exactly how much he means to me before he went to that bloody Sunday dinner.*

Except he knew in his heart that he wouldn't have done that. He thought of the pressure it would have put Ed under.

I couldn't do that to him.

If Ed came back and announced he was moving back home, Colin wasn't sure what he would do. He *did* know it would just about break his heart.

The intercom buzzed. Colin went over to the front door and pressed the button. "Hello?"

"Well, buzz me in, then. Who else d'ya think it was?" Ed sounded cheerful. "Unless you're expectin' someone else, that is?"

Colin laughed as he pressed the door release button. "Get your arse up here." But Ed had already gone.

Colin opened the door and listened to the smooth whirring of the elevator's gears. When Ed emerged, grinning widely, Colin couldn't help smiling.

He tapped his watch as Ed stepped into the apartment. "What time do you call this?"

Ed pouted. "Aw, did ya miss me?" He took off his leather jacket and hung it on the coat rack. Colin followed him into the lounge and watched as he sprawled out on the sofa.

"Just how long does it take to have Sunday lunch, followed by a family discussion?" He didn't mean to sound like a shrew, but it had been a very long, stressful afternoon. "It's five o'clock."

Ed snorted. "Lunch was the quickest part of it. The discussions took a bit longer." He beckoned with his index finger. "Come 'ere, you."

Colin joined him on the sofa. Ed moved closer and cupped his nape, pulling him into a long, sensual kiss, tongue licking at the seam of Colin's lips. Colin opened for him and Ed dived right in, exploring him with soft moans, his hand stroking Colin's hair.

Fuck, the man can kiss...

When Ed broke away and sat back, Colin grinned. "That was quite a welcome."

Ed smiled. "God, I missed you today."

Colin reached across and stroked the soft beard. "Yeah, me too." He sat back. "So... how did it go?"

"Well, the main thing is, Mum is seriously considerin' movin' to Kent to live in a granny annex with me sister Yvonne an' 'er 'hubby Dan. Oh, and she's gonna be a grandma." He beamed.

"That's great!" Relief flooded through Colin. *Oh, thank God.* Colin felt so light, he was almost giddy. "And how did everyone take your announcement?"

Ed exhaled. "They were great. I got asked a ton of questions about ya, though." He winked. "They can't wait to meet ya."

Colin became still. "You're taking me to meet your family?"

Ed was suddenly equally still. "Of course." He tilted his head. "You don't 'ave a clue, do ya?"

"About what?" Colin's heartbeat quickened.

A gentle smile spread across Ed's face. "'ow I feel about ya."

"That might be because you've never actually told me," Colin chided him. His whole body tingled.

Ed raised his eyebrows. "An' you've told me 'ow *you* feel, of course." There was merriment in those clear green eyes. Ed bit his lip, smirking.

"Oh, for God's sake," Colin huffed. "I told you already—I want to see where this goes." He locked eyes with Ed. "So tell me."

Ed moved closer. "You mean, you can't tell that I've fallen for ya, you big dope?" His voice was soft. "I wanna see where this goes, too." He took Colin's hand. "This 'ole thing 'ad me 'ead in bits for the longest time."

"What do you mean?" Colin stared at him.

Ed sighed. "Don't get me wrong. From the start, I 'ad no problem with what you an' me did in bed, right? I mean, *that* was the easy part."

Colin smirked. "Yeah, I could tell."

Ed grinned. "Cheeky sod. Nah, for me, it was this 'ole *am I gay, am I bi* thing. Apart from a year of uni where me an' Derek sucked each other off, I was strictly one for the birds."

"Can I just point something out here?" Colin interjected. "Liking having your cock sucked doesn't make you gay. What man doesn't like having his dick sucked, I ask you? But giving blowjobs and *liking* it? That is *not* the action of a straight man." He smiled sweetly.

Ed shook his head. "Let me finish, yeah? There 'ave been a lot of women, all right? But the other day I did some thinkin' 'bout all those birds, an' the conclusion I came to was that I never really connected with a woman on an emotional level. We'd fuck, we'd go out on dates, but that was as far as it went. I got me itch scratched, an' that was it." His face fell. "Which makes me sound about as deep as a puddle."

Colin cupped his face. "It was always there, you know, deep inside you. The knowledge that this wasn't who you were supposed to be. It just took a while to surface, that's all." He kissed Ed on the lips.

Ed regarded him keenly. "An' then you show up. An' yeah, you fuckin' blew me mind with the sex. Like I said, I 'ad no problem with *that* part. What took longer to crystallize in me 'ead was the fact that I 'ad feelins for a *guy*." He gestured down to his body. "I mean, look at me. Big guy, rugby player, macho as 'ell, right? An' yet last night, when I was thinkin' about what would 'appen if I 'ad to move back in with Mum?" He shook his head. "Just the thought of losin' you had me shakin'." He smiled. "It was then that I 'ad ta face facts. Whatever 'appens from now on, only one thing matters—that I 'ave you in me life." Ed swallowed. "An' that's all I'm gonna say on the matter, 'cause this emotional stuff does me 'ead in."

Colin returned his smile. "It's a damn good place to start." He leaned closer until their foreheads were touching. "Just so we're clear? I fell for you a while ago. I was just waiting for you to catch up."

Ed closed his eyes and sighed. Colin inhaled, breathing in Ed's scent, letting it fill his senses. He knew how much it had taken Ed to bare his soul like that. And in that moment it would do just fine—for now.

"How does pizza sound for dinner?"

Ed opened his eyes and leaned back. "Pizza? You're thinkin' about *food*?"

Colin chuckled. "No, I'm thinking about having dinner delivered because I want to spend every available second of what's left of today in bed with you."

Ed's eyes lit up. "*Now* you're talkin'." He reached down to where Colin's cock tented his sweatpants. "Can't wait to get this monster inside me."

Colin quirked his eyebrows. "And what if I wanted *you* to fuck *me*?"

Ed lowered his chin and pinned Colin with a look through his lashes. "We're gonna argue about who fucks who? Seriously?" He grinned. "Flip-fuckin' it is, then." He was off the sofa in a flash and dashing into the bedroom. For a large man he moved surprisingly fast. "Last one there gets tied to the bed!" he yelled back.

Colin scrambled off the sofa and gave chase, laughing.

Life with Ed would never be dull, that was for certain.

EPILOGUE

One year later

"Any more eggnog in the kitchen, Col?" Ed yelled through from the lounge.

"There's another bottle in the cupboard under the stairs," Colin yelled back. He took the brandy butter from the fridge and carried it through with the plate of warmed mince pies into the dining room, where the table groaned under the weight of Christmas party food.

Phil was there in a flash. "Ooh, mince pies." His eyes glittered.

Colin laughed. "Phil, I'm sure you have a tape worm, the amount of food you put away." He checked to see if anything else needing replenishing, and then left Phil to his mince pies. In the lounge, Christmas carols played quietly in the background. Ed was busy doing refills of wine and other drinks. Tracy and her partner Chris were sitting on the floor, playing a game with their little girl Mandy. Debs sat watching them, laughing.

Colin went over to where Ed's mum sat by the fire. "You okay there, Mavis? Do you want anything?"

Mavis looked up and smiled. "Nah, I'm fine, thanks, Colin." She looked around her. "I love the new 'ouse, by the way. An' this fireplace is lovely."

Colin sighed. "Thanks. There's still loads to do on it. Ed told me yesterday he wants a hot-tub in the garden—and a deck." He grinned.

Mavis snorted. "He doesn't want much, does he?"

Colin squeezed her shoulder. "Let me know if you need anything."

He wandered over to the window where Yvonne and Dan were looking out over the front garden which was deep in snow. He smiled as he gazed at their baby boy, Ben, all of two months old. Ben was fast asleep in his mother's arms, oblivious to his surroundings.

"Wait until next year," Colin told them with a smirk. "We'll have trouble keeping him away from the Christmas tree, you'll see."

Yvonne smiled. "It was lovely of you and Ed to have everyone here for Christmas Day."

Colin shrugged. "Well, it was the least we could do after you put up with us staying at your place last Christmas. Especially after that unfortunate accident...." He bit his lip, his cheeks heating up.

Dan snorted. "Hmmm. I'd still like to know exactly how you two managed to break the bed." His eyes sparkled.

"Oh, is that someone calling me?" Colin said quickly. Both Yvonne and Dan laughed.

Colin circulated around the room, checking if Ed's family needed everything before going in search of his lover, who'd disappeared. No Ed in the kitchen, nor in the dining room. After deciding that everyone was happy, Colin climbed the stairs.

He found Ed in their bedroom, hastily tucking something under the bed.

"And just what are you up to?" Colin teased.

Ed gave a start. "Shit, you made me jump, creepin' up on me like that." He gave a mock scowl. "An' why aren't you downstairs, takin' care of our guests?"

Colin pushed the door shut behind him, walked over to his lover and took him in his arms.

"I could ask you the same question," he said softly, before kissing Ed on the lips. Ed lost no time in responding, his arms winding around Colin, pulling him tighter against that gorgeous body.

"This is *soooo* wrong," Ed murmured into his mouth. "What if someone comes in?"

Colin laughed quietly. "It's not like I'm about to undress you and make passionate love to you on the bed right now." *God, but* there's *a lovely thought....* He released Ed reluctantly. "You're right, I suppose."

Ed's eyes gleamed. "Save it for tonight, yeah? When people leave or go to bed. Although you'll 'ave to be quiet." He smirked. "Whose bright idea was it to put Mum in the room next to ours?"

Colin chuckled. "I could always gag you," he suggested with a grin.

Ed's face was a picture. "You're a wicked man." He broke away. "I actually came up 'ere to talk to Blake, but it can wait 'til later. They've prob'ly got their 'ands full with little Sophie." A gleam came into his eyes. "An' I wanted a word with you, an' all."

Colin gulped dramatically. "Sounds like I'm in trouble."

Ed narrowed his gaze. "It's about my Christmas presents."

Colin opened his eyes wide. "Didn't you like them?" he asked innocently.

"They were all little stuff," Ed groused. "An' after all the trouble I went to for *your* present...."

"Which you haven't given me yet, I might add." Colin let out a sigh. "Oh well, I *suppose* I could give you your present now," he said with feigned reluctance.

Ed was all but bouncing. "Yes please."

Laughing, Colin went over to the bedside drawer which he'd kept locked. He opened it and withdrew a long white envelope.

"Here you go," he said, handing it to Ed. He bit back his laugh at the sight of Ed's face.

"This?" Ed looked disappointed. He tore open the envelope and pulled out several vouchers. His eyes were suddenly so large and round. "Oh my God. Tickets to the Rugby World Cup—in Australia?" His mouth fell open.

"We'll be staying in a five-star hotel, and I got us an invite to a party with the Australian team." Colin had pulled a few strings to get that arranged—with a little help from Blake. That man seemed to know *everyone*.

Ed flung his arms around Colin and kissed him on the mouth. Colin smiled against his lips. He loved making Ed happy.

"Col, it's a bloody brilliant present."

The look on Ed's face was present enough.

Then Ed chuckled. "An' don't think I don't know the real reason behind this present."

Colin frowned. "Excuse me?"

Ed arched his eyebrows. "Oh, so you think I 'aven't worked out why you were rootin' for Australia that first night?" He grinned. "Just which one of the Australian team did you 'ave the 'ots for?"

Colin placed his hand over his heart and sighed. "I shall never tell." Ed chortled. Then Colin held that hand out. "Okay, you've had *your* present—now where's mine?"

Ed grinned. He put the tickets down on the bed and then reached under it, dragging out a large, flattish parcel. He placed it carefully on the bed and then turned to Colin. "Merry Christmas, Col."

Colin launched himself at his gift, tearing the paper off in long strips, to reveal....

His mouth fell open. "Oh my...."

There were four black-and-white prints in all, dramatically lit, each one showing Ed. One showed his torso, arms flexed, his six-pack making Colin drool. Another showed Ed from the back, him looking off to the left, the camera having revealed that wide expanse of muscle, reaching down to the curve of his delectable arse. The third was Ed in nothing but a white towel, the swell of his erection visible beneath it. But the final print was Colin's favorite.

Ed sat on a wooden chair, those massive thighs spread wide, a dark towel covering his cock. Ed was leaning back, head tilted so that his face wasn't visible. There was the flowing line of his neck, arms stretched up, chest wide, the hair covering his pecs and abs a contrast to the pale skin.

Colin was hard just *looking* at it.

"These are incredible," he said softly, running his hand over the captured flesh. "Who did them?

"Blake's mate, Dave. He's a photographer. I saw the ones he did of Blake last year. Thass' what gave me the idea, so I set up a session with 'im." He stepped closer. "Do you like 'em?"

Colin laughed quietly. "Oh, like is far too weak a word. They're wonderful." He couldn't take his eyes off them.

Ed stood behind him, arms circling his waist. "Love you," he whispered. He kissed Colin's neck. "An' you always did love this body of mine."

Colin turned in his arms and reached around Ed to pull him tight against him. "Yeah," he agreed, his voice soft with emotion. "Almost as much as I love you....baby."

Ed's eyes widened. "Ooh, you *are* askin' for it. And when everyone's gone? You are gonna get it."

Colin grinned. "Bring it on."

The End

If you enjoyed this book, then please take a look at the rest of the series. And if you can leave a review, that would be wonderful. Reviews help keep books visible.

And if you keep scrolling, you'll find more about the final book in the series, Personal Challenges.

Personal Challenges

Will and Blake couldn't be happier. They have a beautiful little boy, Nathan, and Sophie finally has the little brother she's been demanding. But all is not bliss in the Davis household. Coping with reality is going to change all their lives.

Rick and Angelo are sick and tired of trying to get a wedding organized. If it was up to them, they'd be married already, but Angelo's mother has plans and they keep getting bigger. Angelo can see problems on the horizon: big, traditional Italian wedding and gay do not go well together.

Something's got to give.

Colin receives an unexpected call from an ex, with bad news. He feels compelled to help, regardless of the consequences. Ed loves Colin's big heart and supports him in his efforts, but when the truth comes out, he finds it difficult to keep a lid on his emotions.

As the coming months unfold, the friends are going to need each other more than ever.

Personal Challenges contains wedding hassles and shenanigans, secrets, heartache, trials and tribulations, and a whole lot of hot loving. Six men, three couples – a family.

<u>Grab your copy here!</u>[1]

---

1.   https://books2read.com/u/bPeZVA

About the author

K.C. Wells lives on an island off the south coast of the UK, surrounded by natural beauty. She writes about men who love men, and can't even contemplate a life that doesn't include writing.

The rainbow rose tattoo on her back with the words 'Love is Love' and 'Love Wins' is her way of hoisting a flag. She plans to be writing about men in love - be it sweet and slow, hot or kinky - for a long while to come.

If you want to follow her exploits, you can sign up for her monthly newsletter: http://eepurl.com/cNKHlT

You can stalk – er, find – her in the following places:

Email: k.c.wells@btinternet.com

Facebook: www.facebook.com/KCWellsWorld[1]

KC's men In Love (my readers group): http://bit.ly/2hXL6wJ

Blog: kcwellsworld.blogspot.co.uk

Twitter: @K_C_Wells

Website: www.kcwellsworld.com

Instagram: www.instagram.com/k.c.wells[2]

BookBub: https://www.bookbub.com/authors/k-c-wells

---

1. http://www.facebook.com/KCWellsWorld

2. http://www.instagram.com/k.c.wells

Also by K.C. Wells

Learning to Love
    Michael & Sean
    Evan & Daniel
    Josh & Chris
    Final Exam
Sensual Bonds
    A Bond of Three
    A Bond of Truth
Merrychurch Mysteries
    Truth Will Out
    Roots of Evil
    A Novel Murder
Love, Unexpected
    Debt
    Burden
Dreamspun Desires
    The Senator's Secret
    Out of the Shadows
    My Fair Brady
    Under the Covers
Lions & Tigers & Bears
    A Growl, a Roar, and a Purr[1]
    A Snarl, a Splash, and a Shock[2]
    Love Lessons Learned
    First[3]
    Waiting for You
    Step by Step[4]

1.   https://books2read.com/u/3JR8lB

2.   https://books2read.com/SnarlSplashShock

3.   https://books2read.com/u/3LwlZD

Bromantically Yours
BFF[5]
<u>Collars & Cuffs</u>
An Unlocked Heart
Trusting Thomas
Someone to Keep Me (K.C. Wells & Parker Williams)
A Dance with Domination
Damian's Discipline (K.C. Wells & Parker Williams)
Make Me Soar
Dom of Ages (K.C. Wells & Parker Williams)
Endings and Beginnings (K.C. Wells & Parker Williams)

<u>Secrets – with Parker Williams</u>
Before You Break
An Unlocked Mind
Threepeat
On the Same Page
<u>Personal</u>
Making it Personal
Personal Changes
More than Personal
Personal Secrets
Strictly Personal
Personal Challenges[6]
Personal – The complete series[7]
Confetti, Cake & Confessions
(FREE)[8]

4.   https://books2read.com/u/bzdA1n

5.   https://books2read.com/u/3JnzKE

6.   https://books2read.com/u/bPeZVA

7.   https://books2read.com/u/mYx6kG

<u>Christmas</u>
Connections
Saving Jason
A Christmas Promise
The Law of Miracles
My Christmas Spirit
A Guy for Christmas
Dear Santa[9]
<u>Santa's Secrets</u>[10]
<u>Island Tales</u>
Waiting for a Prince
September's Tide
Submitting to the Darkness
Island Tales Vol 1 (Books #1 & #2)
<u>Lightning Tales</u>
Teach Me
Trust Me
See Me
Love Me
<u>A Material World</u>
Lace
Satin
Silk
Denim
<u>Southern Boys</u>
Truth & Betrayal
Pride & Protection
Desire & Denial
The Southern Boys Trilogy[11]

---

8.   https://www.prolificworks.com/book/33626

9.   https://books2read.com/u/bMw8E8

10.   https://books2read.com/SantasSecrets

<u>Maine Men</u>

Finn's Fantasy[12]

Ben's Boss[13]

Seb's Summer[14]

Dylan's Dilemma[15]

Shaun's Salvation[16]

Aaron's Awakening[17]

Levi's Love[18]

Maine Men – the Complete Series[19]

<u>Salvation</u>

Wrangled[20]

<u>Second Sight</u>

In His Sights[21]

In Plain Sight[22]

<u>CrossBow Protection</u>

Broken Warrior[23]

<u>Standalones</u>

Kel's Keeper[24]

---

11.   https://books2read.com/u/m2l0NG

12.   https://books2read.com/FinnsFantasy

13.   https://books2read.com/u/md77JW

14.   https://books2read.com/u/m2RjJR

15.   https://books2read.com/u/bQV6pv

16.   https://books2read.com/ShaunsSalvation

17.   https://books2read.com/u/mvWWvz

18.   https://books2read.com/LevisLove

19.   https://books2read.com/u/bMz8J7

20.   https://books2read.com/Wrangled

21.   https://ooks2read.com/u/4NoWOW

22.   https://books2read.com/u/3GGadK

23.   https://books2read.com/u/3R5DwB

24.   https://books2read.com/u/b5vjV6

Here For You
Sexting The Boss
Gay on a Train
Sunshine & Shadows
Double or Nothing
Back from the Edge
Switching it up
Out for You[25] (FREE)
State of Mind[26] (FREE)
No More Waiting[27] (FREE)
Watch and Learn[28]
My Best Friend's Brother[29]
Princely Submission[30]
Bears in the Woods[31]
Holy Hell – with Parker Williams[32]
Teasing Tim[33]
Str8 B8[34]
Anthologies
Fifty Gays of Shade
Winning Will's Heart
Come, Play
Watch and Learn

---

25. https://www.prolificworks.com/book/62550

26. https://www.prolificworks.com/book/74720

27. https://www.prolificworks.com/book/82301

28. https://books2read.com/u/boEK9Z

29. https://books2read.com/MyBestFriendsBrother

30. https://books2read.com/PrincelySubmission

31. https://books2read.com/u/3LRVLX

32. https://books2read.com/HolyHell

33. https://books2read.com/u/bOJRAW

34. https://books2read.com/u/4X0dj6

<u>Writing as Tantalus</u>
Damon & Pete: Playing with Fire[35]